I0542407

Total-E-Bound Publishing books by Robin Gideon:

Passion of Madeline
Ecstasy in Eden

Regency England

SATISFYING OLYMPIA

ROBIN GIDEON

Satisfying Olympia
ISBN # 978-0-85715-086-8
©Copyright Robin Gideon 2010
Cover Art by Lyn Taylor ©Copyright 2010
Interior text design by Claire Siemaszkiewicz
Total-E-Bound Publishing

Published in 2010 by Total-E-Bound Publishing, Think Tank, Ruston Way, Lincoln, LN6 7FL, United Kingdom.

SATISFYING
OLYMPIA

Dedication

This one is dedicated to DPB, who needs to write.

Chapter One

London

"It's good to see you socialising again," Colby Beldon, the Duke of Tasley, said quietly, his green eyes alight with pleasure. "And it's especially nice to see you smiling again. It's been a while since I've seen you enjoying life."

A faint blush coloured Olympia Whyte's cheeks. The duke and several other guests had been subtly flirting with her since the dinner party had begun ninety minutes earlier, and as flattering as it was to receive so much masculine attention from some of London's most charming men, Olympia was out of practice with the art of coquettery. Searching for a response that wouldn't seem either insincerely modest or narcissistic, she finally replied neutrally, "Thank you, Your Grace. It's kind of you to say so."

"Please, it's Colby." His gaze met hers. "We've discussed that."

"But you're a betrothed man, and I could never be *familiar* with another woman's fiancé." Her tone was teasing. After a moment, she added, "Your Grace" with just a touch of impishness. Laughter in the room dispersed Olympia's tension.

"It's still Colby, and there isn't a soul in the *Ton* who doesn't know that my engagement was arranged years ago by my mother and Francesca's father, that I had no choice in the matter, and that I will seldom, if ever, see my wife." His gaze went slowly over Olympia. "Now if you were my wife, it would take an act of supreme willpower just to leave home for the office each day." The duke was something of an oddity in the *Ton* in that he actually worked for his money, and didn't hide the fact that he took pleasure in his labours. His voice dipped low as he added, "Rest assured, if I had *you* waiting for me, I would be home every night."

The timbre of his voice touched Olympia invisibly, and in ways she hadn't anticipated. She looked at the man seated next to her and reminded herself once again that he was one of the more notorious rakes in all of London, a man whose sexual exploits were infamous among the *Ton*. Even more significantly, he was engaged to be married to Francesca LeMorneau, one of the *Ton*'s most beautiful debutantes. Though Olympia was getting back into society after her period of mourning for the death of her husband, men like the notorious Duke of Tasley were undoubtedly tempting.

"My good Lord, your statements are flattering, but I know for a fact that you are far too promiscuous for a woman of my sensibility to give serious consideration." She grinned to soften her words. "However, it does my heart a world of good to be the *temporary* recipient of that charm."

Though Olympia was only twenty-one, cruel fates had already made her a widow. It had been fourteen months since her husband, a lieutenant in the British Navy, had been accidentally killed when a cannon discharged prematurely as he led soldiers into battle against Napoleon's troops.

Nigel Sanders, Olympia's older brother, gave Colby a smile and said, "Save your breath. My sister's on to you, my friend. She's too intelligent to have anything to do with you."

"But what about me?" chimed in Prince Leland Mallory, seated beside Nigel. He had been just one of many men casting the young widow a flirtatious eye. "Is she too intelligent for me, or do I make the grade?"

"Sorry, my friend, but I'm afraid you come up short of the mandatory requirements. My sister prefers the road less travelled, and as much of London and many other cities can testify, you definitely are not that." He turned his gaze towards Olympia, smiling proudly. "For my sister, only the best will do. She doesn't have to settle for anything less."

Uncomfortable with the intense scrutiny and the conversation's topic, heated embarrassment coloured her bosom, throat, and cheeks. "Nigel, when you talk like that you make it seem like I'm a prized brood mare up on the auction block. I am a twenty-one-year-old widow who is just getting out into society again. And as we all know, the duke is spoken for, and the prince is one of the most eligible bachelors in all of England. Eligible bachelors simply do not marry widows."

Leland, a slender, handsome man with coal black hair curled over his carefully tied cravat and strangely piercing silver-blue eyes, flashed the smile that had seduced countless men and women across England and the Continent. "Who says they don't?"

"My darling prince," Olympia answered without hesitation, setting down her fork and adopting a professorial tone, "you have been my brother's friend for many years, which means I, too, have known you for many years. It also means that I have witnessed — on more occasions that I can count or wish to remember — some of the most interesting people in all of London shamelessly throwing themselves at you. The young and the not-so-young, married and unmarried, have been less than demure in their desire for your…" She paused, searching for an acceptable word, '*companionship*'. She gave the word a distinctly libidinous inflection. "Since I am privy to the well-substantiated rumour that you never say 'no' to admirers, and since you are still a bachelor, the evidence suggests that you are not, as the saying goes, on the marriage market."

"The lady's logic is flawless!" Nigel exclaimed, clapping his friend playfully on the back.

Col. John Newton, the only military man at the dinner party, tapped his wine glass with a spoon to draw attention, then smiled warmly at Olympia. He had been her husband's commanding officer. "They're all wrong about you," he said in the quiet, authoritative way of his profession. "The only man worthy of you is I. When your dear husband was killed, I was the one who you knew you could count on for support. And when your period of bereavement has passed, logic and reason dictate that there is only one man who should stand at your side, and I am that man."

"No doubt you are accustomed to giving orders," Prince Leland said to the colonel. "But you seem to have forgotten that we're not under your command."

Olympia, sensing the long-standing tension between the colonel and Leland, said quickly, "Though I think we all can admit that these dinner parties do sometimes resemble a battlefield."

When she received laughter, Olympia felt much more at ease. She had married at eighteen, wedding a young career military man without trepidation. But almost immediately he was assigned to be second-in-command of a division, and the one thing that Olympia hadn't counted on when becoming a wife was spending so much time without her husband. When her husband was killed almost two years to the day after their wedding, Olympia could count on one hand the number of months they had spent together.

Olympia's gaze turned towards Lady Darcia Firth Caldwell. Though there was a significant age difference between them—the duchess was thirty-six—the two women had been together at several society functions recently, and they were forming a close friendship. One thing the two women had in common was their misfortunes. Darcia's elderly husband had recently been thrown from his horse and killed. Olympia wanted to show her emotional support for the duchess, but privately when the two of them would not be overheard.

Olympia watched as Darcia suddenly rose from her chair, then walked from the lavishly appointed dining room with a purposeful stride.

Always a woman to consider the feelings of others carefully, Olympia wondered for a moment whether or not Darcia would appreciate a show of emotional solidarity, or if she'd find it unsettling. She sat for several seconds, unsure of the proper action to take.

"If you'll excuse me for just a moment," Olympia said at last, sliding her chair back. Before she had moved it far enough to stand, both Colby and Leland had bolted to their feet and were politely assisting her. "Thank you," she said to them both, hoping they wouldn't inquire as to what she was doing. "I'll be back in just a moment."

With a conscious effort, Olympia did not hurry so much that she drew attention to herself. By the time she reached the dining room doors—which were opened for her by a liveried butler with no expression on his face whatsoever—and stepped into the hallway, all she saw of Lady Darcia was a flash of an emerald green velvet gown disappearing around the corner near the stairway. Though Olympia had not hurried, it appeared that the same couldn't be said for the duchess. Wherever she was going, she intended on getting there quickly.

By the time Olympia reached the top of the stairway, Darcia was nowhere to be seen.

"What's she in such a hurry for?" Olympia muttered aloud as she raised the skirts of her Grecian-style gown and petticoat, then descended the stairs quickly.

She reached the ground floor, and as she headed for the heavy, twin oak front doors, she heard the sound of a door closing behind her. Olympia was confused because it seemed that Lady Darcia—one of the wealthier titled women in London—was headed for the servant's rear entrance.

Not entirely well-versed with the structural design of the manor, especially not in areas more commonly associated with the servants than with the well-heeled guests, Olympia flailed about before finally catching sight of her new friend once again.

And once she did find her new friend, she wished she hadn't.

Olympia had gone out a rear servant's door of the estate, and as she hurried in the darkness, she looked into the side window of the carriage house. Inside, barely illuminated by just a single lamp, she found Darcia standing beside a big, black lacquered carriage. Short but extremely curvaceous and swathed in a Grecian-style gown created by the famous modiste Elizabeth Saxby, Olympia was certain it was the duchess even though she couldn't see her face. She couldn't see Darcia's face because the woman was sandwiched between two men — one very tall and muscular, and the other shorter with a more trim physique. Lady Darcia was taking turns kissing one man then the other.

"Oh...my...God," Olympia breathed, her heart suddenly racing, her nose nearly touching the window pane.

Olympia's throat felt constricted. She tried to swallow, but her mouth had suddenly gone so very dry. When she tried to moisten her lips with her tongue, it accomplished nothing. Her breath came in quick, shallow gulps. And though everything in Olympia's upbringing whispered — no, *screamed* — that she should run from the lurid scene and return to the dining room and the oh-so-civilised dinner party, she simply couldn't turn away from the window. She could hardly blink. Olympia made a silent promise to whatever gods were looking down upon her that she would never tell a soul about what she witnessed, and hoped that would exonerate her voyeurism. She would keep this moment a secret in her heart forever.

But she couldn't possibly turn away. Her feet wouldn't move, and her heart wouldn't stop racing.

Inside the carriage house, Darcia's encounter, which Olympia now suspected had been planned and was no spontaneous tryst, became even more heated. The burly man had turned her so that Darcia's back was against his chest, her face angled upward and to the side so that she could receive his open-mouthed kisses. While this was happening, the slender liveried servant was busy pushing up her skirt and petticoat as he got down on one knee.

The young man lifted Darcia's knee, sliding his shoulder in beneath her thigh. He leaned into Darcia, and though all Olympia could see was her friend's thigh encased in a white silk stocking and the top of the boy's head, her imagination filled in the details that her eyes could not.

Olympia began to shiver. She felt her clitoris start tingling. The delicate and long-neglected lips of her pussy swelled and became dewy with the nectar of her excitement. Her right hand balled into a small fist, and she unconsciously pressed her knuckles against her mouth for several seconds before biting the side of her forefinger hard enough to leave teeth marks.

She's terrible, thought the young widow, fully well aware of the fact that she really didn't think Darcia was terrible at all. Olympia realised her own jealousy and envy when she felt the evidence of it making her pussy slick and heated. *I never dreamed that Lady Darcia Firth Caldwell would ever be so licentious.*

Olympia watched, wide-eyed with fascination, as the big man's hands groped Darcia's generous bosom. The décolletage of Darcia's dress was fashionably low-cut, and as the coachman's fingers kneaded the pale mounds, Olympia was certain that at any moment her breasts would escape their silken confines. As he administered harsh caresses to Darcia's breasts, he feasted on her mouth, kissing her fiercely, demandingly. On one knee in front of Darcia, the younger coachman's head moved slowly as he administered cunnilingus with what appeared to be spectacular effect. Even through the closed window, Olympia could hear her friend's continuous moans of escalating passion.

Olympia was pulling up her skirt and petticoat before she ever consciously realised what she was doing. For a moment the dark fan of her eyelashes fluttered as an unprecedented voyeuristic thrill took over her senses. She was dizzy, disoriented, light-headed in a way that seemed like intoxication…but that didn't stop her from raising the muslin skirt higher. Small, kidskin-slippered feet separated slightly, and a trembling hand slipped beneath the folds of dress and petticoat. The fingertips of Olympia's right hand brushed feather-soft against the inside of her left thigh, caressing through the sheer barrier of Chinese silk stockings.

Inside the carriage house, the big man curled his fingers inside the bodice of Lady Darcia's gown and, with a forceful tug, bared the quivering mounds of her breasts. The sight of them caused a soft moan to escape from Olympia. She ran the tip of her middle finger over the cleavage of her labia. When her fingertip was moist with her own juices, Olympia caressed her clitoris.

"Oh…" she sighed as heated passion coursed through her veins.

Nothing in Olympia's previous experience could have prepared her for what was happening to her there in the darkness beside a carriage house. Watching Lady Darcia, a woman both beautiful and sophisticated, pleasuring herself in the arms of two men, was beyond anything that Olympia could have imagined was possible. As shocking as it was to discover that Lady Darcia liked her men in pairs was the fact that *watching* her with her lovers was disquietingly erotic to Olympia. Even though she had only been caressing her clitoris for only a few seconds, she could already feel the tightening within herself that warned her an orgasm was fast approaching.

Lady Darcia's arms were outstretched, angling slightly downward, as she kissed the large man bending over her from behind while the smaller man continued with his oral caresses. Olympia tried to imagine what it must feel like to be in the arms of two men, to be simultaneously kissing one man while another was on his knees to administer wicked kisses of a rather more intimate nature.

The thought was all it took to trigger Olympia's climax. She thrust her middle two fingers between the slick lips of her pussy, penetrating herself as deeply as her fingers allowed. The pressure of her palm against her clitoris was firm as the contractions began. Her mouth opened, but not a sound was emitted as Olympia's insides shuddered through four powerful, climactic spasms.

Olympia's fingers were still inside her pussy when, from inside the carriage house, Lady Darcia's short, high-pitched cry of ecstasy signalled her own climax.

Lady Darcia, you're one very lucky widow. No man has ever made me climax.

Breathing deeply through her nose, her eyelashes tapping lightly against her cheeks as she descended from the heights of her self-administered pleasuring, Olympia caressed her pussy lightly, wanting to come down slowly from the summit. Releasing her gown, she cupped a breast in her left hand and squeezed gently. Tingles emanated from her lust-inflamed nipple. Though she had climaxed, she was far from being completely satisfied.

Just as Olympia was about to smooth her gown and petticoat over her legs again in preparation for her return to the dinner party, events inside the carriage house changed her plans. The slender man that had been on his knees suddenly got to his feet, and the big man behind Lady Darcia simultaneously grabbed her by the hip with one hand and used the other to push firmly on her shoulder. She was forced to bend sharply at the waist.

Without being consciously aware of it, Olympia again raised her skirt to allow her right hand to move without restrictions. Her hand resumed its slow, sensual rhythm, two fingers sliding between the lips of a pussy made slick with cream. Olympia's mouth opened slightly, and though moments earlier her breathing had begun returning to normal, she was soon taking quick, shallow gulps of air.

The change in positions among the three people inside the carriage house caused them to be better illuminated by the pale lamplight. Olympia could now clearly see Lady Darcia's profile. Bent at the waist, Darcia's hands were on the slender man's trim waist, her head tilted far back on her shoulders, her lush mouth open in lewd invitation.

A shiver went through Olympia, and she fingered her own slick pussy faster as she watched the men unbuttoning their breeches. Within seconds, both exposed prominent erections. Being as close as she was, Olympia had an unimpeded view of the big man's arousal. For only a moment—for no more than that, since she did not want to miss anything—Olympia closed her eyes and tried to imagine what it would feel like to have an erection pumping back and forth between the lips of her pussy, filling her tight, feminine channel. The fantasy was not without its downside.

It has been so long since I've felt a man inside me, Olympia thought with a touch of melancholy as she watched the big man bring the head of his cock to the lips of Lady Darcia's passion-lubricated pussy.

They entered her simultaneously, the slender man driving his hips forward, burying much of his stone-solid cock into Lady Darcia's mouth, while she was pierced from behind. Olympia watched as her friend's lips tightened around the shaft of the cock, her cheeks hollowing as she drew a firm suction.

She likes sucking his cock, thought Olympia, her own hand beating faster and faster, pumping two fingers in and out of a pussy hungry for stimulation. *It's easy to see, just from the expression on her face, that she loves having his cock in her mouth.*

Behind her, the big man now had both hands on the duchess's hips, the skirt of her gown bunched up on her back. He thrust into Darcia until his pelvis collided with the cheeks of her ass. When Darcia was knocked forward, she choked on the cock, sputtering briefly, her cheeks momentarily puffing out.

They're not gentle with her, but she seems to like it that way.

Olympia felt the passion spreading outward from her pussy, the heat flowing through her veins. The next orgasm would be even more powerful than the first. She was certain of it.

The men inside the carriage house soon got into a steady, timed rhythm, pumping their cocks into Lady Darcia's mouth and pussy at the same time, feeding and filling her with their virility. Olympia watched, transfixed by the visual eroticism of it all, as Lady Darcia's heavy breasts rolled back and forth beneath her as she rocked between her lovers.

Olympia did not hear the man come up behind her. She was transfixed by Lady Darcia's vigorous double-penetration when suddenly a large, powerful hand grabbed her by the back of the neck, and another hand grabbed her arm just above the elbow!

Chapter Two

The hands seemed made of steel. Olympia was so shocked the only sound she uttered was a short, high-pitched gasp that disappeared on the night breeze.

She was forced away from the window an instant later. Olympia tried to maintain her position, but the man holding her — and it certainly had to be a man, since no woman would have hands so large and powerful — pushed her several yards to the side, moving her deeper into the shadows. The hand remained at the back on her neck, holding her so tightly Olympia suspected she would be find bruises in the morning. The darkness was almost total.

Scream! Scream, Olympia!

But she didn't scream. It wasn't that she *couldn't* scream. She just inexplicably…*didn't.*

She was pushed between two saddled horses and thrust against a waist-high pole fence used for hitching guests' horses. The unyielding hand at the back of her neck held her, pushing her so that she was forced to bend over the top pole of the fence.

Scream, Olympia!

The hand came away from her neck, but before Olympia experienced even the slightest relief, both her hands were grabbed at the wrists and wrenched behind her back, then placed one over the other. An instant later, the man held both her wrists with just one hand.

She was bent over the railing with her head down far below the level of her hips. Olympia she could see nothing but the ground. For an instant, the polished toe of a man's boot came into view. Only the toes of her delicate kidskin slippers touched the ground. With a rustle of costly fabric, her gown and petticoat were lifted. The gauzy material was stuffed beneath her trapped wrists.

Olympia felt the evening breeze against her bare bottom. A shiver raced through her, and it wasn't from the cool breeze.

It was all so thoroughly disorienting. One second she had been working two fingers in and out of her pussy and was anticipating her second orgasm in nearly as many minutes, then she was grabbed by a powerful, faceless stranger and bent over a hitching rail. In her mind's eye, Olympia pictured herself, and the image conjured caused a tremor of licentious subjugation to surge through nerve endings and sensory pathways. There she was, exquisitely gowned, her coiffure perfect, bent over a railing, the cheeks of her ass pale in the shadowy moonlight, a faceless stranger holding her as securely as if he had put her in manacles.

Then she felt the head of his cock against the lips of her pussy. As a widow, Olympia was certainly no virgin, but the size of the erection that pressed against her delicate pink flesh seemed significantly oversized. When the stranger added pressure behind his unyielding shaft, Olympia uttered the softest of moans as her body stretched, then flinched as a brief spasm of pain shot through her when she was forced to expand to accommodate the masculine invasion.

He did not plunge full-length into her immediately. Instead, he worked his hips with a slow and smooth rhythm, advancing just a little more deeply into her with each invasion, followed by a smooth retreat. It took a full dozen revolutions of his hips before his pelvis pressed tightly against her bottom. Olympia felt the full length of his enflamed erection pulsing wantonly inside her. He remained motionless for several seconds, pressed snugly against her, his unyielding flesh flexing and throbbing within her silken warmth. A soft sigh came from Olympia before reality forced itself into her consciousness, and she caught her lower lip between her teeth to remain silent.

This was *not* the time to draw attention to herself.

A thousand conflicting emotions bombarded Olympia when the stranger began his next long, slow retreat. The friction from the underside of his shaft against her aroused and elongated clitoris created an intensely and disconcertingly erotic sensation. But even as she was conscious of the slick caress of a man's hard shaft rubbing against the focal point of all her most aroused nerves, she was assailed with the fact that she did not know the identity of the man whose erection so thoroughly tantalised her senses.

Scream! Scream, damn it!

But Olympia's thoughts, however good-intentioned, did not lead to actions. When the stranger had retreated until only the tip of his erection still separated her tingling labia, he paused again. To her horror, Olympia caught herself anticipating the next invasion, her body already hungry for the pleasure of being filled by a man's hard cock.

It was a controlled invasion—measured, slow, and resolute. Olympia felt every inch of him as he filled her, the slick flesh gliding against her creaming clitoris. This time when he reached full-insertion and his pelvis made contact with her bottom, he ground himself against her for several seconds. He then retreated with significantly more swiftness than earlier, paused once again just long enough for Olympia to feel empty and hungry, then thrust into her again.

This invasion was unlike the previous ones. It lacked the civility of being measured, its force ungoverned. The powerful thrust was delivered with little regard to extravagant masculine endowment or normal feminine dimensions.

This time when the stranger thrust, he didn't just fill Olympia...he fucked her.

"Uh!" Olympia gasped. Then, breathily, she sighed on the next jarring thrust that smashed her against the wooden hitching rail. And on the third, her gasp of "Oh...God!" lacked any foundation in theology, but carried with it a marked sense of the divine.

But the fourth hard, invading plunge was clearly the most evocative for Olympia, because when the stranger's pelvis slapped against the cheeks of her ass and his unyielding flesh plunged deep inside her, the voluptuous widow whispered with more candour than decorum, "I'm coming," and began shivering as rolling waves of orgasmic contractions went through her over-stimulated and long-neglected body.

While she had experienced climaxes before, to have an orgasm caused by a man's pistoning erection was unprecedented for Olympia. Even as she was shuddering from one climactic peak to another, in the back of her mind she thought a word she'd never previously spoken aloud. *Fuck!* This word was immediately followed by and clarified with *Fuck me!* And finally, as her wrenching spasms subsided but the thrashing cock continued its blissful assault upon a feminine body vastly over-stimulated and overwhelmed by masculine force, her mind—bidden by urges the ever-proper Olympia Whyte had only moments earlier decided were ungovernable—concluded, *Fuck me to death!*

He didn't, of course. That was just one of many things that later gave Olympia a sense of tolerance towards the stranger. She was even more grateful that the stranger had shown the orgasmic discipline to withdraw an instant before climaxing.

His strangled growl of ecstasy was followed by hot seed splashing down upon her. The first rich eruption hit her buttocks, and though Olympia flinched, her reaction was caused by surprise, not because she was offended by the stranger's slick cum against her skin. The second thick eruption—rather more disconcerting to Olympia in the long run, since it might require the involvement of a chambermaid—spewed into the air, arching over bared buttocks and her exquisite muslin gown, and hit her in the back of the head at the nape of her neck. The sperm, thick as the scented lotion she used on her elbows and heels at night, mingling with her pinned-up auburn curls, playing hell with her coiffure. More of the stranger's gooey seed splashed against her hands, still pinned against the small of her back.

Thank you for not coming inside me, Olympia thought moments later as she rubbed her fingertips with her thumbs. The sperm on her fingers seemed very thick and slippery. *You come enough to impregnate twenty women.* A moment passed before she thought, *What if it's on my dress? Oh, you foolish widow, why did you ever let this happen!*

She could feel his cock slide between her thighs, the shaft pressed lightly against the still-tingling lips of her pussy. She was breathing deeply, still bent over the wooden railing. The hand holding her wrists loosened its grip, but Olympia made no effort to move her hands from the small of her back.

Olympia's feet were together, with the stranger's legs on the outsides of hers. When he withdrew, the slide of his cock between her legs — touching her sensitive thighs just above the tops of her stockings — prompted a low, passionate sigh of discontent to escape her lips. Though she immediately silenced herself, since it would never do to let this man know just how much pleasure he had given her, she heard him chuckle low in his throat. With his hands on her hips to hold her steady, he eased his pelvis forward once again, intimately sliding his cock — the rigidity of which had diminished only slightly since unleashing a torrent of semen — between her thighs again.

A post-orgasmic shiver went through Olympia's voluptuous body, and another sigh worked it way out of her soul. Never in her life had she experienced such forceful climaxes, or so many in so short a period of time.

She moved her hands slowly until her palms were against the hitching rail, and she eased some of her weight off her stomach. As she did this, the stranger tossed her dress and petticoat to cover her bottom and legs.

Now what do I do?

There was nothing in Olympia's previous life experience to prepare her for this moment. What was the proper course to take? Strand up straight, turn around, and politely inquire as to the identity of the man who had just tossed her over a hitching rail and fucked her?

She heard disappearing boot heels clicking against the cobblestone walkway. The wearer was moving swiftly, but not running.

And he was going back *into* the manor.

Unless he was a servant, the stranger was, like Olympia herself, one of Lady Darcia's honoured guests.

Olympia pushed herself slowly to a standing position. Her legs felt weak, and she was a bit lightheaded. Both physical ailments, if one wanted to call them that, she attributed to the frequency and force of the climaxes she had experienced.

Cautiously, she touched the hair at the back of her head, and grimaced when she felt sperm. As best she could without completely destroying her coiffure, she smoothed away the semen, wiping the gooey and cooling cream from her thumb and fingertips onto her petticoat, beneath her gown where it wouldn't be seen. Beneath the skirt of her dress, she could feel more semen cooling, clinging to the fabric of her petticoat. It seemed to Olympia that the stranger had a very powerful, voluminous climax, and she uncharacteristically gave the credit to his orgasmic largesse to her own allure, as though she alone could inspire such a release.

Hurried footsteps—this time sounding like slippers instead of boots against the cobblestones—drew Olympia's attention. Her heart stopped for a moment. Had someone discovered what she'd just done? The last thing in the world she wanted to do was to somehow justify what had just happened. How could she even describe what had happened during the previous ten minutes? She didn't understand her own behaviour, so how could she possibly get anyone else to understand it?

But the footsteps ran parallel to where Olympia stood, and when she saw a shadow pass near the rear doors of the estate, she recognised the flash of green as Lady Darcia's gown.

A smile touched Olympia's lips. Lady Darcia, in a *ménage a trois* encounter with two men from the stables. It seemed to Olympia to be so very gauche...and erotic!

* * * *

At twenty-nine, the Duke of Tasley, was a man who prided himself on never losing his sense of logic and reason. Even when he was thoroughly intoxicated, he never lost his equilibrium, either mentally or physically. And though he'd led a life of profligate excess when it came to women, he always maintained a certain detachment, a degage casualness that let his lovers know he was in bed to give pleasure and to receive it, but he wasn't in any bed permanently. Colby was a man with an excess of sexually willing women in his life, and he took full advantage of the bounty.

So why had he stalked Olympia Whyte, and forcefully taken his pleasures with her? Though he was experienced enough to realise that she had climaxed because of him, the fact remained that her allure had stripped him of his civility and turned him into something feral...and dangerous.

As he neared the rear doors of the estate, he paused a moment, inhaled deeply, then let the breath out in a long, hissing sigh. He closed his eyes and in his mind the image of Olympia's lovely face was as clear as if he was looking at her in person. He saw the startling violet eyes that shimmered with amusement when he said something clever, and the full-lipped mouth that he hadn't kissed but desperately wanted to. He saw the rounded mounds of her breasts, temptingly put on display in her fashionable

Grecian-inspired gown, and the dramatically sweeping curve of her hips that had played with his libido like a dangerous drug.

But most of all, he saw a beautiful woman who wanted nothing to do with him because he was a man engaged to be married.

With the casual disregard of marriage vows typical of his class, Colby felt it utterly ridiculous that Olympia should let marriage get in the way of their having an affair. Most of the women he slept with were married. Being a practical man in matters regarding sex, he knew that a married woman — particularly a woman who had married into a sizeable fortune — was less likely to create a fuss when he decided to end their affair.

He sighed again, opening his eyes to make the young widow's image go away. For months now, Colby had been unable to get Olympia out of his thoughts. Several weeks earlier, when he was with Lady Penelope Fitzsimmons, a voluptuous woman who had let Colby know that he could have her anytime, anyplace, and in any manner that he wanted, he had taken her up on the offer. But to his horror, as he was making love with Penelope, he found himself fantasising about Olympia. The two were about the same height, and both possessed blatantly feminine curves. It wasn't a great leap of the imagination for Colby to think of Olympia as he had sex with Penelope.

But it was the first time he'd ever had sex with one woman while envisioning another. Olympia had created a precedent — and Colby didn't like it at all. His neatly ordered world had a moment of spontaneous chaos, and what frightened the duke most of all was that he had been powerless to *stop* the chaos. For a man who had arranged his life precisely to his liking, a man to whom ducal privileges were second nature, such chaos was a major threat to his peace of mind.

He sighed once more, shrugged his powerful shoulders beneath his finely tailored cutaway jacket, and came to the conclusion that what he needed most to banish Olympia from his thoughts was bourbon. The only question to be answered now was just how much bourbon would be necessary.

He had nearly reached the steps leading up to the rear doors when a figure moved silently out of the shadows ahead. As a powerful businessman in the world's most dynamic city, Colby had made plenty of enemies over the years, in London and elsewhere. Enemies were the price a man paid for being successful, and it meant his senses were always attuned to danger. When the figure stepped out of the shadows, Colby's first instinct was to draw the slender, stiletto-bladed dagger that was hidden inside his right boot.

"Easy, my friend. I mean you no harm."

Colby recognised the voice. It was Prince Mallory.

"In that case, I mean you no harm as well. Now if you will please excuse me, I'm already late for an appointment with a decanter of bourbon."

Colby stepped closer, and when Leland moved to his left, he could finally see the handsome young man's almost delicate features: the slender nose, the mouth that turned upward at the corners as though in a perpetual, sardonic grin, the arched brows. Though not predisposed to seeing beauty in men, Colby discovered he was not immune.

"She never said a word," the prince stated matter-of-factly. He smiled then at Colby's startled reaction, his teeth gleaming white in the moonlight. "She didn't make a sound the entire time you were fucking her. Except to moan, of course, when you made her come." His smile broadened. "She seems incredibly responsive...but then, you'd know better than I."

Colby's first instinct was to use his fists. It was a common reaction for him, and one that had gotten him into trouble in the past. The fact that there was a witness to his barbarous actions with Olympia was shocking, but not as threatening as the awareness that Leland intended to use this information. But for what end?

After several seconds of silence, Colby blandly replied, "I don't know what you're talking about."

"Let me refresh *our* memory." Leland took a half-step closer, and when he spoke, his voice was just loud enough to be audible. "Just a few moments ago you grabbed Olympia Whyte from behind, you bent her over a hitching rail by the carriage house, and you lifted her skirts to expose that delicious-looking ass of hers. You then proceeded to fuck her into an orgasm, and showed the good sense to not climax inside her. Rather gentlemanly of you, especially under the rather...um, shall we say *vigorous* ?circumstances of the encounter?" His smile was devilish. "Yes, vigorous is a suitable word to describe what you threw at her."

Though he was unaware of it, Colby's right hand clenched into a fist. He was only slightly taller than Leland, but he was significantly more powerfully built. He outweighed the prince by two stone or more, and all of it was muscle. In a fistfight, Colby's victory was all but assured.

The duke replied, "It seems you've been slinking around in the dark." A muscle ticked in his jaw. "Nasty habit, that. It's the kind of thing that could get you hurt."

Colton relaxed his right hand. Prince Mallory had a well-documented reputation for sexual excess and business acumen, but not for violence nor blackmail.

"Actually, for a myriad of reasons, I've spent much of my life in shadows." Leland's piercing silver-blue eyes glittered like wet jewels in the moonlight. "Over the years I've met the most interesting people in shadows. You never know who or what you'll end up seeing. Tonight is evidence of that, now isn't it?"

In an icy tone, Colby asked, "Why did you come outside?"

The prince's smile was charm itself, and Colby understood then how men and women were susceptible to seduction by this dashing rogue. "I want to get to know Olympia more intimately, of course. I had hoped to talk to her privately. She seems to have certain doubts as to my character."

"She knows your character quite well. She just finds it lacking."

The tip of Leland's tongue moistened his lips, and Colby experienced a surge of desire course through his system, unprecedented in that it had never before been caused by a man. An aura of sensual wickedness seemed to surround the prince, and no matter how much Colby wanted to ignore this inarguable fact, his body and libido refused. Every move, every gesture made by the prince, seemed to promise illicit ecstasy and unimaginable carnal delights.

"I had intended on using charm to woo the lady," Leland continued, his voice velvety smooth, like an aural caress that trailed lightly along the duke's spine, like the fingertips of a lover. "You chose to use the methods of a barbarian. Not my style, I'm afraid, though I can't argue with the results. Olympia never made a sound the entire time you were fucking her. Well, at least not any sounds of protest, though she did moan and sigh in a way that a beast such as yourself should find quite flattering." His eyes narrowed in assessment. "Though I must confess, after seeing your performance, I do find myself quite curious as to what it would be like to be ravaged by you."

"You can think whatever you like, but guard the way you use your tongue." An overwhelming urge to be *away* from Leland gripped Colby. The dark-haired young man represented a dangerous masculine allure the likes of which the duke had never before experienced. And that allure, quite frankly, frightened him to the marrow of his bones. "Now if you'll excuse me, I'd like to get back to the banquet." Colby took a step to the side, and Leland moved quickly to block his path. "You have a beautiful face, so don't press your luck." Colby's voice was a venomous whisper. "You wouldn't be the first young blade whose nose I've flattened."

The prince's eyes flicked down to Colby's clenched fists, then lifted quickly to meet his gaze. He angled his head slightly to the side, his expression that of a mischievous imp despite the seriousness of the threat he'd just received. "So, what would you rather do, my barbarian friend—fight me…or fuck me?"

Chapter Three

Colby's hands moved as quickly as a striking cobra. He grabbed the lapels of Leland's cutaway coat, determined to bodily toss him aside. The slender prince reacted instantly, grabbing Colby's wrists, stepping back and turning away at the same time. Colby, though heavier and stronger, momentarily lost his balance. Together, the two men stumbled away from the stairs leading up to the estate's rear doors, disappearing into the darker shadows near the ornamental shrubs.

Despite his natural athleticism, Leland backpedalled clumsily, nearly falling, getting stopped by the solid surface of the estate's marble foundation. Colby, still clutching onto the prince's lapels, collided with the smaller man.

They stopped wrestling, their struggle ceasing as quickly as it had started. Colby, several inches taller than Leland, looked down into the prince's silver-blue eyes that shone wetly in the faint moonlight, then down at that moist, sensual mouth that had suddenly proven to be such a temptation.

"Damn you," Colby whispered. "You're the Devil incarnate."

"The hell you say?"

The faintly mocking tone was still there, and it infuriated the duke. "Someday somebody's going to mess up that lovely face of yours. Then where will you be?"

"Perhaps lucky enough to be standing in the shadows with some high-borne barbarian?"

Colby never really intended on kissing Leland. He simply wasn't the type of man who did such things with other men. But the prince inspired urges too strong to resist, and when their mouths came together, it was a bruising, punishing kiss. Colby leant into him, pressing the younger man against the marble wall, his powerful hands crushing the embroidered fabric of Leland's navy blue lapels.

It was an intoxicating kiss for Colby, and searing lust spiked through him, streaking towards his groin. He lessened the pressure against Leland, then tested the young man's mouth with the tip of his tongue. When Leland's lips parted, Colby explored his mouth more deeply, more intimately, with his tongue.

Colby's mind was in a whirl. He was not a man who allowed anyone to taunt him. Some men liked him and other men hated him, but all men were sensible enough to not test his temper. The prince had teased him, but rather than using his fists to get his revenge, Colby was now kissing Leland, their tongues dancing with precision even though this was the first time their lips had touched.

A soft sigh filled with passion reached Colby's ears. It took a moment for him to recognise that it was Leland who had made the sound. He lifted his head, ending the kiss.

"Damn you," Colby said, still whispering, though now there was much less fury in his tone. "Why the hell did I just do that?"

"My God, do you ever know how to kiss!" The words came out a bit breathless, the prince seemingly awed by what he had just discovered. Leland's hands slipped inside Colby's coat to caress the duke's hard-muscled chest. His fingertips sought out responsive nipples through the crisp, white silk of Colby's shirt. "I'm not the Devil, nor any of his minions. And I'm certainly not godly. But if you kiss me like that again, I'll likely think that you are." His right hand slipped down the front of Colby's body, not stopping until his palm was pressed against the swiftly growing bulge in the duke's breeches. Leland's eyes widened dramatically. "So soon? My beautiful barbarian, your powers of recovery truly amaze!"

The fingers measuring his erection added fuel to Colby's burning desire. He felt overwhelmed by the lust that Leland inspired, the feeling so unique that Colby wondered if somehow he had been drugged.

Colby dipped his head to once again taste Leland's lips. This time, when their mouths touched, the waiting lips were parted, and it was the prince's tongue that was exploring Colby's mouth. A low-pitched, groaning sigh of passion rumbled out of Colby's chest as he felt himself tumbling headlong into a new world of sensuality. As he kissed Leland, sucking on the young man's tongue, he felt the buttons of his breeches coming unfastened. It wasn't long before the placket of his breeches fell forward, and his flaring erection, fully formed and pulsing with virility, sprang free.

Straightening, Colby ended the kiss. He looked down at Leland, aroused by the young man's beauty and enraged at the prince's propensity to inspire unbridled lust. Leland could infuriatingly make Colby simultaneously feel powerful and helpless.

Leland's fingers curled around the shaft of his cock, and for a moment Colby's eyes closed as surging desire emanated outward from his groin. He sucked in his breath and unconsciously held it for several seconds. The hand on his erection began moving slowly back and forth while twisting, and Colby's hard flesh reached full extension.

Uncurling his fingers, he released Leland's lapels. His palms turned to press flat against the prince's chest. Then, with deliberate sloth, his hands inched upward. Their gazes met as countless questions remained unspoken in the weighty silence that surrounded them. As a long-fingered hand moved smoothly along Colby's arousal, the duke's hands slipped around Leland's neck.

"I know you'd like to strangle me," Leland whispered in the darkness, a faint smile curling his lips, "but that's not the only thing you'd like to do to me, now is it?"

Colby's emerald green eyes gleamed with fury and lust, and a muscle twitched in his jaw. He bent low to kiss Leland once more, though briefly this time. His pushed the fingers of his right hand into the prince's unfashionably long, coal black hair at the top of his head.

"Down," the duke said through clenched teeth. "Down, damn you!"

With his back to the marble estate, the prince slid until he was on his knees in the grass.

"Beautiful," Leland whispered, stroking Colby as he cupped the heavy, low-hanging testicles in his other palm. "You're absolutely — "

Colby stopped him from saying more. The warm, moist breath against the head of his cock was far too arousing for him to be patient. With a thrust of his hips, he buried his erection in Leland's mouth, silencing any further words of praise. He did not stop his initial plunge until he was pressed tightly against the back of the prince's mouth.

"Fuck!" the duke whispered as Leland drew a firm, wet suction on his cock.

The hair entwined in his fingers was as silken as any the duke had ever felt. The warm lips and frisking tongue, as enticing as any he'd ever experienced. He spread his feet a little wider apart so as to be at exactly the right height, and began pumping his hips, sliding his cock in and out of the prince's mouth with a slowly increasing tempo. Looking down, it was shockingly erotic to watch his erection sliding deep into the mouth of one of London's most infamous rakes. Leland's soft moans, and the occasional sputtering noises emitted when Colby thrust too deeply, heightened the duke's pleasure.

"Deeper," Colby growled, pushing between the prince's lips until the crown of his cock was wedged tightly against the back of Leland's mouth. "Take it all."

Despite his proficiency in such matters, the prince was incapable of swallowing Colby whole. When the breath gushed from the prince's lungs, Colby withdrew quickly, experienced with lovers trying and failing to take all he had to offer. He smiled in the darkness. Irrationally petty-minded, he felt he'd achieved some small victory over the prince.

Colby looked down into Leland's upturned face. The prince's gaze was locked with Colby's as he lewdly flicked his tongue against the slitted tip of the saliva-moistened erection. With Leland's ebony hair still wrapped around his fingers, Colby gave the prince's head a quick, punishing shake. It was a threatening gesture meant to dominate, meant to enforce the prince's submission. The prince's answering moan signalled his willingness to be dominated.

The sounds of hurried, soft footsteps caused both men to freeze. In an instant, all of Colby's newfound fears of being caught sexually with another man bloomed instantly to life in his chest. He put his left forefinger to his lips to indicate the necessity of silence. Both men were mostly concealed in shadows, but they were less than twenty feet from the rear doors to the estate. Colby had been caught *in flagrante delicto* on several occasions in the past, but he'd always been caught with a man's *wife*, never with the man.

The moving figure that had nearly made Colby's heart stop beating turned out to be Olympia Whyte. He watched the movement of her voluptuous curves as she ascended the steps, holding her skirts high, her glorious breasts bouncing and swaying with her hurried movements. She looked neither right nor left as went up the marble steps and disappeared back into the estate.

Only when the door closed behind her did the duke finally resume breathing.

When he looked down, Leland was looking up with a wicked smile curving his much too kissable lips. Colby realised the prince's reputation for simply not caring what anyone said or thought of him was richly deserved.

"You're utterly without shame," Colby whispered before filling the prince's mouth with his erection once again. "Now finish."

A short time later, after ecstasy built upon ecstasy and the pressure to explode could no longer be suppressed, the duke's powerful body shivered as the lust raced through him. Though he had climaxed only a short time earlier with Olympia, he released a floodtide of sperm against the prince's frisking tongue. When he was empty, his chest heaving as he breathed deeply, Colby unlaced his fingers from Leland's hair, then took a faltering step backward.

He could hardly believe what he had just done.

"You are the Devil," he whispered.

Still on his knees, the prince replied, "And you're a brute and a barbarian. And just so you know, I'm yours whenever you want me." His grin suggested he was only too willing to introduce the duke to carnality that he'd never known. "However you want me." His gaze dropped to the duke's hands as he tucked himself back into his breeches and began fastening the buttons. "Now don't you think we'd better get back inside before Lady Darcia sends out an expedition to find us?" He sighed, looking up into Colby's face. "There's the very real chance, my barbarian friend, that you've spoilt me for anyone else."

* * * *

Someone in this room made love to me an hour ago.

Olympia looked at the half dozen men standing near the fireplace, each with a brandy snifter in one hand and a cigar in the other, chatting quietly among themselves. To a man, their tailoring was faultless, their style impeccable. The impact of Beau Brummell, the regent prince's extraordinarily influential good friend, on style among the haute monde was in full effect. At Lady Darcia's insistence, the men and women did not segregate into separate rooms when the meal ended. However, just because all the dinner guests remained in the same room, that didn't mean the men and women mingled. All the men were on one side of the room, and all the women on the other.

After a moment, Olympia amended her initial thought with, *No, it wasn't making love. It was…fucking. For the first time in my life, I was thoroughly and completely fucked — and my orgasms were more powerful than ever because of it. My God, how does Darcia handle it when she's making love with two men at once?*

A tiny shiver slithered along her spine.

"Olympia, my dear, what are you thinking?"

Drawn from her thoughts, Olympia gave Darcia a sheepish smile. "Nothing."

"Nothing? It must be something because you just had the strangest expression, and unless I'm very much mistaken, you're blushing. Well, you're quite flushed, anyway." She raised a single, slender eyebrow. "If you've finally decided to entertain a gentleman caller and you haven't said a word to me about him, I'll be terribly disappointed in you, my dear."

"Errant thoughts," Olympia replied, having no intention of confessing her recent history of voyeurism. "Perhaps later in the Season I'll consider making a change to my social state."

"I've watched the way the men have looked at you," Darcia said, keeping her voice low. "It would be good for a young woman like you to take on a lover, and there are some of the finest studs in all of London in this very room. All you have to do is let your intentions be known, and you'll have more offers than you'll know what to do with."

Uncomfortable with the conversation's topic, Olympia took another sip of champagne and emptied her flute.

"Let's get you another," Darcia said quickly, ever the gracious hostess. "Have you noticed how Count von Krueger has been looking at you? He's back on the marriage market since the death of his wife, you know."

Olympia shook her head, sending the matching curls of auburn hair swirling at her temples. "That man is definitely not a possibility for me. As I understand it, he had six children with his wife, and he has another four or five with at least two different mistresses."

"Men of the *Ton* have always had children on the side," Lady Darcia replied dismissively. "I have few illusions and even fewer high-minded expectations regarding gentlement of my set." She sighed ambiguously. "What about Leland? He has title, more money than you could ever possibly spend, and he's exactly your age."

"The prince is a rake whose most noteworthy ability is to make straying husbands as happy as their straying wives. How on earth does he manage that, I wonder?"

"Don't wonder too long, my dear. What about the Duke of Tasley?"

"A rogue who happens to be engaged to Francesca LeMorneau." She nibbled on her bottom lip. "He dislikes Francesca now, and he's not yet married. I shudder to think what his emotions will be once she's living at Tasley Manor. Francesca cares not one bit for anyone but herself."

"Forget about Francesca, and think about the duke, why don't you?" Darcia gave the young widow a frown. "My dear, you've been celibate far too long. You're too beautiful to remain that way — and besides, you'll become dull and morose if you don't take a man, even if it's just on the sly."

Looking at her friend brought on the memory of seeing Darcia romantically entwined with the two men in the carriage house, and a rush of warmth flooded her pelvis. What would it be like to simultaneously have two men to pleasure and be pleased by? Though Olympia desperately wanted to ask an assortment of intimate questions of her friend, she couldn't possibly admit to earlier playing the voyeur.

She took a moment to look around the room. One of the men in the room had grabbed her from behind, bent her over a hitching rail, then fucked her without saying so much as a single word. Who could have done it? The remarkably virile Count von Krueger?

There are several men in this room who could have done it. And why didn't I make a sound while it was happening? He didn't threaten me, didn't do a thing to keep me quiet. He just knew what I would do…knew what I wanted…knew what I wouldn't do…did he know that I would come?

"I think I'll have another glass of champagne after all," Olympia stated emphatically. Her petticoat was scratchy against the back of her right thigh, where the cum had dried in the cotton. "Darcia, you're the finest hostess in all of London. Your banquets are *sooo* entertaining!"

Chapter Four

Francesca LeMorneau put her fists on her slender hips, and without raising her voice declared hotly, "Goddamn it, Daddy. I want to live in Tasley Manor, and I want to live there *now!*"

Claude LeMorneau sighed and looked out the window of his sitting room. He'd had this conversation with his headstrong and wildly impulsive daughter before. Curiously, she always talked about wanting to live in Tasley Manor, but never said anything about living with Colby Beldon, the Duke of Tasley.

"Would you please be more careful in your choice of words? Sometimes you sound like you've come straight from the dockyards." His tone was long-suffering, and obviously didn't help Francesca's mood. "Perhaps if you were more ladylike, the Duke of Tasley would be more inclined to have a speedier wedding."

"What you should say is: Perhaps if I was *less* ladylike, the duke would want to marry you." She issued a bitter laugh. "I'll fuck him and give him a son, but the instant he has his heir is the last time he'll ever touch me."

"Oh, how I hate it when you use language like that!" He was nearly shouting. Though by nature an even-tempered man, Francesca had a profoundly negative influence on him. "And please tell me you haven't told him of your plans for celibacy." His tone softened considerably, and his face blanched. "Have you?"

"I'm not stupid, father." Her tone indicated she didn't think favourably of her father's intelligence.

"Well, if he got you pregnant, then he'd have to marry you fast as a clipper ship."

"Colby's fucked more women than he can remember," Francesca explained. Her father cringed at her coarse word for fornication. "Once I lose my virginity to him, I'll lose a lot of my appeal. Trust me, I know the duke and his ilk better than they know themselves. I'll make him marry me before I'll let that rutting goat in my bed." She shivered visibly. "Does he really have to stuff that thing up my guts?"

"Without that marriage, all my plans for the future will be for naught. Once you're the duke's wife, it'll open a thousand doors that now are closed to me." He shrugged his shoulders and looked out the window again. "Would it be so bad to"—he searched for a word less crass than the one his daughter had used—"let the duke have your virginity before marriage? If he got you pregnant, that would guarantee a speedy wedding, and you wouldn't have to touch him ever again."

"Awww!" Francesca growled, her slender hands clenching into fists. "Daddy, he's a man! Once he fucks me, he may never want to fuck me again! Men like Colby live for new conquests!" She laughed softly. "I enjoy saying the word 'fuck,' I just have no intention of doing it more than absolutely necessary. Understand this, dear father — once I am married and produce the required male heir, I shall forever be known as a duchess, and I will never again allow myself to be touched." She smiled triumphantly. "Best of all, I will have access to one of the largest private fortunes in all of England." She made a derisive sound in her throat. "I've thought this whole thing out very carefully. Your assistance is hardly necessary."

"I carefully arranged that wedding with the dowager duchess," Claude explained. "I suggest you either learn some patience and wait for the Little Season, or you get yourself pregnant." His eyes narrowed and took on a hard, objective glint as he looked at his daughter. "The more he thinks about the union, the less enthusiastic he may be. Many debutantes have tried to rein in the Duke of Tasley, and all have failed."

With escalating anger, the virgin replied, "Sometimes you think so small, Daddy! Please leave now. He'll be coming to see me very soon." Like an actress on a stage, she smiled prettily and said, "I must repair my mood to be my loveliest when he arrives. Men are swayed by their first sight of a woman."

Whenever Francesca got angry, she had an unattractive habit of clenching her teeth. A year earlier she'd glimpsed her reflection in the mirror when in such a rage, and when she saw the cords in her neck sticking out, the ruddiness of her complexion, and the pinched and nastily thin slash of her mouth, she promised herself then and there to never let anyone — other than the servants, which she didn't really consider real people anyway — see her angry.

* * * *

"She's in the sun room, Your Grace."

Colby gave the young chambermaid a smile, and the girl blushed. She was the newest of Francesca's servants, and he found her presence a bit surprising. Francesca usually didn't like to have attractive women anywhere near her. A debutante, Francesca knew that the only acceptable competition was no competition at all.

He followed, enjoying the sway of the chambermaid's hips. When she stopped outside the slightly open door to the sun room, Colby came to a stop, treated the girl to one of his more charming smiles, and muttered, "I don't suppose you'd consider hiding me from Francesca, would you?"

The girl grinned and blushed, looking away quickly. Colby hoped that Francesca wouldn't be too cruel to the girl. Francesca's history of treating her servants abominably was well-known.

He stepped into the sun room. Francesca was sitting in a chair near the open windows, looking delicate and pretty as ever. Her golden blonde hair was pinned up perfectly, with tendrils falling down her temples in artful disarray. In her morning clothes, her prim white blouse was buttoned to her throat, and her skirt and jacket were an off-cream colour. She looked pale and lovely in the sun, naturally poised though she was not a true-born debutante of the *Ton*. Her father had made a hasty exit from France at the tail end of the revolution, avoiding the guillotine where so many of his brethren had not.

"Good afternoon, Francesca," the duke said as he crossed the room.

She smiled at him as though somewhat surprised to see him. Colby knew it was an act because she had summoned him with a letter.

"Good afternoon, Your Grace," Francesca replied, giving him a pretty smile that held just a hint of pointless flirtation in it. "I'm so glad you've come to see me today."

The chambermaid had followed Colby into the room. Francesca looked at the girl and said in a dictatorial tone, "Bring the duke some tea." She looked at him and asked, "Or perhaps you've care for something a bit stronger?" Her tone was ambiguous as to whether 'something a bit stronger' appealed or appalled her. "The choice is yours."

The thought of fortifying himself with some whisky to deal with his fiancée wasn't the worst thought of the day, but he rejected it just the same. "A bit early for me," Colby said, dissembling only a little as he took his chair at the small table where Francesca was seated. "I'd appreciate some tea."

Francesca turned to the servant girl. "And bring some of those small cakes that the cook made this morning." She patted the back of Colby's hand. "You'll love them. They're delicious."

Pausing a moment to study the young woman seated with him, Colby wondered what was really behind Francesca's friendly demeanour. Not for the first time, he questioned the wisdom of his mother, who had arranged his marriage to the LeMorneau family.

"Don't look at me that way, darling." Francesca pouted prettily. "Sometimes you can seem so cold."

"What did you want to see me about?"

He saw her react to his blunt question. She was taken aback, but only for an instant. "You never use any soft love words with me. And don't tell me you're no good at love words. I've heard too many stories of the ladies you've made swoon. I harbour no naive notions of what manner of man you were," she paused, and the smile that suddenly curled her lips suggested a secret victory, "Before you met me."

The right side of Colby's mouth pulled upward in a half-smile. His sex life was an open secret within the haut monde, and given the rate at which gossip circulated among the debutantes and married ladies of the social set, he was quite certain that Francesca was well versed with his carnal activities.

"Love words, Francesca? You really don't want love words, now do you?"

"What fiancée wouldn't?"

The chambermaid showed up with a fresh pot of tea and a cup and saucer on a serving tray. Colby waited until he had a cup in front of him and the girl had left before he turned his attention back to Francesca.

"What is it you want?"

"Civility."

"I've always been civil with you."

"Let's not argue." She folded her slender hands and placed them in her lap. "I asked you to come here because I want to talk to you about our wedding. It's only loosely scheduled for the Little Season. I think we could push that date forward by weeks, or even months."

I'll bet she's out of money. She loves to gamble, but she's lousy at it, thought Colby, wondering who was holding her markers.

"It's early July now," Colby explained. He was hellishly curious as to why Francesca was impatient about the wedding. "I've agreed to a wedding in the Little Season — between September and mid-November. If we push the wedding date ahead, then every tongue is going to be wagging, and you're not going to like the tenor of the gossip." He looked into her eyes. She looked back with brow furrowed in confusion, but he could tell she was feigning innocence. "Everyone is going to think we're getting married early because you're enceinte. But you didn't need me to tell you that."

He watched as her blue eyes turned to chips of ice. "Don't tell me what I know. And since when did you ever care about what anyone said?"

"Are you pregnant, Francesca? Is that why you need a quick wedding?" It didn't seem a likely event to the duke, but he couldn't resist asking.

"Of course I'm not, you impossible man!" Her small hands clenched into fists briefly before she relaxed them in her lap. "I'm pure. You know that." She looked up into his eyes. "You *do* know that I'm a virgin, don't you?"

The urge to taunt Francesca was strong but it was also small-minded, and Colby tamped it down, but with some difficulty. "Yes, I know you're a virgin. What I don't know is why you're so insistent upon getting married to a man you clearly do not want in your bed."

"Darling, our marriage will be perfect for both of us. You need a wife, and you need an heir. I'll be the perfect hostess for all the social affairs required of a man of your power and influence, and you know that. My father has a thousand plans in the works. Once we're married, you and Daddy will conquer London, he says."

A faintly amused smile touched Colby's lips. It wouldn't particularly surprise him if her father was behind the push for an early wedding.

Francesca sighed with weary resignation. "Colby, if sex is so all-fired important to you, I'm yours."

This prompted a full smile from the duke. "You'll forgive me if I'm not terribly aroused. Your entire lack of enthusiasm doesn't exactly set my blood to boiling. But you needn't worry. I won't take you up on your offer. I'm not short on bed mates."

"I'm serious, Colby. You *can* have me." When the duke chuckled dismissively, Francesca's face went pale. She squared her shoulders and cleared her throat, a gesture she invariably made just prior to making an announcement she felt was of profound importance. "I know you'll never be faithful to me, so let me be honest with you. I'll give you a male heir, but I'm telling you now, the minute you have your son, that's the last time you'll touch me. You can sleep with those sluts you seem to find so amusing, I suppose, but you *must* be discreet. I won't let you flaunt your indiscretions." She cleared her throat. Her eyes never strayed from the tall man. "You need a wife who understands the necessity of putting forth the proper appearance. I fill that requirement perfectly. Admit it, we'd be perfect together. You don't want to touch me any more than I want to be touched. If you married a woman you loved, you'd crush her heart with your shameless promiscuity." Her gaze went up and down over the duke very slowly as though measuring the man with new vision. "And one more thing, I'm going to need a wet nurse."

"Oh?" Colby lifted his brows.

"I'll fuck you as often as necessary to give you a son, but you're delusional if you think I'll let some baby feed off me." A shiver went through her, and her lips curled unattractively. "It disgusts me to think of some baby sucking on my breasts like an infantile vampire." She paused for several seconds, and when the duke didn't reply, she added, "I mean it, Colby. I mean every word I said."

"I don't doubt that for a second." Colby rose to his feet, now towering over his seated, delicate, cold-blooded fiancée. "Our marriage was arranged between my mother and your father. I wasn't happy about it when I first found out about it, and I'm not happy about it now, but I also understand that sometimes there are obligations that mustn't be shirked. We'll get married during the Little Season...or not at all." He turned and took a step towards the door, then immediately turned back to the ashen-faced woman. "Perhaps you can think about a price. You can blame me for the marriage not going through. You can say about me whatever you want. Think of a price, Francesca. You could end up with a lot of gold, and still keep those thighs of yours clamped shut."

He turned on his heel and walked out of the sun room before his opinion of Francesca sank even lower. He had known all along that she was a bloodless virgin, but her outburst had shocked even him, who had almost no favourable opinions of her. Women of the *Ton* had never been known for their maternal instincts, but Francesca was not simply indifferent to the role of mother, she was openly hostile to it.

As he stepped through the front doors to the LeMorneau estate, Colby banished Francesca from his thoughts. Tonight he would see Olympia again, just as he had seen her almost every night since their encounter in the shadows at Lady Darcia's. He wouldn't see her alone, unfortunately, but he would be part of a group that would stroll through the walkways of Hyde Park.

Adding to his anticipation was the awareness that Prince Leland would be there. Since their fevered encounter two weeks earlier, the handsome prince had been playing hell with Colby's peace of mind. A hundred times he recalled how erotic it had been to push the prince to his knees to feel the taboo pleasures of receiving fellatio from a skilled and enthusiastic practitioner of the sensual art. But since that time, though he'd seen Leland often, he hadn't been able to have a private moment with the prince.

As he stepped into his private carriage, Colby felt his cock start to harden once again.

He pulled the gold watch from his waistcoat pocket and opened it. It was barely twelve-thirty, and he wasn't expected at Hyde Park until six-thirty or seven. It would be a long wait, but he was enjoying the anticipation of seeing Olympia and Leland once again.

* * * *

"What gown will you be wanting?" Missy asked.

Olympia turned towards her elderly maid, pursing her lips. "You decide for me."

"Are you expecting a special man in the Park? Someone you want to notice you?"

Standing in her chemise, petticoat, and short-stay corset, Olympia turned away from Missy towards the mirror. "Maybe," she said after a moment.

"Maybe yes or maybe no? There are two types of maybes when it comes to men, m'lady. Who might this gentleman be?"

"I don't really know. There are so many dashing men in carriages going around and around Hyde Park, and they're all from the best families."

Missy smiled merrily, and her eyes nearly disappeared behind folds of flesh. "If you want to be noticed, let's go with the new turquoise gown that Mrs. Saxby done for you."

"The Saxby?" Olympia replied, a bit shocked. Elizabeth Saxby was one of the most famous modistes in England, her services in much demand among the ladies of the *Ton*. One only wore a Saxby for special occasions.

"The very one," Missy declared. The gown was of the finest Chinese silk trimmed in white lace, and its décolletage was perhaps the most daring and yet flattering of Olympia's collection. "Nobody but me an' Miss Saxby seen you in that dress. If it's attention you want, you'll get it tonight in that gown. And we'll put you in new gloves and slippers, too."

Olympia smiled. Missy had been with her for years, and after the death of Olympia's husband, she had been gently and not-so-gently hinting that it was time to get out in society again.

Chapter Five

"You look utterly ravishing tonight, my dear," Col. John Newton said, smiling down at Olympia, his dark gaze lingering on her exposed bosom. He bent low, put his lips near her ear, and added, "And the day will come when I'll be the one to ravish you."

"Oh, you!" Olympia replied sotto voce, and made a playful motion as though she would jab the handsome officer in the immaculate red uniform with her parasol.

Before she could say more, both Colby and Leland turned their attention away from each other and towards her. Their scrutiny made it impossible for her to speak privately to the colonel without being overheard.

Olympia gave the men a smile, and when they went back to their quiet conversation, she murmured under her breath to the colonel, "You really mustn't say things like that."

"Why not?" His eyes flicked in the direction of the Duke of Tasley. Olympia could tell the colonel disliked Colby.

When he turned his gaze back to her, his eyes weren't quite as teasing as they had been earlier. "It's true, you know," he said in a serious tone. "I've had my eye on you for longer than you could know. I couldn't do anything about my feelings earlier, of course, because you were married. But you're no longer married, my dear, so that means you're available" — his eyes narrowed and his voice lowered intimately, his tone intense—"and that means you're *mine*."

A shiver went up Olympia's spine at the last comment. Lately, the colonel had taken almost every conceivable opportunity to let Olympia know that he was something more than just an ardent suitor. His advances had become more openly bold and less couched in socially acceptable mannerisms...since the dinner party at Lady Darcia's.

He could be my mystery man, Olympia thought, recalling how her body had shamelessly betrayed her on that night, when she had been bent over a hitching rail and ravaged by a stranger. *He's strong enough to have been the mystery man, and he certainly has the personality of a man who simply takes what he wants.*

"I've been patient with you, my dear, but don't imagine that I'll be patient forever," the colonel continued. "When your husband was killed, it was only reasonable that you should spend a year in mourning. But he has been gone for nearly two years now."

"I-I made it known that I'd need two years to recover from my loss," Olympia replied, hardly speaking louder than a whisper. "I made that very clear. I haven't been misleading with you."

"And I've seen the fetching looks you've been giving to that insufferable prick, Prince Mallory. That'll have to stop immediately."

"Oh?" Olympia asked, raising a slender eyebrow. Despite the almost universal subjugation of women to men in society, she never responded well to commands from suitors. In a tone tinged with sarcasm, she asked, "Am I really forbidden to smile?"

"The man," Col. Newton's lip curled derisively, "is the very embodiment of dissoluteness. There's hardly a matrimonial bed in the *Ton* that he hasn't been invited to. Apparently he likes to entertain both members of a marriage."

"Yes, I've heard his skills are much in demand," Olympia said, aware of how her observation would rankle. "With the prince being the man he is, that means my smiles are all for naught, since I am a widow. The dissolute prince can't possibly be interested in me as I can fulfil only half of his desires." Olympia saw the flash of annoyance colour Col. Newton's dark eyes, but she refused to be intimidated by his mood. Still rather irked by his presumptuousness, she couldn't resist twisting the knife a little more. "If I'm going to get back into society, then who better to practice my long dormant skills of coquettery with than our own darling Leland, Prince Mallory himself? By your own admission, he's immune to me."

"You mock me."

"Yes, I do."

Coldly, the colonel replied, "Some day you won't."

She saw it then, mostly hidden but still recognisable there in his eyes—suppressed violence. The colonel was not accustomed to anyone standing up to him, most certainly not a woman. Olympia was thwarting his wishes and not showing the deference and respect he felt he deserved, and this was an offence he refused to tolerate. Another shiver went through Olympia, and fear knotted her stomach. Though earlier she had been open-minded about the possibility of Col. Newton being her mystery lover, she now hoped that he hadn't been the man.

Laughter drew Olympia's thoughts away from the colonel. Lady Darcia walked into the room, flanked on either side by Colby and Leland. Her laughter was open, without guile, and as Olympia looked at her friend, she once again remembered how erotic it had been to watch her being pleasured by two men simultaneously.

"Olympia, darling, what is all that whispering about?" Lady Darcia called out, clearly enjoying being the centre of attention with the two handsome men. "Come closer and defend me. These rascals have me outnumbered."

Two men isn't too much for you, dear friend! I've seen that with my own eyes!

Pleased to have an excuse to step away from Col. Newton, Olympia wedged herself between Lady Darcia and Colby.

"Excuse me, Your Grace," she said, smiling up at Colby, "but my friend has requested that I rescue her."

"Has there ever been a more misunderstood man than the Duke of Tasley?" he replied with an expression of theatrical sorrow. A deep dimple formed in his right cheek when he smiled a moment later. He put out his elbow, and Olympia slipped her arm around it. "I'm as harmless as a lamb."

"Ha!" Olympia chided. She gave his arm a playful squeeze, and was suddenly conscious of how the side of her plump breast pressed against the solid surface of his biceps. "There isn't a woman in all of London who is unaware that the Duke of Tasley is *anything* but harmless."

Leland said, "She's got your number, old fellow. Her brother was right when he said you weren't up to scratch with his sister."

"In Nigel's opinion," Colby replied, clearly not offended by the comments, "there isn't a man this side of heaven worthy of his sister." He chuckled lightly, looking from Leland down to Olympia. "And for once, your brother and I are of a similar opinion." He eased her hand from around his arm and extracted his pocket watch. "But I'm afraid that a previous engagement makes it impossible for me to stay longer. My good friends, if you would all please excuse me, I'll be off."

The abrupt departure of the Duke of Tasley surprised Olympia, and for several seconds she watched his retreating figure as he headed towards the long line of carriages on the western edge of Hyde Park.

"That man is a charmer," Lady Darcia said, slipping her arm around Olympia's. "It's easy to understand why he has the reputation he has."

"The man's a barbarian," Leland chimed in. When Olympia and Darcia reacted, he smiled warmly and added, "A beautiful barbarian, but a barbarian nevertheless."

With a sly grin touching her lips, Olympia said nonchalantly, "Well, being a barbarian isn't necessarily all bad."

"And this from the woman who let it be known that she wouldn't be socialising for at least another year?" Lady Darcia replied, giving Olympia's arm a squeeze. "It seems like I should stick close to you, my dear. I get the feeling your life's more interesting than mine."

Not likely! Olympia thought, then blushed guiltily upon remembering the licentious pleasure she'd taken in voyeurism. *I don't take on lovers two at a time!*

* * * *

Leland watched the taut trembling of Olympia's breasts as she laughed, then looked away and squeezed his eyes tightly shut for several seconds. Olympia's bosom drew his gaze with an almost mystical force, and the young prince's cock was already half-erect and threatening to grow to full stature. If he couldn't get his thoughts directed *away* from her enticing charms, it would be impossible to hide the erection trapped inside his breeches.

"Is something wrong?" Olympia asked in a low voice.

"Not a thing," the prince replied. He patted the back of her gloved hand resting on his forearm. "I had something in my eye, that's all."

Col. John Newton, walking to Leland's left, made a derisive snorting sound and said, "You've got a weak constitution, that's what it is. If you were in my outfit, I'd make a real man out of you, a true soldier."

A muscle flickered in Leland's cheek when he clenched his jaws, his contempt for the colonel ratcheting up several notches. It was bad enough watching the Duke of Tasley flirting with Olympia, but to see a cretin like Col. Newton looking at her hungrily and talking to her as though she was already his possession, was simply outrageous to the prince.

"My constitution's perfectly fine, Colonel," Leland replied in a droll, faintly condescending tone—one that the prince had perfected while still in his teens. "The only skills you might teach me are of the killing kind, and that hardly strikes me as necessary for someone of my," he looked directly into the colonel's eyes, the challenge undisguised, "station in society."

Simultaneously, Olympia and Darcia uttered a short, startled gasp, and Leland felt a strange sense of victory go through him. He had publicly let the distinguished Col.

Newton know that he most definitely was *not* a member of the peerage. No matter what his rank in the British Army, and no matter how successful he was in battle, there were doors which would always be closed to the colonel that were opened wide for Prince Mallory.

When he saw Olympia turn her face away so that the colonel couldn't see her smile, Leland knew that he'd achieved a great victory—and the day would come when he'd have to answer for publicly humiliating the colonel.

"And on that note, since violence would be an unfortunate ending to such a lovely evening," Leland continued, completely ignoring the glowering colonel as he bestowed his charm upon Darcia and Olympia, "I bid you ladies good night. I hope to be blessed by your companionship once again very soon."

He gave a quick, short nod to the women, then turned and walked westward, his spirits soaring. Though Col. Newton hadn't intended it, he had given Leland the perfect opportunity to insult him, and an excuse to leave the soiree at precisely the right time.

There was a bounce to the prince's step, and he had to consciously slow his stride so as to not draw attention to himself. Though long accustomed to being the epicentre of attention—and sometimes of matrimonial conflict—in almost any social setting, and infinitely comfortable playing the starring role on the stage of life, tonight of all nights, the prince had to be as anonymous as possible.

He looked to the west. The sun would be down within minutes, and with it, the foot traffic in Hyde Park would come to an end. The carriages would continue to circle slowly for another hour, or so, as the last of the haut monde made sure they were seen by those who counted.

The prince approached the line of carriages, most of them open landau models, all of them black and highly polished. Among the *Ton*, a family's carriage was one of numerous indicators of just where in the highly stratified London society a person belonged. Showing up at Hyde Park in a muddy carriage, or worse, a carriage showing the wear and tear of time, would be a black mark that would not easily be expunged.

As important as the carriage were the horses. Though many of the carriages were two-wheeled models requiring only a single horse, the larger landau and cabriolet models harnessed with two horses made it necessary to have a matching set. The cost of a good coach with a matching set of geldings exceeded the incomes of only the wealthiest Londoners.

Leland spotted the big, fully enclosed, four-wheeled coach among the significantly smaller landaus and berlins. One coachman, a broad-shouldered man who had the appearance of also holding the duty of bodyguard, sat at his post in the front seat of the carriage, reins for the four horses held negligently in his beefy hands. Another coachman, much smaller but wearing identical livery, was polishing the black lacquered side door.

"Gentlemen, I assume you've been expecting me," Leland said as he approached.

The smaller coachman smiled and nodded. "Yes, my lord. The duchess said there's champagne on ice inside and that you're to quench your thirst, but keep the curtains closed."

A faint smile touched Leland's mouth. He had gone to see Lady Darcia three days earlier and together they'd schemed and planned, but only now, as he was about to get into her magnificently appointed carriage, did he really feel confident about the plan.

As the slender, young coachman opened the door, Leland decided that Lady Darcia deserved a truly special gift for helping him this evening. He had planned all along to give her a pair of emerald earrings, but now he was thinking she was deserving of that pair of blue-white diamond ear bobs he'd seen at A.J. Carruthers Jewelry on Freemont Street.

With the side curtains down, the interior of the large carriage was very dark, but not so dark that Leland didn't realise instantly that he was not alone.

"Hello, Leland. I'd ask what brings you here, but I'm sure I can guess."

"Hello, Colby. I didn't expect to see you here."

The carriage was one of the roomiest that Prince Mallory had ever seen. It was larger than any of the three he owned. He had the option of sitting beside Colby near the rear of the carriage, or on the rearward-facing seat near the front.

"Lady Darcia has champagne on ice, but I've got a flask full of rather smooth single malt whisky." The duke's teeth flashed white in the darkened interior. "It would seem that Lady Darcia's got a devilish sense of humour."

"It would seem so." Leland took a seat beside the duke. It was the closest they had been together since their feverish encounter in the shadows two weeks earlier.

Colby asked, "What do you know about this?"

"A couple of days ago I went to the duchess and told her I'd like to have some time alone with Olympia. I've spent plenty of time with her in groups, but I haven't been able to speak to her alone." Heated memories of being kissed by the duke streaked through his memory. His scalp tingled at the thought of Colby grabbing him by the hair once again and forcing him to his knees. "My style of seduction is rather less forceful than yours, I'm afraid. Mine requires conversation, and perhaps some flirtatious looks that tease the imagination. Hard to accomplish in large groups."

"Lady Darcia sent a note stating she wanted to talk to me," Colby said. "When I arrived at her estate, she was cryptic, not saying much other than she would be escorting Olympia here tonight, and her coachmen would let me in. The idea of surprising Olympia appealed to me." His eyes narrowed as he looked at Leland. "I didn't plan on you."

"As I recall, you didn't plan on me two weeks ago, either." The prince's eyes had adjusted to the darkness, and he could see Colby much more clearly now. The duke's nearness, his ostentatious virility, tantalised Leland's libido. "I guess some surprises are more entertaining than others."

The duke reached into his pocket and extracted a silver flask. He took a hefty swallow, coughed softly, took another swallow, then offered the flask to Leland.

"Does Olympia know you were the man in the shadows?" Leland took a sip of the whisky and was pleased with the crisp burn of the liquor as it went down his throat. "I've been watching her these last two weeks when we're all together, and I've seen the way she's studied us. I don't think she knows."

Colby shook his head, and rubbed his eyebrows with a forefinger and thumb. "She doesn't know." He sighed. "Tonight I intend to tell her."

"Tonight I intend to seduce her." When Colby's gaze met Leland's, the prince smiled wickedly. "Perhaps, my beautiful barbarian, I should take a page out of your book. Lord knows, the lady responds to a commanding touch." He caught his lower lip between his teeth and nibbled flirtatiously. "And so do I...as you well know."

Leland could sense the duke's anger and desire. He could almost smell it. He had taunted Colby before, which resulted in a forcefully physical response that didn't disappoint the prince. But the duke wouldn't be the first man to trespass into forbidden sexual territory, only to never again sail in those waters...and Prince Mallory wasn't finished with the big man.

Not yet. Maybe not ever.

Chapter Six

With her arm looped through Darcia's, Olympia approached the duchess's enormous, well-sprung carriage with a light-hearted sense of a well-spent evening coming to an end.

"What do you think of Colonel Newton?" Olympia asked, recalling how he had spoken to her more luridly, and in a more dictatorial manner, than ever before. "He's always made his intentions known, but tonight he was more demanding than usual."

"When he flirts, he can be quite charming. But don't be fooled by his smile, my dear. Men do not reach his rank in the military without being as much politician as soldier. He doesn't so much as comb his hair without having an ulterior motive." Darcia adjusted the strap of her bonnet beneath her chin, then took Olympia's arm once again. There was a mischievous curl to her lips, but Olympia resisted the urge to ask what had put it there. "I have it on good authority that not only does the colonel already have children with mistresses, he's also got a fierce temper, and he's known to use a dagger or his fists if he doesn't get everything that he wants."

"I suspected as much."

"For now, try to not think about the colonel. By the way, have you been formally introduced to my coachmen?"

It seemed a rather strange thing to ask. As servants, the coachmen would be expected to know the names — and especially the titles — of all of the duchess's friends, but they would never be referred to by name by any guests. In London's stratified social structure, a servant seldom warranted a proper noun.

Odd…unless, of course, Darcia saw me watching her in the carriage house with those gorgeous men. This angst-ridden thought was followed almost immediately with, *Don't be a fool! She doesn't suspect me. More likely, she's just playing a little game to amuse herself.*

"I'd like to meet them," Olympia said, determined to appear casual, though the thought of looking directly into the eyes of the men she had witnessed behaving so brazenly with the duchess was altogether unsettling. "They seem very competent."

Darcia smiled softly and replied, "Yes. Quite. Amazingly so, in fact."

As they approached the carriage, the coachmen flanked the door in preparation to greet their employer. Olympia tried to banish from her thoughts the memories of seeing them in all their virile glory, their cocks hard and glistening moistly in the pale lamplight as they pleasured the duchess.

"Good evening, Your Grace," the larger and older of the two coachmen said sharply.

"Good evening, Addison." She made a motion with her gloved hand. "Olympia, these are my coachmen, Addison and Jacob."

The shorter and more slender of the coachmen touched the tip of his tricorn hat, "It's an honour, m'lady." He bowed even more deeply than Addison.

Darcia asked the younger man, "Is everything set?"

"Yes, m'lady. We've followed your instructions to the letter."

"Excellent!" She patted Olympia's hand and gave it an affectionate squeeze. "Now into the carriage, my dear," Darcia said, an undercurrent of amusement laced through her words.

"You have so many smaller carriages, why did you choose this leviathan? It needs four horses just to move it along." Olympia put her foot on the bottom run of the entrance ladder. "Must cost a bloody fortune to maintain your stable."

"Some things are worth the expense. Now in you go."

The sun had nearly set, and if it wasn't for a single candle, placed in a holder attached to the front wall of the carriage, the interior of the carriage would have been black as coal. As it was, there was enough light for Olympia to clearly see Leland and Colby sitting in the rear seat of the carriage.

"What the—?"

"Oh, do take a seat, Olympia." The duchess's glee was undisguised now. "I suspect you're all rather curious as to just what is going on, so it's probably best if I do some explaining." She sat in the front seat and with her parasol tapped the ceiling. "Let's go, Addison!"

As the enormous private carriage began rattling down the cobblestone street flanking Hyde Park, Olympia, Colby, and Leland all demanded answers of Lady Darcia.

It wasn't until she had gotten the three to stop talking that she finally began giving them answers.

"Leland, please do be a dear and pour me some champagne." When she received the glass, she took several small sips, and Olympia suspected the delay was intentional to heighten the suspense. The duchess loved being in the eye of a storm. "Two weeks ago, I held a dinner party which all of you attended. Since that time, I have learned several things from various members of my staff that, I must say, has surprised me greatly." She turned to Olympia and smiled. Olympia folded her gloved hands in her lap to keep them from trembling visibly. "You see, my dears, I am a widow, and until quite recently, my life had very little excitement in it. Then, rather by accident, I took a lover. Actually, two lovers."

"Two?" Leland exclaimed, his grin handsome and lascivious. "Lady Darcia, have I been negligent in never seeking your charms?"

"Prince Mallory, my lovers are my coachmen. They're quite enough for me, though I thank you for your interest. It does this old heart good." She turned and looked at Olympia, remaining silent for several agonising seconds. "I enjoy my lovers two at a time...as you well know, don't you, dear friend?"

Olympia put a hand to her mouth, her eyes opening wide. *Oh, God! She knows! She knows I was hiding in the shadows watching her!*

Speaking slowly and precisely in the dimly-lighted carriage, the duchess explained how she had deduced the scandalous events of a fortnight earlier.

After admitting that she enjoyed *ménage a trois* encounters that must be hurried and are semi-public, the duchess explained how she had returned to her own dinner party and found that several guests had gone missing. At first she wasn't particularly interested in this seemingly inconsequential fact. To tell bawdy jokes, the men often retreated to the billiard room or stepped outdoors.

But then, later in the evening, she noticed that Olympia was a bit flushed, and though she was trying to appear casual and elegant, her agitation could not be disguised. This nervous disquietude was what first drew the duchess's suspicion. What prompted Darcia's focused attention was when she noticed on Olympia the irrefutable evidence of sexual intercourse.

"We were talking," the duchess explained, "and you turned to look around at the men in the room. It wasn't just a casual glance. It seemed to me at the time that you were searching for someone, or something specific. I wasn't sure exactly what you were searching for, but you were looking at the men much too acutely. And it was while your back was partially turned to me that I noticed," her smile broadened naughtily, "a drop of semen on the back of your neck."

Olympia's hand once again flew to her open mouth. The blood drained from her face.

"Don't try to deny it, my dear. I know what a man's come looks like when it's fresh." She took Olympia by the wrist and lowered her gloved hand. "Did you watch me with Addison and Jacob?"

Seconds passed before Olympia finally nodded. "I-I wanted to talk to you privately so I followed you from the dining room. I didn't mean to…spy."

"I wondered if you'd seen me." She made a passing motion with her hand as though to wipe away the social infraction. "It wasn't until later, when Colby asked if I might arrange a private meeting with you, that I began to suspect him as your lover. But then Leland had been showing you such attention this past fortnight, that I began to suspect him." She spread her hands out, circling them. "And then there is the matter of what might or might not have happened beneath the windows of my pastry cook's bedroom. You see, she is not on duty during the evenings, only during the day, so on the night of my banquet, she was in her room...and do you want to know what she heard?" The duchess laughed softly. "I was making inquiries of my servants to learn what they had seen, and it was clear that little Penelope had something to tell me, but was too embarrassed to put what she knew into words. Her face was red as a beet when I finally got her to say that she heard someone giving someone else fellatio right outside her window."

Some of the story made sense to Olympia, and some of it did not. She did not know whether it was Colby or Leland who had ravaged her in the shadows. For two weeks, the prospect of learning who had fucked her into such wrenching climaxes had caused her alternating bouts of anticipation and anxiety, but now that she could actually put a face to the actions, the reality of it was too lurid for Olympia to accept.

These people were dangerous. They were dangerous because they were alluring and charming and wickedly tempting. They understood the rules of a game Olympia now realised she had no business playing.

She had to escape. Now.

Olympia bolted for the door, determined to open it wide and leap out even as the carriage rolled on.

"Stop her, you fools!" the duchess snapped.

Olympia's hand was on the handle of the carriage door when Colby knocked her onto her hip on the thick wine-coloured Persian rug on the floor.

"Stop fighting!" The duke hissed as he took her by the wrists and twisted her arms behind her back.

It's him! It was the duke who ravaged me in the shadows! thought Olympia as, for the second time in two weeks, her arms were forcibly wrestled behind her back.

"Leland, use your cravat and tie her wrists! This vixen's not leaving until she hears what I have to say!"

* * * *

The Duke of Tasley's cock was already half-hard and making swift progress towards being a full-grown erection by the time he hauled Olympia off the floor. He sat on the back seat of the carriage while the infuriated widow squirmed on his lap, her hands securely bound behind her back.

"You've got to listen to me," he said, distinctly aware of the rounded globes of her ass pressing against his burgeoning penis. "What happened at the duchess's—I never planned for that."

"So it *was* you!" Olympia spat. "I should have known!" She made an indignant, huffing sound. "This is the second time you've put my arms behind my back, but at least last time you didn't feel the need to tie me up."

"Tonight I need more time," Colby replied, his tone more cool than his libido, every nerve in his body tuned to the erotic, tactile stimulation provided by the voluptuous woman on his lap. Olympia's full breasts in the low-cut décolletage were dangerously close to his face. He felt her bound hands against his torso, propitiously close to his sex. The awareness did nothing to slow the lengthening of his cock. "And since I don't trust you for a second to not try to run, I'll just leave you tied up for a while."

"Trust? Ha! You're one to talk about trust!"

It was at that moment he saw her eyes widen, and he knew she was now aware of his arousal. He smiled and said, "Yes, Mrs. Whyte, you excite me. Even more now than when I caught you fingering that sweet, little pussy of yours as you hid in the shadows and watched the duchess with her lovers!"

It was the duchess's turn to gasp and say, "You masturbated while I was with Addison and Jacob? Oh, dear, you are *not* the dried-up widow I was afraid you might be!"

"I've wanted you for a long time," the duke continued, "but you wouldn't have anything to do with me because I'm engaged." Surging lust raced through his system even as he struggled to calmly find the exact words for Olympia. "Even as we speak, I'm taking steps to rectify that woeful situation with Francesca."

"But you...you and the prince..."

"Leland and I have been talking." He looked at Leland, who was still kneeling in the centre of the carriage after having wrestled Olympia into submission, his tussled hair and missing cravat testimony to her high-spirited escape attempt. "I'll explain all of that later. But for now, what you need to know is that I believe we're a three-legged stool that cannot stand if any one of the three legs is removed."

While the widow hotly defended herself with a flood of words, Colby watched her mouth, remembering how much he had wanted to kiss her that first time when they were together in the shadows. And on the ensuing evenings, during the almost nightly gatherings at the duchess's, at Leland's grand palace, or at his own Tasley Manor, he had watched her lips as she talked and laughed — the lips he had never had the chance to taste, even though her exquisite charms had brought him to orgasm.

Olympia looked into his eyes and stated, "Oh, for God's sakes, Colby, do you really think the three of us — "

He looped his hand around the back of her neck and pulled down, pressing his lips demandingly against hers, silencing any further words of protest. The kiss was long and commanding, and the more Olympia squirmed in his lap, the more heated his blood became.

It took a full twenty seconds for Olympia's frantic struggles to begin abating. He held her tight with her shoulder against his chest, one hand to the back of her head, the other around her middle. Before the first kiss had ended, his prodigious cock had reached full extension, trapped within the tight-fitting confines of his black linen breeches, warmed and aroused by the delectable cheeks of Olympia's virgin ass.

When her struggles weakened, the duke tasted her lips with the tip of his tongue. She resisted for a second or two, then parted her lips. Colby's tongue eased into her mouth, gliding against her tongue. A low, throaty moan of desire came from the duke, and seconds later, a similar moan — though distinctly feminine — came from Olympia.

The kiss ended, but before Colby could say anything, Olympia flinched in his lap.

"What are you doing?" she demanded, the whispered words hushed as she looked at Leland.

"Nothing you won't like," the prince replied as he grabbed Olympia by an ankle, pulling her leg to the side.

"Colby! Leland! You don't understand! I don't do that! Lady Darcia, why are you just sitting there? Help me!"

Chapter Seven

Olympia tried to kick Leland, but his reflexes were lightning fast, and though he wasn't nearly as brutishly powerful as Colby, he was by any measure lean-muscled and very strong. When he grabbed Olympia's ankles and began to pull them apart, she struggled mightily but in vain.

"Trust me, you don't want to stop him," Colby said with a laugh, his breath warm against her cheek. He held her tight to his chest, a long arm around her waist. "The prince's tongue is ecstasy itself."

These were not the words that Olympia wanted to hear, though that didn't stop her body from responding favourably. She was shocked at her own wanton receptiveness to forbidden pleasures. Liquid heat rushed to the lips of her cunt. Her juices flowed freely. She tested the silk binding her wrists, found herself securely trussed, and her clitoris tingled even more because of her own defencelessness.

Leland spread her legs wide, crawling forward on his knees, pushing the hem of her gown and petticoat higher with his chest. He exposed her silk-sheathed legs up past her knees where the white silk garters encircled her thighs at the tops of her stockings.

"I'll bet you're delicious," the prince purred, his exotic silver-blue eyes shining wetly in the candlelight. "Fresh and sweet as a raindrop!"

Scream! Scream, Olympia! her better judgement silently cried out. But like a fortnight earlier, her well-intentioned thoughts could not be translated into action. The prince was wickedly arousing under any circumstances, but seeing his face — the handsome features finely chiselled, his mouth pink and moist and animated — between her thighs, his raven-black hair erotically contrasted with her white silk stockings, was a visual temptation that caressed Olympia to the core of her soul.

She looked towards the front of the carriage. If she thought she might find an ally in the duchess, such hopes were immediately dashed. Lady Darcia had pushed the neckline of her gown beneath her breasts to expose lust-hardened nipples, and she was watching the activities on the opposite side of her lavish carriage with the unblinking intensity of a true voyeur. She was slowly raised the hem of her gown.

"Ohhh... Please..." Olympia purred as Leland raised her legs even higher, spreading her ankles as he bent low at the waist.

She watched him kiss the inside of her left knee, his lips warm against her skin through the sheer silk, his hands like steel manacles surrounding her ankles. When the prince bared his teeth and bit her through the stocking, Olympia let out a shocked squeal of surprise and pain.

"Oh, m'lady, I do indeed intend to please," Leland said, then licked the area he had just bitten. "I'm going to please your pussy until your whole world turns inside out." He inhaled deeply through his nose, a bit theatrically, then smiled. "The scent of you makes my cock turn to stone!"

It was concurrently tawdry and wildly erotic to watch and feel Leland ease his moist, snakelike pink tongue far out of his mouth, then follow the edge of her stocking top with the tip of his tongue. He licked her naked thigh with a slithery touch that made the slick nectar of her passion flow even more freely to her labia. Olympia was almost dripping she was so aroused, so ready for whatever these men planned to do to her next.

Colby drew her attention away from Leland by forcibly turning her head, then pulling her in for another demanding kiss. His lips were feasting on hers, his tongue exploring her mouth, when Leland slipped her legs up over his shoulders, then planted a moist kiss on her pussy. Olympia flinched, whimpering softly as she sucked on Colby's tongue. A moment later, the prince's tongue spread the lips of her cunt briefly before making a slow circuit of her pussy. He licked up and down one pink sex petal, then the other, before finally grazing over her clitoris. Olympia began to understand why Lady Darcia took her lovers in pairs.

These men were powerful, dominating, and it was their command over her that fuelled her feverish excitement to incandescent levels. Though her loving husband had pleasured her with his tongue in their matrimonial bed, Olympia now realised his skills in the sensual arts were significantly inferior to the decadent prince's. Nothing her husband had done ever felt as stimulating as having the prince's tongue wetly caressing the lips of her cunt. *Nothing.*

As Olympia kissed Colby, her tongue dancing intimately with his, Leland teased and tormented her by repeatedly circling her clitoris with the tip of his tongue without ever actually licking the pink nub. By avoiding direct contact, he caused Olympia to squirm and tremble, shivering as she moved her hips, searching for the oral caress she had learned to crave in an instant.

Leland slipped his arms around Olympia's naked thighs, reaching between her legs until his fingertips were at her cunt. He carefully pulled the labia apart to expose the pink, sensitive inner tissue, then applied a series of licks and sucks with the skill of a connoisseur. Within seconds, Olympia was gasping and panting. All thoughts of "escaping" would have to wait until *after* she experienced the orgasm that was rushing towards her at a stallion's gallop.

While still holding her head with his right hand, the duke used his left to tug down the muslin décolletage of her gown to expose her breast. When he found her passion-elongated nipple and gave it a firm pinch and twist, Olympia moaned loudly, the sound of intemperate passion getting swallowed up in his kiss.

This is insanity, thought Olympia as she felt the swift, relentless tightening within her pelvis that signalled an onrushing climax. *I'm shameless! Only a shameless woman would be aroused by two men at once! I am so wicked! Truly wicked!*

The censorious thoughts did nothing to dampen the fiery lust consuming her body and soul. With each passing second she was bombarded by more sensations than she could comprehend. Her nipples were tight and tingling. Colby's kisses were intoxicating. The prince's tongue was a frisking, restless serpent that had been sent by the devil to strip her of any inhibitions she still clung to.

The duke ended his kiss, and Olympia opened her eyes. She blinked several times, pre-orgasmic and disoriented. It was difficult to focus her vision in the moving carriage's dark interior. On the opposite end of the carriage, Lady Darcia was entertaining herself. Her dress was up to her stomach, and her legs were spread luridly apart. On the plush leather seat beside her were her discarded above-the-elbow gloves.

Watching Lady Darcia's hand moving rapidly between her thighs caused a fresh surge of nectar to moisten Olympia's cunt.

Olympia had slid down a little on Colby's lap, and only now — with her climax just seconds away — did she realise that her hands, bound behind her back, were on the hard, throbbing shaft of the duke's arousal. She squeezed his cock firmly through his breeches, and in response she felt him pulse with lusty life. When Colby dipped his head and captured the crest of her exposed breast between his lips and began sucking hungrily, a myriad of emotions and sensations exploded like fireworks in Olympia.

She arched her spine as the spasms began. Strong, climactic surges went through her, followed by a series of lesser ones. Dancing across the passion-dazed surface of her consciousness was the fear that her skin would literally burst into flames.

When the contractions subsided, she felt weak and drained. She stammered, "P-Please…stop! I-I can't take any more."

The prince took his arms from around Olympia's legs as he lifted his head and shoulders, though he remained on his knees. In the pale, flickering candlelight of the carriage, his lips and chin glistened with the juices of Olympia's passion. His mouth was quirked in that self-satisfied, faintly imperious manner that was so much a part of the prince's personality. Seeing the prince on his knees between her own spread thighs, his mouth still shimmering from her feminine honey, was the guilty evidence that though she had been bound and helpless against his lusty advances, her traitorous body had responded with a greedy acceptance.

"Can't take any more?" Leland asked in a faintly mocking tone, his pale, slender fingers deftly unfastening the twin vertical rows of buttons holding the fall of his breeches in place. "I'm willing to bet I can change your mind about that."

With his placket unfastened, the cloth dropped away from his erection. He was generously endowed, and his cock was fiercely rigid, angling sharply upward from his loins. The flesh over the crown appeared so taut it seemed ready to split wide open. When Olympia saw the prince's arousal, a low moan worked its way out from her chest. She tested once again the silk cravat surrounding her wrists, and like earlier attempts, found that she was securely bound and would remain so until either the prince or the duke released her from captivity.

She'd had her climax, so now it was time for the prince's. And after that, there was the duke. A shiver worked its way through Olympia as she came to this awarenes.

"Oh…oh, God," she whispered as Leland moved closer. He rubbed the plump crown of his erection up and down over the entrance of her pussy.

She was not a virgin, but she'd never before witnessed a hard cock forcing the lips of her pussy to separate, never *watched* while she *felt* her body accepting a man's pulsing erection. As the prince began his slow invasion, Olympia involuntarily clamped her thighs tightly around his lean hips, as though trying to stop his forward thrust. As quickly as she had closed her legs around Leland's torso, she spread her knees apart. Olympia was a woman in a pitched battle…with herself.

The hard, slick slide of cock into pussy created the most blissful friction, eliciting tactile sensations that were significantly enhanced with voyeurism. Despite her earlier proclamations to the contrary, when Olympia watched the crown of the prince's cock forcing her pink lips to separate, then disappear into the smooth embrace of her femininity, all she felt was bliss. The upper surface of the unyielding shaft rubbed smoothly against her clitoris, her pussy still wet from his oral caresses.

"Tight," the prince sighed, sliding his hands around her curving hips to cup her buns, pushing the skirt of her gown even higher. His withdrawal was as slow and measured as his invasion. But when he entered her a second time, his lean hips pumped forward more forcefully, and he buried his entire length.

Olympia's mouth was open, but her eyes were closed as she concentrated on the feelings created by the prince's pistoning erection. He filled her completely, his length and girth thick enough to accept without either pain or a sense of "something lacking." Each forward thrust was a little harder, a bit more intense, than the preceding thrust. When his pelvis smacked against her own, it put the heavy mounds of her breasts in motion, sliding to and fro above the lowered bodice of her gown.

"Hurry along, my friend," Colby said. Though the words were cordial enough, his tone hummed with sexual tension. For good reason, the Duke of Tasley had never been known as a patient man, especially when his libido was involved. "If I don't free my cock soon, I'm going to pop the buttons of my breeches. Lady Olympia has bewitched me."

"As she has me," the prince replied.

Olympia gave the duke's imprisoned erection a firm squeeze. In response, he cupped her chin in his palm, angled her face upward and sealed his mouth over hers. She was sucking on his tongue when she felt Leland's moist, warm mouth fastened on her left breast. Her nipple burned with desire when the prince suckled.

I'm so wicked to enjoy this! I've never felt more helpless, nor more alive!

It was a jarring awareness to have while being buffeted by the prince's churning hips, his cock lancing deep inside her cunt with steadily increasing speed and ardour. To feel Leland's sharp teeth nipping at her breast while she lustily danced her tongue with Colby's was utterly disorienting to a woman who, prior to her encounter with the duke in the shadows near Lady Darcia's carriage house, had only made love to one man in her entire life.

The prince released her nipple from his oral embrace with a moist popping sound. His hands were tight on her lusciously curved hips. When the duke ended his kiss, Olympia looked at Leland. In the pale candlelight, she could see that his face was flushed with lust and exertion. His hips pistoned faster and faster, driving his cock between the pink lips of her cunt, filling her completely. She could tell that he would soon release his seed, and a tiny, still-rational part of her brain whispered that she should warn him to not climax inside her.

Whatever sense of reason Olympia suspected she still possessed vanished only seconds later when her clitoris, which was still highly sensitised from the tongue-lashing that the prince had so generously and skilfully administered, seemed to literally explode. The climax that shuddered through Olympia hit her with unexpected swiftness and shocking force. She started to cry out, but a wide-palmed hand clamped hard over her mouth to silence her. Her body trembled through a series of climactic spasms.

She heard the prince groan "Fuck!" an instant before he withdrew from her velvety embrace.

Leland stroked his detonating erection as streams of semen shot from his dusky-hued crown. The cum was thick and glistened lewdly white against the emerald green of her Saxby gown. The sight of the cream's presence on the exquisite fabric was both damning and erotic to a young widow frighteningly new to illicit pleasures.

"I've never...come so hard...in my life," the prince admitted between deep gulps of air, a weary half-smile on his lips. He squeezed the shaft of his cock firmly, working a final drop of sperm from the tip. He rubbed the pearl of cream off onto Olympia's auburn pubic curls. "I damned near turned inside-out."

Olympia wanted to say that she, too, had never come so hard. But since there was still a cravat tied tightly around her wrists, and because she was at least nominally trying to defend her honour by putting forth honest resistance against these men, she kept her silence.

The widow was aware of her own sexual hypocrisy, though she wished she wasn't. A lifetime of inhibitions weren't easily abandoned, no matter how persuasive a prince and duke could be.

Olympia's hopes of having time to collect her senses were dashed only seconds after Leland's climax subsided. The Duke of Tasley lifted her as though she weighed nothing at all. In a move that bordered on violence, he spun, depositing Olympia so she knelt on the floor of the carriage with her head and shoulders over the seat cushion. A moment later, his fall had been unbuttoned and an enormous erection was jutting out from his loins, fully formed and distinctly menacingly.

On her knees with her exposed breasts compressed against the leather seat cushion, Olympia asked in a whisper, "Again?"

She received her answer in a manner characteristic of the duke—with action. She felt the bulbous crown of his erection pressing against the lips of her pussy. An instant later, the duke's cock was thrust into her. She tossed her head up and uttered a short, high-pitched gasp of pain.

"Oh, God!" she whispered as the duke forced her to accept nearly all of his arousal. "You're just so…big!"

His withdrawal was slow, and with the next thrust Colby put an end to any words Olympia may have wanted to say. It was impossible to form words when her tender body was being forced to stretch to capacity to accommodate the length and width of the duke. His retreat allowed her to inhale quickly, but in the next instant he invaded again, this time fully. When his torso collide with the cheeks of her ass, and she felt the entire throbbing length of his cock filling her…Olympia gritted her teeth and began coming once again.

Could a woman die from too many orgasms in a single evening?

It was an intriguing concept for Olympia to consider. The climax prompted by the duke's brutishly thick cock was her fourth—or was it the fifth?—in a shockingly short period of time. For a woman accustomed to going months without experiencing a orgasm—and even then they were always self-administered—to suddenly be dancing erotically from the summit of one climax to the summit of another was a surreal experience. One of which she suspected mere mortal women weren't supposed to have firsthand knowledge.

Her eyes drifted shut as she began the slow descent from her orgasmic highs while still feeling the seesawing thrusts of her lover. Colby's hands, broad-palmed and powerful, were on the cheeks of her ass, holding her tightly. She felt the slap of his torso against her as he forcefully thrust full-length into her. She heard his rapid breathing as he laboured behind her, his unyielding cock advancing and retreating, advancing and retreating....

Time passed. Not much, but it was enough for her to wonder if she might not come yet again. But then she heard the leonine growl an instant before he withdrew, then felt the heavy splash of his passion's release. A weary, satiated smile curled her mouth as the eruptions rained down upon her. When she felt his cock touch her hands, she curled her fingers around the shaft and squeezed firmly. The last of the duke's slick, erotic discharge splattered into her palm and trickled between her fingers onto the small of her back.

As though from a great distance, Olympia heard a high-pitched moan, and knew that Lady Darcia had masturbated herself into another climax.

Chapter Eight

Olympia pulled up her left stocking and adjusted the garter high on her thigh, but didn't have enough energy to pull up the other stocking, which was crumpled around her ankle. She slumped back in the carriage seat sighing with a blissful combination of satisfaction and exhaustion. Her exquisite gown — the only Saxby she owned — was on the floor of the carriage, love stained beyond repair. Also on the floor were her chemise, petticoat, and underbust corset. The petticoat was stained in a fashion similar to the gown. The chemise had been torn in two, the victim of masculine impatience. There was also a considerable assortment of men's clothes, all hastily discarded and trampled underfoot.

Seated between Leland and Colby, naked save for the single stocking, Olympia purred kittenishly as she basked in the afterglow of multiple orgasms and an unprecedented *ménage a trois* more uninhibited and satisfying than she had thought physically possible.

She put a hand modestly between her legs, then crossed her other arm over her breasts in a futile attempt to hide their naked extravagance. Seated on the opposite side of the carriage was Lady Darcia, who was fully dressed, and smiling serenely with pleasure.

"I had so hoped this would work out well," the duchess commented. She used a tone of voice identical to one used to describe a pleasant tea party. "You're a lucky woman, Olympia, to have such handsome and virile lovers. If I wasn't similarly blessed, I'm afraid I'd be quite jealous of you."

The conversation's topic was unsettling for Olympia. The urge to deny the voluntary nature of her own actions was strong. She could say, and not without some justification, that she hadn't actually been a willing member of the *ménage a trois*. The duke and prince had, after all, wrestled her to the floor of the carriage when she tried to escape, and used a cravat to tie her hands behind her back.

"Never in my life," Olympia said softly, wearily, "did I ever think something like this would happen to me." She glanced at Leland and Colby, then looked at Darcia. "And I never dreamed I would come that many times. I never thought it was possible."

The duchess smiled knowingly. "It was a treat for me just to watch you." She sighed. "But, alas, there is only so much pleasure a woman can provide for herself, even if she's being given a beautiful performance from only a few feet away."

With the passion abating, Olympia's self-consciousness was returning regarding her own nudity. She started to lean forward, wanting to retrieve her petticoat from the floor, but Colby put his arm out to block her.

"Don't," he said quietly. There was a covetous quality to his tone. "I like looking at you." He gave her a rogue's smile. "And I'm not finished with you yet."

"Nor I," Prince Mallory piped in quickly.

As a compromise, Olympia crossed her legs at the knee, then folded her arms over her bosom. "How did you know that I would...?" she began, then stopped when the words became too embarrassing. She looked into her lovers' eyes before guiltily avoiding their gaze. "How did know that I wouldn't be able to resist you? How could you know that I wanted you both, when I couldn't even admit that to myself?"

The scrape of a boot against the cobblestones outside drew Olympia's attention. Once again she started to reach for clothing to cover herself, and once again Colby stopped her with his arm.

The door opened and Jacob, Lady Darcia's coachman and lover, stepped up into the carriage. Olympia felt her cheeks flame with embarrassment, but the handsome young man never so much as glanced towards the rear of the carriage.

"For Your Grace, as requested," he said with a dramatic flourish, placing a large wicker basket on the floor of the carriage at her feet. "Mrs. Davies wasn't too happy about being woken at this hour, but I gave her an extra half crown for her troubles, and she brightened right up. She's provided a nice bottle of port, along with whisky, cheese, sausage, and a loaf of bread from this morning."

"Excellent, Jacob. You never fail to perform miracles." The duchess's gaze was a bold caress. "Please tell Abbott that we'd like to continue our journey through the streets of London, and that I'll," she smiled, and its libidinous message was unmistakable, "attend to *his* needs later. Then hurry back to me." She glanced at Olympia before turning her attention back to the liveried coachman. "I have need of the pleasure you dispense with such enthusiasm."

"Yes, Your Grace. I live to satisfy your wishes."

Jacob left to do as instructed. Despite all that had happened during the past few hours, hearing Lady Darcia's bold declaration shocked Olympia.

"Dearest friend," Olympia said, trying hard to not sound critically judgmental, "are you really going to have the pleasure of that young man right here in the carriage?"

Lady Darcia nodded slowly. "If the sight of me offends you—though I know it does not—just look the other way. If not, you're welcome to watch, as I must confess that I rather enjoy giving a private theatrical show, if the circumstances warrant it." The handsome lad soon stepped into the carriage and closed the door. "Jacob, you naughty boy, get on your knees," the duchess said with mock sternness as she stretched her right foot out, toe extended. "You can start by kissing my ankle. I'd like my first climax to be caused by your tongue." She laughed softly as the boy began kissing and nibbling his way from ankle to calf. "We'll figure out what to do with that glorious cock of yours when the time is right."

The carriage was not well lit, and Jacob's back was directly to Olympia, which prevented her from actually seeing his giving the duchess cunnilingus. Nevertheless, just watching Jacob's head moving between Lady Darcia's pale thighs provided a voyeuristic thrill that caused Olympia to feel her own passions to once again begin to simmer.

The duchess's sighs filled the heated carriage, the sounds an illicit caress to Olympia's newly-freed licentious imagination. With her legs crossed at the knee, she squeezed her thighs together, and the added pressure against her clitoris caused her to issue a sigh. A moment later, when Colby slipped his hand between her legs and pulled to the side, she didn't resist, letting him spread her knees wide.

"*Yesss,*" Lady Darcia said through a moan, her head angled back against the padded backrest. "Right there! Just...just like that. Oh, yes, my darling Jacob. Just...like...that!"

So entranced was Olympia that she could hardly blink as the duchess lowered her bodice so that she could caress her own nipples. Without looking, Olympia uncrossed her arms and reached for her lovers. Leland and Colby were both fully aroused, their lusty cocks standing up in straight columns to fill her hands. She stroked her lovers, running her fists up and down over their lengths.

She looked at Colby and was only a little surprised to see that he was staring just as hungrily at the activities occurring on the opposite side of the carriage as she had been only seconds earlier. Briefly, jealousy came to life in Olympia's bosom before she tamped down the unwarranted emotion.

"She has lovely breasts, does she not?" Olympia asked in a whisper. She wasn't entirely certain she wanted to know the duke's answer. The past hours of intense lovemaking had made her possessive.

"Yes." He put a hand to the back of her neck, his finger sliding into silken auburn waves that had long since come loose from the pinned-up coiffeur she had begun the evening with. "But no lovelier than you."

When Colby began pushing Olympia down and to the side, she did not resist. Bending at the waist and twisting her upper body, she brought her lips to the plum-sized crown of the duke's erection.

"Don't you ever get tired?" she said with false censure, speaking to the lust-hardened flesh as though it was an independent entity separate from the man.

Colby chuckled, and when he put more pressure at the back of Olympia's neck, she dipped lower and captured the head of his cock in her mouth. Tightening her lips around the broad shaft, she drew a firm suction, her cheeks concaving as her tongue swirled against the tip.

Nodding up and down, Olympia let her mind wander as she pleasured her lover. How strange it all seemed that she should be giving fellatio to a handsome man while there were so many other people in the carriage with her! Actions and behaviours she would have considered unimaginable only a day earlier now provided the sweetest, most orgasmic pleasures.

After several more revolutions, she released Colby with a slurping sound, and sat upright in the carriage seat. On the opposite side of the carriage, Jacob was still on his knees, but judging from the way his right arm was pumping in short, herky-jerky movements, he was fingering Lady Darcia as well as licking her. And if the duchess's increasingly frantic moans and sighs were any indication, another climax was in the offing.

Twisting on the seat, Olympia bent low again, this time taking Leland between her lips, nibbling down the shaft until the crown pushed firmly against the opening of her throat. She bobbed slowly, feeling the manly flesh pulsing with strength and virility. When a salty drop of fluid seeped out, Olympia trembled softly, aware that what she'd been given was only a small sample of what would be hers when she'd administered more pleasure than the prince could withstand.

By the time Olympia was sitting upright in the carriage seat again, her eyes were glassy with lust. Though she had never before taken great pleasure in *giving* pleasure, she did so now. In only a handful of hours, her life had changed so completely it was difficult for her to remember the woman she had been. What kind of woman, she wondered, delighted in sucking on not one cock, but two?

Lady Darcia's wailing cry of climactic release drew a chuckle from the voyeurs in the carriage. While the duchess begged for young Jacob to stop licking her--she had murmured indistinctly about becoming too sensitive for continued activity--Olympia slipped off the seat, to kneel on the carriage's thick woven rug. She faced her men with a sensual smile curling her lips.

"Sit closer to each other," she said. When the men were hip to hip, she straddled their touching legs with her knees. Taking their solid cocks in her hands, she purred, "Such a bounty I have! It should be a crime for one woman to have *sooo* much."

She took turns with the prince and duke, sucking on one then the other, sometimes nibbling lightly with her lips, at other times drawing a firm suction, working the men steadily closer and closer to climax. When she sensed that Colby might soon unleash the torrent of sperm he released with each orgasm, she abandoned his erection and turned all her attention on Leland, licking and nibbling on his rigid penis, occasionally tucking his testicles between her lips to suck on them lightly, one at a time.

From above, she heard Colby say in a low growl, "Get down there with her."

A frisson of excitement went through her. Was she to share Colby's abundance with Leland? It seemed a truly wicked thing to do...but then, Olympia was quickly developing an appreciation for the truly wicked.

"Move over a little, precious," the prince said as he got down on his knees beside Olympia. "You're not the only one who enjoys what the duke has to offer."

* * * *

Col. Newton finished cleaning the last of two matching pistols, and set the weapon reverently down beside its mate on his desk on a soft cloth. The pistols were newly loaded in perfect working order, but if his rather rapidly evolving plans unfolded properly, he wouldn't need firearms. Still, it was always best to be prepared.

For the kind of killing the colonel intended, his razor-sharp, double-edged dagger would do the dirty work. It could slice to the bone and did its killing silently.

The colonel had killed several men already. There were those three Frenchmen his men had captured. They were low-ranking foot soldiers who spoke guttural French. They had thought it funny to call him a "British pig-fucker" and joke among themselves that he "got buggered by the crazy king." What they hadn't known was that Col. Newton spoke French quite well.

On trumped up charges of spying, he had them tried and convicted in a makeshift military court. For execution, he had them stripped naked to heighten their humiliation. The colonel put the nooses around their necks himself. One by one, he kicked the chairs out from beneath the trembling men. He left their corpses hanging in the tree as he led his soldiers out of the territory.

But killing three of Napoleon's poor soldiers wasn't the same as killing fellow countrymen. Furthermore, the men he intended to murder weren't just Englishmen — the Duke of Tasley and Prince Mallory were members of the aristocracy. The duke's bloodline could be traced back to the Norman invasion. The prince's genealogy was unbroken for several hundred years. Both men came from powerful families, and were powerful in their own right.

Men like that didn't die without a thorough governmental investigation.

The colonel smiled as he thought about the ramifications of getting rid of his competition for Olympia Whyte's affections. After two successful tours on the continent fighting Napoleon's troops, he was stationed in England now for the foreseeable future. Perhaps, if he positioned himself properly, he might be assigned to head up the investigation of the murders of the Duke of Tasley and Prince Mallory.

Wouldn't that be just so wonderfully ironic?

* * * *

"Isn't he huge?" Leland whispered almost conspiratorially, speaking only loud enough for Olympia to hear. He had his right hand wrapped around the base of Colby's shaft. Olympia's hand, much smaller than his own, was also around the pulsing shaft, more towards the dusky crown. "It's a good thing I didn't lose my virginity to him. He'd have torn me in two."

Olympia watched, hardly breathing, as the handsome prince leant forward and licked the taut knob. She could tell that he was pleasuring the duke in a theatrical manner, as much intending on providing a show for her as giving stimulation to Colby. When Leland opened his jaws wide, taking the hard flesh deeper, Olympia purred her approval, then wedged her face in between thickly muscled thighs. As Leland sucked, Olympia licked the duke's shaft, then began sucking lightly upon his egg-shaped testicles.

From the front of the carriage, Lady Darcia's panting gasps were punctuated with the slap of pelvis against pelvis. After her first orally-stimulated climax, her handsome coachman had freed his erection and was putting it to good use working the duchess into a libidinous frenzy. When Olympia looked in that direction, she was given the almost comical sight of Jacob's naked buns pumping furiously as he threw every ounce of energy at, and into, the duchess.

Releasing Colby from his oral embrace, Leland kissed Olympia's mouth softly, then said, "Are you ready for something special?"

The light in his eyes was mischievous, hinting at forbidden pleasures. A shiver went through her, and for a moment she closed her eyes and rested her cheek lightly against the duke's naked thigh.

"I-I'm not sure," she whispered. "This is all new to me. I've never..."

"Shhh," the prince replied, putting a finger to her lips. "Trust me. I know what you need."

Olympia hadn't drunk too much champagne that evening, yet when the prince spoke, she wondered whether she was intoxicated. It seemed as though her brain was spinning, all her thoughts and emotions in a chaotic swirl. Prince Mallory asked for her trust. Could she give him that?

As though answering her internal question, Olympia lifted her head off Colby's thigh, opened her eyes, and said to Leland, "Trust you? To be honest, I'm not sure that I do. But what I'm confident of—confident beyond question or measure—is that there isn't anyone in the world who knows more about giving pleasure to women than you two." She kissed Colby's thigh, licked it and tasted the tang of his perspiration, then sighed. To Leland she said, "My darling, decadent prince, there has to be some reason that so many couples want you in their bed. So, if you would be so kind, would you please teach me why you're in such high demand?"

Olympia was only a little surprised to see how readily Colby abdicated his dictatorial role and followed, without question, Leland's direction. While Lady Darcia moaned with pleasure, and her young coachman lover let out a low groan as he released his seed upon her stomach, the Duke of Tasley stretched his big, powerful body onto the floor of the carriage while grumbling about the costly clothes being crumpled beneath him.

"Now straddle his hips," the prince instructed, "but keep your knees beneath you with your bottom raised up a bit. Don't put your weight on him. You want to let him move beneath you."

She took the time to kiss Leland's mouth. Glancing towards the front of the carriage, she found Lady Darcia smiling serenely in post-orgasmic bliss while stroking Jacob's hair as she held his face between her breasts. Olympia lifted a knee over the duke's waist. He held his erection in one hand, aiming it towards her pink lips.

"Let him inside," Leland said in a purr, his breath warm against Olympia's ear as he moved into position behind her.

The prince slipped his arms around her body to give her heavy bosom a quick squeeze. Olympia looked down at Colby's face, saw that he was flushed with passion once again despite the times she had satisfied him already this evening, and with some difficulty resisted the urge to bend down sufficiently to give him a deep, tongue-entwining kiss. She hesitated because the conical crest of the duke's erection was pressing against her labia, and there was always a momentary stab whenever she took his steelish flesh inside.

"Ohhh!" she sighed when she felt her body being forced to open, to expand, to accept. "Your cock fills me so completely."

As the duke cupped her breasts and lifted one towards his mouth so that he could suck on her nipple, Olympia began bouncing slowly, raising and lowering her shapely hips to work the tingling lips of her cunt over more and more of his length. So great was the pleasure she received from Colby that she was hardly aware of Leland rummaging through the clothing on the floor of the elaborate carriage, mumbling something about needing to find his 'lotion'.

"You're too far away," the duke complained, abandoning Olympia's erect nipple in favour of her mouth. "It's a crime for me to be this deep inside you and not taste your kisses."

A short, joyous laugh erupted from Olympia's throat as she lowered herself onto Colby's powerful body, her breasts compressing against the heated, solid surface of his chest. Her tongue had just slipped between his lips to explore his mouth when she heard Leland exclaim, "Aha!"

It should have been sufficient forewarning, but passion had focused Olympia's perceptions to such an extent on the duke that she was only marginally aware of what had preoccupied the prince.

Until she felt the Prince Mallory slather a liberal amount of "lotion" onto her anus!

"Leland—"

"Shhh! My love, didn't I ask you to trust me? And didn't you give that trust?"

"No...I didn't."

The prince kissed her cheek, then shoulder, and whispered, "But you should have, and that's what matters." As Olympia sank onto the duke, taking the full length of his cock inside her tight sheath, she felt the prince's finger nudging, prodding, seeking entrance to her forbidden passage. "Let me have it." His voice was a narcotic that went straight to her pleasure receptors. Forbidden desires danced at the edge of her consciousness. She wanted the unthinkable, even if it frightened her. "Give it up, precious. You want me to have it."

"But I've never..." Her words were barely a whisper, equivocation ringing clear in each word. She shivered. "It'll hurt."

"Give me your ass." His tongue, warm and wet, swiftly traced the circumference of her ear. "Yes, it'll hurt...the kind of hurt that makes you come." He bit her shoulder lightly, his teeth sharp, hinting at pain. "Imagine having two cocks inside you at the same time. Imagine what that'll feel like."

She felt his finger slip past her resistance, the digit slippery with the prince's special lotion. The invasion, despite her virginity, was smooth and painless. The sensation of having a finger seesawing in her ass was unlike any she'd previously experienced. She whispered "Oh, God!" when he withdrew, then shamed herself by sighing loudly as the finger returned, sliding in even more deeply the second time.

Unconsciously, Olympia began raising and lowering her hips, impaling herself upon the duke's cock, taking pleasure in the upstroke nearly as much as when she slide down the shaft, feeling his strength and hunger filling her to capacity. As she enveloped Colby, Leland's finger pistoned between her cheeks, and the combined feelings of having men tantalising her pussy and ass simultaneously made her shiver with escalating passion. She squirmed in Colby's embrace, pressing her breasts tight against his powerful chest. She kissed him greedily, mashing her lips against his, sucking his tongue into her mouth.

A stab of pain went through Olympia when Leland thrust a second finger inside her, moved it with deliberate force, then added a third digit. The sensations going through her rapidly overheating body were dichotomous, in direct conflict with each other, strangely enhancing the effect of both. Pleasure and pain mingled, entwining to such an extent that she could not tell where one feeling ended and the other began. Colby's hard cock filled her cunt, gliding against her clitoris to send ecstasy coursing through her body. And at the same time, three slick fingers pumped hard and deep between the cheeks of her ass, stretching delicate tissue that had never before been used sexually.

Olympia experienced momentary relief when the fingers were removed, but almost instantly she had the prince on top of her, his naked chest against her back, the head of his cock nudging her tight, lotion-lubricated opening.

Wrenching her face aside, Olympia ended the kiss with Colby and was just about to tell Leland that she couldn't take him there — when he plunged deep into her bottom!

Olympia's orgasm hit her the instant the prince thrust between the cheeks of her ass. To have two gorgeous men filling her completely, thrusting hard cocks deep into her body fore and aft, to have the pain of Leland's erection pumping into her bottom while Colby's huge cock filled her pussy, was more than she could withstand without climaxing.

In the intellectual and emotional fog following a wrenching orgasm, Olympia was only distantly aware of what was being done to her. The hard, manly flesh continued spearing into her, forcing her to expand, to yield. The sounds of men labouring furiously, and the wet slap of perspiration-moistened flesh striking flesh, filled Olympia's ears. She felt the heat of Leland's breath and the pounding of his heart against her back as he groaned and huffed, plundering her bottom. Beneath her, Colby soon let out a loud growl. He arched his back, pushing deep into her. Then, with his hands on her hips, he held her up as he descended, withdrawing completely from her sheath. When he relaxed his arms, Olympia crushed down upon him, his freed erection trapped between their bodies as his passion was released.

Seconds later, with Leland still inside her and Colby's cock pressed against her abdomen, Olympia kissed the duke's sweaty shoulder. She could feel the men — *her* men — getting softer. Full consciousness, complete awareness of herself and her surroundings, returned to her slowly. Her body tingled all over, her ass throbbing a bit unpleasantly, her vagina pulsing joyously from vigorous use and multiple climaxes.

"How are...you doing?" the prince asked, easing his chest off Olympia's back as he withdrew from her bottom.

"I didn't die," Olympia replied. She felt both men become tense. With a smile, she added, "Try as you might, the two of you couldn't fuck me to death after all."

Lady Darcia laughed softly, drawing Olympia's attention, and murmured, "Dear friend, now we share secrets that must never see the light of day!"

Chapter Nine

The Duke of Tasley looked at the mantle clock above the fireplace in his office, saw that it was nearly three o'clock, and silently cursed himself. Most men of his social set were content with amusing themselves by spending their vast fortunes. The duke, like his father before him, believed that no man could oversee his numerous business interests as well as he.

Ordinarily, Colby took pride in his work and in the effort he put forward. His father had inherited a vast fortune, and over the years built it into an even larger one. Colby took his ducal duties with a seriousness seldom seen in the aristocracy, and took pride in his personal involvement in the expansion of the family's finances. But on this Friday, nearly four weeks since he and Prince Mallory had huddled in the dark carriage at Hyde Park waiting for Olympia to return with Lady Darcia, what he really wanted to do was shirk all of his responsibilities and go to his lovers immediately.

Leland and Olympia were already at the prince's lavish country estate, where the servants were accustomed to the master of the manor coming home for protracted periods of time with men and women in tow. Their loyalty to the prince was unwavering, though this sentiment, however genuine, was no doubt augmented by the extremely generous salary he bestowed upon his staff. The fact that Leland liked to bring home a wife *and* husband simultaneously was conveniently and self-servingly overlooked by maids and butlers alike, no matter what their personal opinion regarding such licentious conduct. Prince Mallory was well aware that money had a way of creating temporary blindness to iniquitous behaviour.

For four weeks the three of us have been together. A smile curled Colby's lips and warmed his eyes. *Only four weeks. It seems so much longer than that. Like I've been with Olympia and Leland my entire life. I went from bed to bed, not knowing that I was looking for Olympia and Leland all along....*

With his quill still in hand, Colby let his mind wander. Leland and Olympia now seemed to accept his leadership. Though he hadn't instantly recognised it, over the past weeks the duke had become aware that Olympia and Leland were looking for guidance in their lives, for a strong man to give them direction — and those were traits the Duke of Tasley had in abundance. Once he had taken the dominant position in the trio, Leland confessed that he no longer felt compelled to find an unending string of married couples to bring back to his estate. And Olympia had seemed to discover within herself a highly passionate and responsive woman who blossomed with confidence, sexual and otherwise.

For the duke, the once-unsettling fact of Leland's masculinity made less and less of a difference to Colby until finally it meant nothing at all.

The clock began chiming, signalling three o'clock. The duke sighed. He had to stay in the office until six o'clock. Only then would he be free to leave London and all his responsibilities behind so that he could spend two heavenly days with Leland and Olympia.

He would have his black Arabian mare saddled. She was a runner, and he could make much better time getting to the prince's estate on horseback than in a carriage.

When he was separated from Olympia and Leland, time meant everything.

* * * *

Col. John Newton was doing all he could to keep his temper reined in as he dealt with Claude LeMorneau.

"You wanted in on this business. You damned near begged me to let you buy in," the colonel said sharply, standing in Claude's sitting room, his hands on his hips as he glared at the frightened entrepreneur. "Now you're telling me you haven't enough gold in reserve to make your next quarterly payment. Let me advise you of something, my good man—if you fail to make your quarterly payment, you're out for keeps. And you can forget about getting back any of your previous investment, because that just isn't going to happen. If you're in arrears, you forfeit all previous payments."

A pasty-faced Claude LeMorneau held his hands out and almost shouted, "But that's not fair! I've already invested thousands of pounds!"

"You wanted in on initial shares of the British-India Tea Company, and you got in with your eyes wide open. Nobody begged you for money, and you knew exactly what you were signing on for. In order to get the tea from India to England and turn that tidy profit we're all waiting for, we have to lease the ships. That means quarterly payments from you, me, and everyone else who has a stake in the company."

Claude looked as though he would continue defending himself, but a cold-eyed glare from the colonel silenced further protests. It appeared that he might become physically ill at any second.

A great deal of Col. Newton's frustrations with Claude LeMorneau stemmed from the colonel's almost nightly soirees with Olympia Whyte. While several weeks earlier it had seemed as though there was some thawing in the voluptuous widow's attitude towards him, lately she appeared significantly more aloof. To stoke the fires of the colonel's anger even further, she appeared to find the conversations of Prince Leland Mallory and the Duke of Tasley to be witty beyond measure — utterly and unequivocally enchanting. Her laughter often rang like music through the early evening air at London's most famous haunt for those wishing to see and be seen, Hyde Park.

Considering the fact that the colonel had secretly modified a cannon to cause the "accidental" death of Olympia's husband, Col. Newton considered — and not without considerable justification, he believed — the woman to be his property. He had, after all, killed for her, and there weren't a lot of suitors who could honestly say that. To have Olympia, with her period of mourning now behind her, directing her laughs, her smiles, her quick-witted rejoinders, to men other than the colonel, was a horrific injustice and an indisputable miscarriage of The Way Things Ought to Be.

Turning chilly eyes upon Claude, the colonel asked, "You've been talking about business arrangements with the Duke of Tasley. What's become of them?"

Claude cleared his throat nervously. "As soon as my daughter marries the duke, I'll have a hundred new business opportunities." He smiled avariciously. Everyone in England knew of the advantages of marrying into the peerage, particularly in London. "With the Duke of Tasley as my son-in-law, the bankers are going to want be in my good graces. I'll be able to pick my projects and have the financing for then instantly." He smiled tightly. "The British-India Tea Company will be only one small source of gold for me."

"If that's the case, then you'd better get that daughter of yours married off fast, because you're running out of time." The colonel rose abruptly to his feet. He wouldn't be talked down to by Claude LeMorneau. "I don't care how you do it, but get the duke churched and do it quick." He half-turned on the heel of his brightly polished boot. "Have a talk with your daughter. See that she understands all that's at stake here, Claude. The Duke of Tasley's fucked a thousand debutantes. Maybe if Francesca isn't such a miser with that precious virgin cunt of hers, she'll be able to get him to commit."

* * * *

By the time Claude LeMorneau strode through the front doors of his house, he knew what action needed to be taken. His mind had been racing throughout the carriage ride he took to clear his mind after seeing Col. Newton. Everything he had struggled so hard for, everything he had plotted and planned and dreamed of was on the verge of collapse. He was now—finally!—on the perimeter of real wealth. Soon he would no longer be living on the fringes of the aristocracy. As the father of a duchess, he would *almost* be one of the *Ton*. His familial proximity to the Duke of Tasley via marriage to Francesca would open the floodgates of opportunity.

But only so long as Lord Beldon married Francesca, and did it soon.

Claude had no naive notions regarding the colonel's honesty. He knew the man was a consummate liar. But what Claude was absolutely certain of was that should he miss his upcoming payment to the British-India Tea Company, Col. Newton would consider all of his previous payments forfeited. If ever there was a cold-hearted bastard, it was the colonel.

So that meant Francesca wasn't going to wait several months to get married. She wasn't even going to wait several weeks.

A maid stepped out of the sun room carrying the remains of tea time on an ornate silver platter. When she saw the master of the manor striding so purposefully towards her, she blanched and stepped quickly away from the door.

"Is she in there?" Claude asked sharply. When the maid nodded, he replied, "See that we're not disturbed."

He found Francesca seated at the windows. In the chair beside her was Amanda Mecklenburg, a friend of many years. Amanda had married a baron of some substance during the Little Season the previous year, and she was already heavy with child. Seeing the young woman, married to one of the wealthier members of the aristocracy despite being of low rank in the peerage, heightened Claude's fury. Better to be a low-ranking aristocrat than a foreign-born outsider who was known to have fled France during the Revolution for fear of the guillotine.

"Darling Daddy, what brings you here?" Francesca's smile faded quickly when she took note of her father's demeanour. In a voice that strained for bonhomie, she added, "Amanda has just been telling me how wonderful life has been since she got married. She's hoping she'll have a boy."

"Amanda, you'll have to excuse us, but I have some important things to discuss with my daughter." Claude turned sideways and waved with his hand towards the door. Baroness Mecklenburg's jaw dropped open, and she put a hand to her mouth. People simply didn't *dismiss* her like she was some servant no longer needed in the room — but that's exactly what Claude was doing. "I don't mean to be uncivil, but I must speak with my daughter. I have a carriage outside that can take you home."

With some difficulty due to her pregnancy, Amanda rose to a standing position. What had initially been shock and embarrassment had evolved rather quickly into upper-class fury.

"I don't need your carriage," she said as she passed on her way towards the door. "I don't need anything from you at all." At the door she turned, her dark eyes narrowed with contempt. She studied Claude for several seconds, as though weighing her next words. "It's too damned bad they didn't guillotine you like they did so many of your kind. You half-monied French never learned your place, and yet you come here to England and think you're still someone important."

The instant the door closed behind Amanda, Francesca bolted to her feet. "Daddy, how dare you talk to my friend that way?"

Claude pivoted swiftly, and every impulse in him screamed to put a fist into his daughter's face. How many times in his life had he endured her looking at him with smug indifference or open contempt? No one would fault him for just one punch to the nose for all those countless offences she had heaped upon him since she was a little girl, he reasoned.

It was only his sense of purpose and profit that stopped him from striking her now. He needed her looking pretty. More pretty than ever...if she was going to get impregnated by the Duke of Tasley.

"Francesca, sit down, you stupid, insipid bitch, because I've got something to say to you, and every word's the gospel truth, so you'd better listen carefully." It was only after his daughter returned to her chair that Claude unclenched his fists. "The Duke of Tasley will probably be at Hyde Park tonight. I want you to meet him there and bring him back here. When he gets here, you're going to seduce him."

"Daddy—"

"You're going to fuck him and with any luck at all, you're going to get pregnant. Either way, I'm going to barge in on you the instant he's finished fucking. I'll have some friends with me from the club, so there'll be plenty of witnesses that the duke won't be able to bribe, so it won't just be his word against mine." He paused a moment, taking a calming breath. "Then he'll have no option but to marry you immediately. He may be a duke, but I'm the father of a daughter, and I've still got a good name, and that counts for something with the courts and with the church."

"You're overreacting." Francesca leant back in her chair and delicately crossed her legs at the knee, then adjusted the folds of her skirt. "And I don't fuck on command. I thought you knew that I—"

Claude's hand lashed out, his fingers instantly clamping tight around his daughter's throat, cutting off her breath. She grabbed his wrist with both hands, but he continued squeezing.

"You're going to get pregnant even if I have to tie you to a bed and let every stevedore on the docks fuck you 'til sperm dribbles out your ears." He released Francesca's throat, pleased that he finally saw primal fear in the depths of her eyes. She massaged her throat, but her eyes never left his, and she didn't say a word in complaint. "You're getting pregnant, one way or another. You might as well let the duke have his fun." He smiled with vicious triumph. "It isn't an idle threat, Francesca. If I have to, I'll have stevedores lined up around the block just waiting to stick a cock in you. Think of that as motivation for getting Colby back here where he can get caught with his pants down."

* * * *

"If I may say so, my lady, you look particularly delightful tonight."

Through the reflection in the mirror, Olympia looked at the man who had complimented her. His name was Dennard, and he was one of Leland's most trusted servants. He was also openly homosexual, completely dedicated to his employer, and an absolute genius at arranging a woman's coiffure for the evening.

"Thank you." She smiled at him in the mirror, then turned her head a little and looked at her coiffure in the reflection. For the evening, Dennard had pulled her hair back in a loose chignon while allowing curling tendrils to fall down her temples. Woven into her silky auburn tresses were a string of small but exquisite diamonds that caught and reflected the light like stars. "How did I ever get ready for an evening without you? You have positively spoilt me, Dennard."

He smiled, and though Olympia couldn't be certain since she hadn't known him that long, she thought his blush was genuine embarrassment at the fulsome compliment.

"Can I ask you a personal question, Dennard?" Olympia saw his immediate, wary reaction, and she quickly made a dismissive motion with her hands. "It's not about you." There was no need to ask about his sexual orientation. The butler's preferences were plainly written in every gesture he made. "You've been with Leland a long time, haven't you?"

"The prince took me in when I was quite young. He...he got me away from people I shouldn't have been with. I'll be forever indebted to him."

Olympia nibbled on her lower lip thoughtfully for a moment, uncertain of how far into privileged territory she could trespass. "Since Leland has been bringing Lord Beldon and me here to his home...has he brought anyone else?"

Dennard studied her for a moment before saying diplomatically, "Prince Mallory has many residences, my lady, and this is just one of them."

Olympia turned to face the servant directly. "And you're not supposed to talk about the prince's activities, are you?"

"Of course not, my lady. The prince trusts me and everyone in his employ to be the soul of discretion." He smiled then, and an amused twinkle came into his eyes. "But if I *were* the kind of man who would speak when he should remain silent, then I'd say that since m'lady and Lord Beldon have been frequenting this estate, Prince Mallory's fidelity has been without blemish." He raised an eyebrow waggishly. "And I know for a fact that he hasn't brought anyone home to any of his other estates, either. It seems that my employer's search for contentment has come to a successful conclusion."

Olympia's smile could have lit the room. "Dennard, you've made me so happy I could kiss you!"

"Please don't, m'lady, as I'm not that kind of man," the young valet replied with mock seriousness. "However, if you have a handsome lad in your employ who seems a bit lonely, I won't object to an introduction." He raised his hand to curb Olympia's laughter and said, "Lord Beldon should be arriving shortly. I assume you'll be taking a carriage to Hyde Park again?"

"Yes, I believe those are the plans."

"Then if you'll excuse me, I'll see to my duties." He paused, his smile genuine. "And again, you're looking especially lovely tonight, m'lady. Lord Beldon and Prince Mallory will be swept right off their feet."

After the valet had exited, Olympia turned to the mirror. The men — *her* men, she thought with both possessiveness and pride — hadn't yet seen her in this pearl-coloured muslin gown, trimmed with stunning Italian white lace at the cuffs, skirt hem, and along the fashionable, yet daringly low-cut, neckline that nearly skimmed the upper edge of her areolas and put her generous bosom flatteringly on display.

The gown was an Elizabeth Saxby, paid for by Colby and Leland. Olympia shuddered at what it must have cost her lovers to get London's most exclusive modiste, along with an entourage of nearly a dozen of her finest fitters and seamstresses, to make a spontaneous house visit. Elizabeth Saxby's services came at a hefty price, but even more importantly, a client had to have the right connections and influence to catch her attention. Even then, an at-home visit was usually booked several months in advance.

Apparently, Lord Beldon and Prince Mallory had those connections, and the money that went with them, in abundance.

After the marathon session of lovemaking in Lady Darcia's enormous carriage, where both prince and duke showed the orgasmic discipline to never climax inside Olympia, the Saxby gown she'd worn that evening had been stained beyond repair. Colby and Leland, who were known for their largesse, went beyond lengths either had previously gone with their other lovers. Elizabeth Saxby, London's finest and most expensive dressmaker, was called for. As she took Olympia's measurements, with both prince and duke in attendance, they insisted that this fabric or that style were simply too perfect for Olympia for them to not have the gowns made.

For her part, Olympia said she would not be treated like a courtesan, and that she could purchase her own evening gowns. She might just as well have been speaking in Greek for all the good it did her.

If Leland liked a velvet gown in ruby red, Colby thought it would look better in black. Rather than arguing the point, they ordered both. If Colby thought a gown's design would be best in silk, Leland was intractably convinced Olympia would look better if the gown were in satin. Again, both were ordered. On occasion, the men agreed that the fabric should be muslin — and with a grin they agreed that the more sheer the muslin, the better — but then their arguments centred on whether the gown should be trimmed in a matching colour of lace, or make a more dramatic statement by being red, gold, or a royal purple.

By the end of the fitting, the men ordered what amounted to a lady's entire evening wardrobe of Elizabeth Saxby dresses.

For the modiste, though it was clear that she was thankful for the extraordinary order she had received, it was necessary for her to explain that she simply *couldn't* deliver all that had been ordered within a week. When the men looked disappointed, the modiste promised that she would be bringing on new staff first thing in the morning. The men smiled and thanked Elizabeth Saxby, who was already issuing commands to her workers on what she expected of them in the coming weeks, and muttering under her breath that she would have many angry customers whose orders *would not* be filled on time because of the impatience of the Duke of Tasley and Prince Mallory.

Olympia, alone in her private suite of rooms at the estate, looked at her reflection in the mirror and thought about what Dennard had said. The word he had used was 'delightful.' Olympia had rather he'd said 'ravishing,' since being ravished was exactly what she was hoping for.

Chapter Ten

Olympia walked out through the side door of her dressing chamber and into the library. She had taken just one step into the room before she was stopped by the sheer physical beauty of the man leaning negligently against the fireplace mantle, a brandy snifter in one hand, a slender cigarette in the other. Prince Mallory was in a black cutaway jacket with a white shirt, a red waistcoat, and an artistically arranged cravat that touched his chin. His hair, as ebony black as his jacket and breeches, came down over the back of his collar in loose, silky curls.

He wears his aristocracy without ever being aware of it, thought Olympia, standing motionless. *Beautiful...too beautiful for his or my own good...and he's decadent...in the best and most skilful of ways.*

However decadent the prince, his dissolute qualities were what promised Olympia the most exquisite sensations. One look into his silver-blue eyes seemed to guarantee complete sexual fulfilment. As she gazed at him in regal repose, Olympia's body reacted instantly, instinctively, a sudden rush of warmth heading straight for her groin. The lips of her pussy began tingling, her clitoris pulsing, her entrance moistening in anticipation of penetration.

The young prince turned his face towards her slowly and delivered that devastatingly handsome half-smile. In the large, high-ceilinged room, his voice echoed faintly as he said quietly, "Good evening, Olympia." His gaze went unhurriedly up and down over her. He took a puff of his cigarette and blew the smoke towards the ceiling. "I'd tell you how lovely you are, but the words wouldn't do you justice." He sipped his brandy. "Besides, you're much too sexy to merely be referred to as 'lovely.'"

The urge to cross the room in a rush and throw herself into his arms was nearly overpowering. In the past month, Olympia had discovered what complete and utter enchantment was possible when in the arms of two skilled, unselfish lovers, men who were aficionados of the art of delivering orgasms almost at will. It was because of their devotion to seeing that *she* was satisfied with their encounters that made her so determined to make sure *they* were completely satiated when their lovemaking ended. The arrangement worked to everyone's advantage.

"How is it you alone can wear your hair that long and still look gorgeous?" Olympia asked, searching for something innocuous to discuss with her lover until Lord Beldon's arrival. "You need a haircut."

"Say the word, and I'll have a barber brought to the manor in a heartbeat."

"Don't you dare!" As she moved closer, she became distinctly aware of her body's movement, and of the faintest pressure against her clitoris caused by her stride. "I love your hair just the way it is." Her gaze met the prince's startling silver-blue one. "In fact, there isn't anything about you that I would change."

She watched as his eyes once more took her in slowly, appraisingly, starting with her face, moving downward to linger for several seconds upon her bosom, then going all the way down to the toes of the white kidskin slippers that peeked out beneath the bottom hem of her gown. By the time his eyes met with Olympia's again, there was a distinct swelling in the crotch of his black satin breeches.

Leland pulled a golden watch from his waistcoat pocket and opened the lid. "I wish Colby would get here." There was tension in his voice. He flicked the remains of his cigarette into the fireplace with a touch of irritation.

"I'm sure he'll get here as quickly as he can." Olympia's tone was similarly constricted. They had made a pact that there would be no romantic encounters unless all three of them were present. With newly discovered worlds of rapture in her hands, Olympia was determined to see that there would be no odd man out. "God, I hope he gets here soon." Her gaze drifted down to the bulge in Leland's breeches, and her lips parted just slightly for several seconds. Despite wearing a chemise beneath her underbust short-stay corset, the fact her nipples suddenly became erect was blatantly evident in the pearl-coloured muslin. In a tone similar to a prayer, she breathed, "Very soon."

When she looked into the prince's eyes, the effect on her body was very much the same as when she'd looked at the erection imprisoned beneath the fall of his breeches. Her body responded receptively to Leland's presence. It was with some difficulty that she turned away from him.

"Perhaps a brandy would help to settle your nerves?" the prince suggested. The air between them was thick with sexual tension. For the past month, neither had been forced to curb sexual impulses. Restraining them now took an act of will. "Lord knows, I could use another drink."

"Yes. Yes, I think a brandy is what we both need." She turned and looked into his eyes, paused because the breath caught in her throat, then added, "At least until Colby gets here."

Olympia had tried to sound casual, or at least faintly humorous. She failed on both accounts. When she followed Leland to the liquor cart, the scissoring of her thighs was a gentle caress, and she worried that her pussy would get so wet the honey would actually dribble down her thighs. New to sexual excess while the lovers in her life were artisans of the craft, Olympia was joyously doing what she could to make up for lost time.

At the cart, Leland poured brandy into a snifter glass and handed it to her. When Olympia's fingertips touched the prince's, it was as though an electrical current had passed between them. When she brought the snifter glass to her lips, the sip she took was closer to a gulp. She coughed softly for a moment as the brandy, though of the finest quality, sizzled from her throat all the way down to her stomach. Almost instantly, she felt the liquor warming her blood.

"I knew that Saxby would do you justice. She's a wizard with fabric," the prince said, his voice a sultry purr in the enormous room. "But not even I dreamed she would bring this much out in you."

Olympia looked down at her own bosom, daringly exposed, and blushed a little. "I'm afraid Miss Saxby has put my charms so much on display that if I bend over, there's a very real chance I'll fall out completely."

"My father was stationed in the late 1790s in St. Petersburg, and he said that at one formal governmental ball there were several ladies with a décolletage that came under their breasts." When Olympia's eyes widened in shock, Leland smiled wickedly. "I'm serious. Their corsets actually held their breasts up as though putting them on a pedestal, naked there for all the guests to see."

Olympia looked at him sceptically out of the corners of her eyes. "Seriously? You're telling the truth?"

"Absolutely. It was a court function of some sort for Czar Alexander. The bare-breasted ladies were French and Russian."

"No Englishwoman would be so daring, I would hope." Olympia felt a sudden pang of guilt. Who was she to disparage women for showing their breasts when she was in a *ménage a trois* love affair?

"My father never said anything about Englishwomen, but then, we can be a priggish lot." He lifted his hand and, with just the very tip of his right forefinger, touched Olympia on the shoulder where the puffed sleeve came upward. His slid his finger directly downward, simultaneously touched skin and muslin. "Imagine, my dear, what it would be like to be at a formal ball with the Czar...with all the most important men and women in attendance...and you with your lovely breasts on display." His finger reached the bottom of the vertical line of muslin. From there, the fabric went straight across the mounding swells of her breasts.

Olympia could hardly breathe, and her heart throbbed in her chest.

"Think of all those men looking at you, lusting after you. Just imagine that, Olympia. And think of all those women looking at you, jealous of you because of the beauty of your breasts." His finger began moving sideways, his touch feather-light and yet inordinately evocative.

Olympia's clit pulsed with tension.

"But not all of the women would be jealous."

Olympia brows furrowed. "Oh?"

"There would be those women who would wonder if your breasts were as delicious as they looked, if your nipples were as responsive as they appeared." His finger dipped into the tight cleavage of her bosom.

Olympia's long, dark lashes fluttered against her pale cheeks briefly, and for a moment she caught her lower lip between her teeth.

"Those women would want to suck on your nipples...but they wouldn't do it better than I can."

"Of course they wouldn't." An immediate reply. She knew the rapture Leland was capable of giving.

"I can make you climax," the prince said, his silver-blue eyes promising ecstasy, "just by sucking on your nipples."

If another man had said such a thing, Olympia would have laughed. What a ludicrous boast to make! But Prince Mallory was not like other men. He was uniquely skilled, particularly with his oral caresses. Sweet enchantment, utter bliss, *and* a satisfying orgasm, were standing directly in front of her, all in the guise of a darkly handsome man named Prince Leland Mallory.

His finger caressed along the entire upper edge of Olympia's gown, from shoulder to décolletage to shoulder. As his finger made the reverse voyage, it paused between her breasts. While looking straight into her eyes, the prince eased his finger between her breasts, sliding it portentously between the pale mounds. Olympia's mouth opened as she gasped softly, and for a moment her knees trembled, threatening to fold beneath her.

"Would you like that, my love? To feel my cock sliding between your breasts? Can you imagine me making love to your breasts?"

Olympia moistened her lips with a furtive swipe of her tongue. For a moment her lips moved as though she was trying to speak. Finally abandoning verbal communication, she simply nodded. Curling tendrils of auburn hair danced at her temples.

While moving his finger through her cleavage, the prince asked, "What about Lord Beldon's cock? He's twice the man I am."

Olympia shook her head instantly. "You're wrong. He's not twice the man. He's just twice your size. But trust me, my darling, dissolute prince...your cock satisfies me. In fact, for the past month I have found virtually everything about you to be...*sinfully multi-orgasmic*."

She delivered the last two words slowly, one syllable at a time, and with stunningly erotic effect. Despite years of profligacy, the prince uttered a short gasp, and for several seconds he breathed deeply through his nostrils in an obvious effort to control riotous emotions. Olympia considered his turmoil a personal victory. She might be new to this game of erotic duelling, but she was a fast study, and a woman who liked to win.

Leland slid his finger up and down between Olympia's breasts for a moment longer, then brought the finger to her mouth. "Suck it," he whispered in a hushed, fevered tone. "Pretend it's my cock. Get it wet so I can fuck your breasts with it."

These were intoxicating words for Olympia to hear. The urge to touch herself, to finger her pussy, was nearly overpowering. Better still, she could beg the prince to do it. The man was endlessly willing to satisfy carnal cravings he himself had brought to life.

When the prince brought his forefinger to Olympia's mouth, she parted her lips in abject surrender to the wanton desires coursing through her veins. As the single digit entered her mouth, her eyes closed and she drew a light suction, her cheeks caving inward as her tongue swirled against the fingertip. Leland pushed his finger deeper into her mouth, and Olympia moaned softly, her mind in a dizzying whirl, aware of just how lewd a portrait she must be presenting to the prince, wishing desperately that it was his erection and not his finger that she was orally caressing.

In her right hand was the brandy snifter, but as she sucked on the undulating finger, Olympia's left hand slipped up her body until she cupped her right breast. Slender, pale fingers pressed into the extravagant, responsive mound, and the warbling moan that came from Olympia whispered of a feminine soul teetering on the brink of sexual oblivion.

"Don't touch yourself," Leland commanded as he withdrew his finger from her mouth. "You mustn't climax." His smile was the epitome of refined decadence. "At least not until Colby gets here."

With a moue, Olympia let her hand fall away from her breast. When Leland held his hand up, she saw that the entire length of his forefinger was shiny with saliva. He brought the finger to the juncture of her breasts, and this time when he pushed it between the mounds, the digit slid more smoothly.

It shouldn't feel this good, thought Olympia as a shiver went through her. *It's just his finger, and he's not even touching my nipples.*

But it was the lasciviousness of the action, the way in which the prince could make even the most mundane things become supercharged with eroticism, which made all her nerves crackle with energy. Her cheeks were flushed pink, and her breathing was erratic.

The sound of the door opening caused Olympia to flinch. She turned to see Lord Beldon step through the threshold, all big-shouldered and brawny beneath the silk cutaway, his cravat perfectly tied at his throat, a tall hat in one hand and his cane in the other.

She crossed the room at a dead run, with Leland matching her stride for stride.

Colby Beldon, the Duke of Tasley, didn't stand a chance.

* * * *

At the exact moment that Olympia, achingly close to the first orgasm of the evening, was rushing across the expanse of Prince Mallory's library, Col. John Newton was walking slowly in Hyde Park with Lady Darcia Firth Caldwell. His mood was significantly different from Olympia's, and he most certainly was *not* on the brink of an orgasm.

"I haven't seen Olympia around lately. Has she been well?" the colonel asked, his tone bland.

"Yes, quite well," Darcia replied, giving the colonel a smile that was polite, but nothing more. She closed her ornately painted fan. "I spoke with her just the other day and she seemed in the rose of health."

"She used to come here to the park with you."

"Yes, well, she has so many philanthropic responsibilities, you know," Darcia replied. "Helping the downtrodden and those less fortunate takes up much of her time."

The colonel scratched his chin. He knew that Olympia had pet causes that she championed, but she didn't have so many that she couldn't see to the social obligations of the leisured class.

"What about Lord Beldon and Prince Mallory. I've seen neither in quite some time."

The colonel had wanted the question to appear innocuous, but the quick sidelong glance he received from Darcia said she knew he was fishing for information. This was not idle chatter.

After some hesitation, the duchess replied, "I really can't vouch for the duke or the prince." She made a vague gesture with a gloved hand. "You know how those rakes are. They never stay anywhere, or with anyone, for very long."

"Yes, of course," was the colonel's indifferent reply.

But he could feel his blood heating as a slow-burning rage took to flame in his stomach. Colby and Leland not attending their de rigueur obligation of being seen in a carriage ride or a walking stroll around Hyde Park was easily accepted. Both men had reputations that made their absence easily understood. Olympia Whyte's reputation was quite to the contrary. Since she had begun socialising again after her period of mourning, attending pro forma social events was strictly maintained.

As a military man, the colonel was instinctively and professionally distrustful of anything that smacked of coincidence. Olympia not attending the nightly soirees at Hyde Park while Leland and Colby missed them as well simply could not be written off as mere *coincidence*.

So who was courting her? The dissolute duke? Or was it the profligate prince?

I didn't kill Arthur Whyte to let some high-borne prick take his widow to bed.

The thought of Olympia in bed with any man other than himself brought a shudder of revulsion to the colonel.

He had killed before for Olympia, and it seemed that the fates had deemed it necessary he kill again.

* * * *

The prince's bed was in a shambles. Olympia's naked and lusciously rounded body glistened in the lamplight with perspiration. The perspiration was her own, as well as Colby's and Leland's. Under less amorous circumstances, the urge to bathe would have been overpowering, but with the aroma of lovemaking thick in the air, Olympia wore the perspiration as a badge of honour.

She was sitting cross-legged at the foot of the bed, leaning back against one of four enormous, elaborately carved posts of black oak. She was completely naked, breathing softly in post-coital, orgasmic lassitude. She combed her fingers through her auburn tresses in a futile attempt to put the strands into some semblance of order.

The previous three hours had been spent in such vigorous sexual excess the actions had bordered on violence. But Olympia—as the almost continual centre of sensual attention—wouldn't have changed a thing. She bore the mien of a woman who had been thoroughly ravished. It was not a deceptive appearance.

Colby was on the right side of the bed, on his back with one arm tossed beneath his head. His cock, seemingly tireless, was at half-mast. Looking at it, recalling all the pleasure it had given her over the past month—and the past three hours in particular—Olympia wondered if that delicious flesh was on its way down, or on its way back up.

Leland was on the left side of the bed, his slender body all rippling, graceful muscles. He was leaning back against the carved headboard, smoking a cigarette. In spite of all that had transpired over the past hours, his erection, though not nearly as massive as the duke's, was again in full bloom.

"Don't look at me like that," Olympia said to the prince, seeing the desire once more begin to smoulder in his eyes. "If you keep making love to me, I'll be dead by sunrise."

"No, you won't," Leland replied, his voice hushed, the undercurrent sensual. "I would never do anything to hurt you, and neither would Colby." He dropped his cigarette onto a glass tray, and languidly moved towards Olympia. He had a way of moving that reminded her of a cat stalking. "The night's still young."

With little conviction, Olympia shook her head. Her unbound auburn tresses swirled over her shoulders, and her naked breasts bobbled tautly from side to side. She raised a hand as though to defend herself.

"Leland, I need more time." Even Olympia heard the equivocation in her tone. She had unconsciously gone from *no more* to *not right now*. "It's not fair. You've got me outnumbered."

"Let's play a game," the prince said as his fingers curled around her ankle and began straightening her leg. "Let's see if I can change your mind." This was a game where he was a master.

"Don't you ever listen?"

"I *am* listening," the prince replied as he slid onto his stomach on the mattress while straightening her leg and pulling her ankle to the side. "I'm just not *obeying*."

All women should have such disobedient lovers.

It was a startling thought for Olympia. Sometimes she envisioned Leland and Colby as a single entity, which enabled her to conveniently skirt the unconventional nature of her relationship with two men. After all, it was hardly a comforting notion to think of herself as a woman who accepted lovers two at a time. What would the fine women of the *Ton* say about that? Decorum and propriety meant everything to the aristocracy.

I don't care what anyone else thinks. I love them both, and there's nothing that gives me more pleasure than to be with them, making love to both of them at the same time, feeling their....

The reverie came to an abrupt end when Leland's moist, pink tongue snaked out of his mouth and slipped between the tender, tingling lips of her cunt. Olympia was not at the most advantageous angle to be pleasured, and though she had one leg straight and out to the side, she lifted up onto the opposite knee.

"That's my lady," Leland purred as he rolled onto his back, his ebony hair spreading out on the mattress, in stark contrast to the white silk sheet. "Now lower yourself to me," he said as Olympia moved slightly to be in the proper position above him, "and let me taste your pussy."

Lowering her hips, Olympia mumbled, "Oh, fuck!" when the prince put his lips and tongue in motion on her pussy, sucking lightly on her clitoris. She repositioned herself so that she had both knees beneath her and, looking down between the trembling mounds of her breasts, she saw Leland. As he pleasured her pussy and reawakened her libido, all she could see of his face was his chin. Her gaze went slowly down his naked body, moving leisurely, taking in the visual delights of his hairless chest, his flat stomach with the clearly delineated muscles, and finally his cock, fiercely erect, pointing towards her as though beckoning, a rigid sceptre of masculinity.

"I'll do anything you ask, anything you say," Olympia whispered as she lowered herself onto the prince, her heavy breasts pressing against his abdomen, flattening and expanding under the pressure as she brought her lips to the crest of his arousal. "And if you fuck me to death...what better way to die?"

A pearl of fluid glistened on the slitted tip of Leland's cock. Olympia curled her right hand around the base of his shaft and squeezed, and the droplet grew in size, threatening to dribble down from the crown. The sight of her lover's cream heightened Olympia's passion. A month earlier, the notion that she might delight in pleasuring a man with her lips and tongue would have been unthinkable. With the advent of a rakish duke and prince into her life, she now took satisfaction in seeing the responses she could draw from them when she administered — with steadily improving skill — the pleasures of fellatio.

With a flick of her tongue, Olympia licked the pearl from the tip of Leland's cock. The nectar was salty, and not entirely pleasing, but this didn't stop her. She licked the tip again, then pushed her lips over the flaring crown. She began nibbling slowly down the shaft with her lips, not stopping until she felt his knob pushing firmly against the opening of her throat. The prince's low groan let her know he was pleased, and she felt him devouring her rapidly overheating pussy with even greater vigour.

Moments later, Olympia felt the mattress move. She didn't need to open her eyes to know what had happened. Colby had gotten off the bed, but she wasn't dismayed. He wouldn't be gone for long. Not if she had any understanding of Lord Beldon and his passion.

The bed dipped again, only this time the movement came from behind her, at the mattress's edge. A broad-palmed hand caressed her back and shoulders briefly. Then, as Leland's tongue slithered over her clitoris, she felt the broad head of a large erection pressing against her labia.

Her moan signalled her emotions, though the wetness of her pussy had been evidence enough to let her lovers know of her readiness.

This was how she loved it the most. Though all the other positions of lovemaking were thrilling, this was how she climaxed the hardest, with the prince beneath her giving cunnilingus while the duke knelt behind her, pumping that enormous cock of his deep inside her. The combined sensations of having Colby's cock pumping into her hard and fast while Leland's tongue worked on her clitoris created a plethora of sensations that no single man could possibly provide.

She came twice and was working on the third climax before Leland's passion splattered against her tongue, and Colby's hot release left lines of semen from her shoulders to her buttocks.

Chapter Eleven

Col. Newton had been at Rosalyn's for an hour, and he still didn't have an erection—a fact which had pushed him into a state of near-hysteria.

First it had taken nearly a half hour for him to pick out a prostitute from the line-up at Rosalyn's. Usually, he preferred his hired women to be slender, young, and with the distinct though false appearance of innocence. But on his last two visits he had made a specific request for an auburn-haired woman with a voluptuous figure.

"She's gotta have tits. Big ones," he had said, slurring his words only slightly.

The colonel always fortified himself with substantial quantities of brandy prior to visiting Rosalyn's. Without the assistance of hard liquor, he had the embarrassing habit of climaxing almost the instant he became erect. Liquor did an acceptable job of substituting for orgasmic discipline.

With troubling thoughts of Olympia playing more and more on his mind—rather poisonously, he was beginning to think—he found himself seeking out the cold comfort that could be purchased for a fairly reasonable price at Rosalyn's. Another factor that weighed on his thoughts was the awareness that his idea of beauty had evolved. Where once a woman pale, short, and slender, with girlish attributes and a quick giggle fired his libido in an instant, now he sought out professional women who had lost the first blush of spring. He wanted women with feminine curves, with breasts that filled the hand to overflowing, and a luscious bottom he could slam into when fucking them from behind.

"Mister, ain't you feelin' anything yet?"

Her voice had the twang of a cockney street vendor to it, which irked the colonel enormously, and dampened any possible sense of eroticism he might have experienced. Looking down at the woman kneeling between his thighs on the bed, the urge to slap her across the face washed over him like a tidal wave. For a moment he closed his eyes, fighting against his own violent urges, knowing in his heart that it was Olympia who was infuriating him—and therefore she should be the one to receive his punishment—and not the plain-faced, plump woman he had procured.

"Just keep sucking," he said with a growl. "And you'd better start doing it right. If Rosalyn hears how bad you're treating one of her best customers, she'll toss your ass out in the street."

The woman resumed sucking his cock, pleasuring flesh that refused to respond.

When I've got my cock in Olympia's mouth, it'll turn to stone. I know it. I fucking know it. When I've got her with me in India, I'll make her suck my cock while the natives watch. First I've got to shut down the British-India Tea Company before the investors figure out its all a sham, then I'll grab Olympia and sail off to India without anyone being the wiser. When she's in India, she'll show me the respect I deserve. I'll see it in her eyes...and in the way she sucks my cock.

The thought brought a smile to his lips, and his penis started to twitch, at last coming to life.

Olympia likes to pretend that she makes all the decisions in her life, but I'll beat that attitude out of her with a razor strop. She was married, so I won't be the first one to fuck her...but I'll bet she's never been fucked in the ass before! I'll bet she screams the first time I ram it up her ass.

Now his erection began growing rather rapidly. He kept his eyes closed, his confidence increasing as he embraced the illusion that it was Olympia on her knees in bed with him, giving him fellatio with energy if not enthusiasm.

"There you go, mate!" The woman's accent shattered any fantasy the colonel had conjured that it was his beloved Olympia performing fellatio. "Now you're right perky!"

His erection evaporated in seconds.

"You bitch," the colonel hissed, then began slapping the frightened prostitute.

* * * *

"What time is it, Dennard?"

"Nearly five, m'lady."

Olympia leant back in the tub, luxuriating in the warm water. When she'd first gotten into the high, slant-backed tub, the water had been so hot she could barely withstand it. But after soaking for nearly thirty minutes, the water had lost much of its heat, and all of it seemed to be stored inside Olympia. She felt as though her bones had melted.

"I suppose I have to get out, don't I?"

"You still have some time, m'lady."

She sighed. "I love it here. I love being with Leland and I love being with Colby and I love everything about this estate." She raised her right foot out of the water, pointing her toe towards the ceiling. Her flesh was normally quite pale, but the hot water had transformed her skin to a soft shade of pink. "I've fallen in love with two men, Dennard. What do you figure the odds are that the *Ton* would understand that?"

"Nil, m'lady."

She looked at the servant and gave him a smile. "That was brutally honest."

"You'll find that polite society is not really very polite." He raised an eyebrow in self-mockery. "And who would know that better than I?"

"You're right, of course...but I wish you weren't."

Dennard shrugged and replied, "I am a realist with few illusions regarding society. Sometimes there is little comfort in being right."

When she had first eased her passion-weary body into the bath tub, there had been a layer of soap bubbles a foot thick. Now there wasn't a single bubble. Olympia sighed again, not so much because she had to leave the embrace of the warm water, but because it meant she had to get dressed to leave the safe haven of Prince Mallory's palatial ancestral estate.

She got her feet beneath her and rose slowly, water streaming down her body. Dennard stood at the ready, holding a hand out. Olympia took it, stepped out of the tub onto the towel on the floor, spread her feet and extended her arms.

As Dennard began wiping her body dry, Olympia asked, "Have you ever performed such services for any of Prince Mallory's other…um…female guests?"

"No, m'lady. You seem to be the exception to all of the prince's rules." Dennard, in full, immaculate livery, was wiping his way slowly up the front of Olympia's thighs. "The staff and I are really quite amazed at the prince's change since you came into his life." He smiled up at Olympia, and she wondered what gift she could give Dennard to show her appreciation. "He has been most insistent that, first and foremost, I am to see to your every wish and need."

"But why doesn't he have that maid from Wales attend to my needs? Marian is her name, isn't it?"

Dennard pressed the towel lightly against the damp, auburn curls at the apex of Olympia's thighs. She smiled at him, but felt not an inkling of passion.

"I'm surprised you have to ask, m'lady, since I thought you already knew."

"Oh?"

"Marian is a woman partial to women. My guess is that Prince Mallory wouldn't allow anyone to look upon you with lust in their heart, so he has given the assignment of seeing to your needs to me." Dennard rose to his feet, tossed the towel to the floor, and unfolded a fresh towel from a nearby table. "A rather agreeable assignment, if I may be so bold."

"You may, Dennard. You may indeed." Olympia raised her outstretched arms a little higher as the servant towelled droplets of water from her breasts, then underarms. "I've had servants my entire life, but already I feel closer to you than to any of the others. And I feel completely at ease being naked with you. Isn't that the strangest thing?"

Dennard smiled, bit his bottom lip for a moment, then said, "Actually, to be brutally honest once again, that isn't the strangest thing...if you really think about it."

Olympia's laughter filled the room as Dennard began drying her shoulders and back. "You're positively priceless! Are you sure I can't kidnap you?"

"I work at Prince Mallory's discretion, m'lady. If he says you can kidnap me, then I guess you'll be my new employer."

As tempting as the thought was, Olympia was too grounded in reality to give the notion serious consideration. Her servants, like virtually all servants with the singular exception of Leland's, were notorious gossips, forever whispering to other servants what was happening in the upstairs rooms. The idea of a gentleman's gentleman taking care of a widow was simply unthinkable, and would surely cause tongues to wag. Being ostracised by the *Ton* would be all but guaranteed, and though Olympia certainly had her disagreements with the haut monde, turning her back on her birthright was too radical a gesture to consider.

While Dennard dried her pink body slowly and thoroughly, Olympia thought back on the days she'd spent at Leland's estate. Though it had taken some effort, she had finally abandoned her belief that falling in love with two men at the same time was innately bad.

It isn't wicked to fall in love with two men simultaneously, she reasoned, with what she hoped wasn't too much self-justification. *It might be selfish, considering the lack of truly splendid men in this world, but it isn't wicked. Naughty? I suppose. But what pleasure is there that doesn't have at least a touch of naughtiness to it? None!*

From behind, Dennard slipped the towel up between her thighs to press it against her labia. Olympia gasped softly, surprised by the contact. She felt a twinge of discomfort. The previous days had been spent in vigorous lovemaking of nearly every variety.

"My apologies, m'lady. I did not mean to hurt you," Dennard said quickly while remaining on his knees behind her.

"It's not your fault," Olympia replied, then blushed a little. "I'm just a little sore, that's all."

In a soft voice, the servant replied, "They love you very much."

"So a little soreness is a small price to pay for such complete satisfaction?"

"Precisely, m'lady."

"That's the way I see it, too." She laughed softly. "Now let's get me dressed before I make a damned fool of myself by begging them to make love to me one more time before I leave."

* * * *

On a west-facing second-floor balcony, just off one of the forty-two bedrooms, Prince Leland Mallory stood in the doorway with a glass of whisky in one hand and a glass of gin in the other, and said aloud, "I've never been so contented in my life. Not ever."

The Duke of Tasley, Colby Beldon, turned in his chair, smiled in that way that always made his dimple appear to be endlessly deep, and replied, "My feelings exactly."

Though protocol dictated the hour was suitable for formal evening attire, both men wore ankle-length royal blue robes of thick Chinese silk. And though they were both on their second libation of the evening, neither man was feeling festive.

In fact, both were quite dour.

"She's not leaving forever," the prince said as he handed Colby the glass of whisky. "And as much as we'd like to keep her here and lock her up forever, we just can't do that."

"Why not?'

Leland smiled. The Duke of Tasley was notorious for rearranging the lives of others to suit his wishes. The privileges of power were not lost on a man of his social rank. Ducal prerogatives in Regency England were almost without boundaries.

"Because we can't. Because she'd be furious." Leland sat in his chair, crossed his legs at the knee, adjusted his robe, and delivered the trump card on the argument. "And because she's got one hell of a temper, and she'd be livid with us if she missed the meeting of the Ladies of Society for the Prevention of Destitution tomorrow morning. She on the board, and they'll notice if she's not there."

"We could send an endowment on her behalf as an apology for her not being there." His smile was beatific, his enthusiasm childlike without being childish. "I'll write a bank draft today!"

The prince chuckled. The masculine love of his life was a man who had rather more than just a difficult time taking 'no' for an answer. The vast range of ducal privileges were ingrained in Colby to the marrow of his bones, and though he of late had learned to be a bit more open-minded about things, doing away with class stratification was not on his agenda.

"Olympia, using only those amazing violet eyes of hers, would cut us to shreds if we tried to keep her from that meeting. She'd take our skin off in strips with little more than a damning glance."

Colby groaned as though in physical pain. "She *can* be difficult at times."

"An understatement of staggering dimensions."

Leland would have said more, but Olympia stepped out onto the balcony. She wore a grey skirt with a matching waist-length jacket, a prim white blouse buttoned to the throat, and a small bonnet. Her auburn tresses had been brushed back and knotted into a tight chignon at the base of her neck, sans the loose temple curls that she preferred for the evening.

"Dennard has done wonders with your hair," the prince said, smiling warmly at the only woman he'd ever loved. "But then, you look lovely even when your coiffure is something less than pristine."

"You only like it looking wild when you and Colby are the ones who destroyed my coiffure."

Olympia pouted prettily, and the prince felt a rush of warmth go through his veins. He was momentarily bewildered by the reality that he couldn't get enough of Olympia Whyte. It wasn't just that he couldn't get enough of her body, he couldn't get enough of her companionship, her conversation, her wit — even her petulance. With a nod towards the door, the wise valet turned on his heel and headed out of the room.

"A crime I'll not plead innocent to."

Olympia's violet eyes narrowed comically. "My darling prince...you and the word *innocent*," she drawled the word out with a libidinous inflection, "are not exactly first cousins. You're not even *distantly*," again, the teasing annunciation with the precise delineation of syllables, "related."

Colby, who had not involved himself in the earlier, light-hearted banter, said in a voice that was low, authoritative, and blatantly sexual, "The scent of lilac in the soap you used during your bath does you justice, but I prefer a more earthy scent on you."

"Earthy, Lord Beldon?" Olympia's right eyebrow arched with amusement. "I'm not sure I know what you mean."

"I prefer you with the scent of perspiration—fresh perspiration, both male and female. And with a faint undertone of pussy and cum." A gasp caught in Olympia's throat, and Colby smiled. "It goes without saying, of course, that the semen must be either mine, or Leland's...or best of all, both of ours."

"Yes, it goes without saying," the prince said quickly, feeling his pulse suddenly accelerate. During his time with the duke, he'd learned to expect the unexpected. They had all agreed that it was time for Olympia to return home, but still...

"Stop that now," Olympia chided. "Haven't you had enough yet?"

"Of you and Leland?" the duke asked, scratching his chin as though giving the matter serious consideration. "No. As a matter of fact, I haven't. And I don't think I ever will."

Like an electrical charge shooting straight into his veins, the prince felt raw lust streak through his body. Though under normal conditions he was the least insecure of men, now that he had fallen in love—and he no longer had any doubts that what he felt for Colby and Olympia was, in fact, love—he sometimes worried that what Colby felt for him was more lust than love. The fact that he had specifically included Leland in his declaration of unending desire gave the prince a heady sense of being protected.

"Sit and have a drink with us before you leave," Leland said. He took Olympia's hand and tugged, wanting to pull her down onto his lap.

"Don't you start that now," Olympia said quickly, slipping her hand out of the prince's grasp. "If I sit on your lap, the next thing that'll happen is that we'll all be making love again. Dennard has done wonders with my hair, and I've just stepped out of the bath, *and* I'm a little sore from all the good loving you two have given me. So I'm not going to sit on your lap, and you can stop looking at me like you're a man who has been deprived of attention." She waggled a forefinger at him. "The carriage should pull up to the front doors for me in just five minute."

"Five minutes?" Colby asked. "I can give a lot of pleasure in five minutes."

When Olympia turned to look down at the duke, Leland felt his erection beginning to form. Wearing only the thin silk robe meant his state of mind was impossible to hide.

Leland added, "An amazing amount of pleasure, and we won't even mess your coiffure."

He slipped off his chair fluidly, kneeling on the balcony behind Olympia. An instant later, Colby was kneeling in front of her. Together, they raised her skirt and petticoat. Her legs, sheathed in white silk stockings, were first revealed to the prince, then the lace-trimmed garters, before the tops of her thighs and the pale, lusciously rounded globes of her buttocks. Her flesh was clean and still warm from the bath, the fragrance of soap delicate and pleasing to the senses.

Olympia spread her feet a couple of inches wider apart. Through the opening of her legs, Leland saw that Colby's was on his knees with his robe open, and his enormous erection was filling his hand.

"You can leave in five minutes," Leland said.

Olympia replied, "Provided I can still walk, that is."

He leant forward, pressing his face into the snug cleavage of her buns, and began tonguing her with gentle strokes.

"Oh, God..." Olympia whispered.

* * * *

They always give more than they take, Olympia thought with a touch of guilt. *I've got to think of something special to do for them, something they'll never expect.*

It was an incongruous sight to look down and see her skirt bulging outward, draped over a big, broad-shouldered man who was, at that moment, sucking very lightly upon her erect clitoris. As the duke used his thumbs to gently separate her labia to have better access to her clitoris, Leland's hands were on her buns, squeezing her as his flicking, frisking tongue tantalised nerve endings unaccustomed to oral caresses.

"That…feels…*sooo*…fucking…good," Olympia whispered, spacing the words out, delighting in the taste of the naughty word. Though she would never use such an obscenity in public, when she was alone with her lovers, it felt natural to be a bit saucy with her words. "Don't stop." She cupped her breasts through her blouse and camisole, pinching the nipples above the half-cups of the underbust short-stay corset. A surge of pleasure went through her when she pinched her nipples. In front and behind, experienced tongues were delivering slick caresses to sensitive tissue. "Don't ever…stop fucking…me. Oh, fuck!"

Olympia said the word 'fuck' at precisely the moment the first of her orgasmic contractions began shuddering through her. Her legs trembled, shaking beneath her as Colby and Leland, aware of what they had caused, tongued her ass and pussy with an even more ardent frenzy.

Chapter Twelve

His name was Sergeant Rogers, and though he wore the uniform of a British soldier, he was in civilian clothing now. He worked for Col. Newton, and he'd been given a very special, secret assignment that had nothing to do with defending crazy King George, the Regent Prince, or England itself.

Standing nearly two hundred yards from the palatial estate of Prince Leland Mallory, his presence hidden by an enormous silver maple tree, a telescoping spy glass to his eye, Sgt. Rogers had a lascivious grin on his lips.

"The colonel's going to be mad as hell when I give him my report," he murmured aloud, squinting through the high-powered optics.

On the second floor marble balcony of the estate, the woman he had been assigned to follow was standing—with the Duke of Tasley and Prince Mallory beneath her skirt!

From such a long distance, the sergeant couldn't see the details, but then he didn't need to see everything to know what those men were doing beneath the woman's skirt.

Like many soldiers, Sgt. Rogers was always looking for ways to make money. Even before he had folded up his spy glass, he was already wondering what the going rate was for the murder of a prince and a duke. Unless, of course, the colonel wanted Olympia Whyte murdered. The sergeant had killed many people in his life, but he'd never killed a woman before. Not that he *wouldn't* kill a woman, he just hadn't had the opportunity, and he'd never been paid to. Sgt. Rogers thought it poor business judgement to kill without turning a profit, and it seemed to him that killing a woman should be a bit more expensive than killing a man, though he couldn't say why he felt this way.

* * * *

Col. Newton's hands were balled into fists, and his jaws were clamped so tightly shut that another ounce of pressure and his teeth would shatter. His eyes narrowed on Sgt. Rogers.

"You're absolutely certain it was her on that balcony?" he asked.

"Yes, sir. I followed the lady's carriage to the Mallory estate and stayed outside to make sure she didn't leave unnoticed. When she stepped out onto the balcony, I could see it was her right away." The sergeant nodded vigorously, as though the gesture somehow added credibility to his observation. "Those blokes just crawled right on up under her skirts and stayed there on their knees. Then some time later a carriage pulled up out front and she left. That's what she done. I saw it all, Colonel."

Col. Newton rose to his feet. From the pocket of his uniform, he extracted a two shilling coin. He dropped it on the much-scarred table and said, "Good work. Get drunk now, if you want to, but I'll have need of your services in the near future."

"Yes, sir. Thank you, sir." The sergeant's grin was tainted with sadism. "You can count on me to do the job up right."

* * * *

Standing shoulder to shoulder with Lady Darcia, Olympia looked at their reflections in the angled oval mirror and said, "That Saxby looks wonderful on you," she said. "But if fashion dictates that the necklines get any lower, I'm afraid we'll both have few secrets left."

The duchess, every bit as curvaceous as Olympia, laughed softly. "Fashions change. It wasn't so long ago that a woman had to have a two-foot-high powdered wig and a painted face in order to be considered fashionable. You're too young to remember, but it was nearly impossible to walk anywhere with all those hoops and whatnot we wore beneath our skirts. I'm so thrilled *those* days are over. Besides, with the high waistlines of the Grecian influence, it enables women like us to hide a few extra pounds."

Olympia twisted right and left, taking careful note of how her robin's egg blue Saxby gown swirled freely around her legs. Then she shook her shoulders gently, studying the taut, swaying movement of her breasts. She smiled sheepishly. It had been a full week since her glorious days and nights of passion with Colby and Leland, and the men were expected to attend this evening's soiree. The host and hostess for the evening were John and Mable Kennerly. He was a member of Parliament, and she was one of the more influential hostesses in London. Making sure that the Duke of Tasley and Prince Mallory were both invited took some doing, but Olympia had managed it without drawing suspicion from the scrupulously proper hostess.

"Fortunately, this country now likes its women looking like real women who actually enjoy a dinner now and then, women who look like women and not like skinny boys," Lady Darcia continued. "So we're all the rage. It seems that whatever the dissolute Prince of Wales likes — and the only women who turn his head are women with curves — the rest of the men on the *Ton* immediately emulate."

The door opened and a woman Olympia did not recognise stepped into the chamber room. After adjusting one auburn curl at her temple, Olympia slipped her arm through the duchess's, and they stepped out into the ballroom.

The orchestra was playing a slow waltz. Of the hundred attendees, perhaps thirty were dancing.

"Don't you wish sometimes that you could bring Jacob and Abbott to these?" Olympia asked, learned towards her friend so she could keep her voice low and still be heard. "Do you know if they dance?"

"The kind of dancing they specialise in doesn't require an orchestra."

Olympia laughed softly, her violet eyes scanning the audience, looking for two very delectable men wearing black cutaways, silk breeches, and immaculately polished boots.

"Abbott and Jacob — they're good to you?"

"Better than good. I've never felt so contented in my life."

"Me, too."

Memories of what Colby and Leland had done to her just before putting her in a carriage to return home came to mind, and Olympia blushed a little.

"What *aren't* you telling me? Come, my dear friend, tell me what's put that blush on your cheeks." She patted the back of Olympia's hand, which rested on her forearm. "After what I've seen you do, secrets seem silly between us."

"Yes, they do." Olympia glanced around quickly. What she had to say *couldn't* be overheard. That's when she spotted Colby's sandy hair in a crowd of men, and her heart seemed to leap in her chest. "Thank God, they're finally here."

"Quick, tell me your story," Darcia prodded. "I'm not turning you over to those men until you let me in on your secret—because judging from that blush in your cheeks, someone was naughty in the best possible way."

Olympia looked from Lady Darcia across the dance floor. Leland and Colby were, as promised, in black cutaway suits, one darkly handsome, the other her blond barbarian in silk. The urge to run straight across the dance floor and throw herself into their arms was powerful, and she had to remind herself that decorum dictated she show her lovers only marginal interest—when in public.

"Olympia, if you don't tell me why you blushed, I'm going to be furious with you. Quickly now. Your men are making their way through this crowd to us."

Turning so that she faced Lady Darcia directly, Olympia leant forward and whispered into her ear, "They're always such gentlemen about using *coitus interruptus* with me, so baths are *really* necessary. Anyway, I had just taken this nice long, hot bath and had dressed to come back home, when Colby and Leland started flirting with me again. I was a little sore from all their wonderful lovemaking and I had told them so, and I was going to be leaving in just five minutes, so I told them I simply couldn't make love to them again. The next thing I knew, I was standing and both of them were on their knees under my skirt."

Lady Darcia's eyes widened and her jaw dropped open. "Both of them at the same time?"

"I had Colby's tongue on my clitoris, and Leland's tongue on my bottom." She closed her eyes briefly, and a shiver worked its way up her spine. "All they did was use their tongues on me, but it was so intense I could hardly breathe. When I finally came, I almost fell over because there wasn't any strength left in my legs." A shiver went through her at the memory. "Oh, Darcia, it was *such* a powerful orgasm."

"Tell me you returned the favour," the duchess said, her expression conspiratorial and sunny. She obviously wanted to hear all the lurid details with graphic precision. "You got down on your knees right then and there, didn't you?"

Olympia nibbled on her bottom lip for a moment before replying, "Was I supposed to?"

Though they were dear friends, and getting closer all the time, the duchess gave Olympia a very stern and slightly condemnatory look and stated, "When men like that get on their knees to pleasure you—front and back, I might add—the least you can do, and the least they can *expect*, is that you give as good as you've gotten." She leant closer to Olympia. "There's nothing like a hot, wet mouth to put the twinkle in a man's eye."

Olympia's brow furrowed. "I was selfish, wasn't I?"

The duchess's expression displayed her surprise once again. "My dear, you may be a widow, but you're hopelessly naive when it comes to certain things. And I wouldn't say you were selfish, just a little addle-brained, but under the circumstances, that's hardly surprising." She put a hand on Olympia's bare shoulder. "It's eight o'clock and this ball isn't going to end until at least midnight. You haven't seen your lovers in nearly a week. I suggest you find a nice, quiet place somewhere on this estate, you get down on your knees, and you start sucking like their pleasure is all you need to be happy yourself."

In a soft voice, Olympia replied, "Thank goodness they're the forgiving type."

"I get the feeling they're only forgiving where you're concerned. Now Leland and Colby will be here soon. They might be a little resentful for your lack of reciprocity, so let them know right away what you intend to do." She smiled naughtily. "Men are far more patient once they've had their first orgasm of the evening."

* * * *

The Duke of Tasley saw Olympia standing on the opposite side of the dance floor, talking with Lady Darcia. It had been nearly a week since he'd last seen her, and during their time of separation he had fantasised about her like a teenaged tyro completely new to sex. To see her now made his heart race and his palms feel clammy. He wasn't a nervous boy…but he felt that way.

"She's lovely," Prince Mallory said quietly, standing at Colby's side.

"You were right about that dress. I didn't think the blue would enhance her stunning looks, but I was entirely wrong."

"Everybody's looking at her."

Colby studied the men in the room. Not all of the men were looking in Olympia's direction, but enough of them were for the duke's jealous anger to flare.

"Has she ever looked better?" Leland asked, drawing the duke away from his fevered thoughts.

"No." He looked at the handsome, slender man beside him, dressed in an exquisite, black cutaway suit, his long ebony hair curling over the high collar of his crisp white shirt. "And neither have you, for that matter." When their gazes met, Colby smiled softly and added, "I'm a lucky man to have the two of you."

"We're all lucky," the prince replied. "Now let's make our way through this crowd as unobtrusively as possible, and see how we can get Olympia alone for a little while."

"How 'little' a while?"

"How does the rest of her life sound to you?"

"Perfection. Absolute perfection."

As titled members of the *Ton* and two of its richest bachelors, Colby and Leland were looked upon by debutantes and their mothers in roughly the same way that a lioness with hungry cubs looks at a limping antelope. They were stopped, individually and collectively, at least a dozen times before they made it entirely around the perimeter of the dance floor to where Olympia and Darcia stood.

"Mrs. Whyte, so good to see you again," Colby said with cordial bon homie, accepting her offered hand. To an observer, he was being polite, but nothing more.

The Duke of Tasley bent over Olympia's hand, kissing the back of it. She wore over-the-elbow white gloves with an off-the-shoulder Grecian-style evening gown of pale blue, trimmed in white lace. Her breasts were on prominent display, held lovingly high by an underbust short-stay corset.

Memories, richly evocative, of feasting on those breasts, licking and sucking on the nipples as she squirmed in ecstasy, came rushing back to the duke, and he felt his penis awaken. Whenever she was in his presence, all his senses were alert to every subtle hint of sensuality that seemed to ooze from her pours. It was like a very heady aphrodisiac that could be inhaled.

"Your Grace," Olympia replied, her violet eyes taking in the big man with slow appraisal, "so good to see you again."

Prince Mallory kissed Olympia's hand next. "My lady, can I say you look lovelier than ever? I didn't think it was possible, but you continue to look better and better and better."

The duke nearly dropped his cocktail when Olympia calmly and conversationally replied, "It must be all that wonderfully hard cock I've been getting from you and Colby. Fucking you seems to have done wonders for my outlook on life."

Under his breath, Colby bent low and replied, "Jesus, Olympia, what are you trying to do? Do you want me to get an erection right here and now? There are a hundred people in this ballroom, and half of them are looking right at us."

Lady Darcia delicately cleared her throat to draw attention to herself. When Colby was looking at her, she said in a low voice, "Olympia has something special she'd like to tell you. She's…well, let's just say she's making up for a mistake she made a week ago."

The duke's eyes narrowed suspiciously. As far as he was concerned, the events of the previous weekend were flawless. No mistakes had been made. He said, "Oh?"

"The duchess is correct. Last weekend, you lovely men gave me a very nice, very erotic climax as sort of a going away present," she said with teasing, false naivete that amused Colby. "I should have known it instinctively, but I'm so new to this game that I didn't realise I should have shown..." She turned to Darcia, a question in her eyes.

"The word is 'reciprocity'," the duchess answered.

"Yes, I should have shown reciprocity to you men." She paused a moment before continuing with comic sincerity. "But I intend to rectify my error as quickly as I can find a place where we can have some privacy. Then I'm going to get down on my knees and..."

Colby felt a tightening in his chest—and in his breeches. He'd been given many bold promises of sexual nirvana in the past, but never by Olympia...and that made all the difference in the world.

"I'm going to get down on my knees," she continued, then took a rather hefty sip of champagne to fortify her courage, "and suck your cocks." Her gaze darted from Colby to Leland, and the duke saw that she was fearful of what she was proposing. The threat of getting caught *in flagrante delecto* carried equal measures of horror and eroticism. "We won't have much time, so don't hold back."

Lord Beldon's erection began flaring to life, stretching and growing, already making a burgeoning bulge in his breeches.

"Damn it, Olympia, when you talk like that, you make me want to push you to your knees right here and now."

"And grab me by the hair, like you've done before?" When the duke groaned his approval, Olympia smiled. "Soon, my precious. Soon. First I have to find a place where we'll have some privacy." She turned to Darcia. "Come, my friend, help me find a trysting spot in this drafty old castle."

Colby grinned, shaking his head slowly in amazement, and asked Leland, "Have you ever met a woman who fascinated you so much?"

"Never. No one else has come even close to her."

"Let's get another drink, and try to think of something else. I don't want to be standing around with a painful erection stuck in my breeches all night."

Chapter Thirteen

Twenty minutes later, Olympia wasn't so certain she'd made the right decision by wantonly promising her lovers pleasures best delivered from a kneeling position. The ball at the Kennerly estate was a fund raiser for the Foundation for the Suppression of Vice, of which Mable Kennerly, hostess for the event, was a founding member and its most vocal supporter. She was a woman who saw vice simply *everywhere*. Of the approximately two thousand families of the *Ton*, no matter what their moral proclivities happened to be, all were interested in being seen as being *against* vice, all who received an invitation to the ball were in attendance. Many with bank draft in hand to donate for the eminently worthy cause.

Which meant there wasn't an empty room for Olympia to make good on her promise of oral ecstasy to her lovers.

I can't believe I'm looking forward to giving blowjobs to Colby and Leland. But I saw it in their eyes — the shock and the excitement when I told them what I was going to do right here during the ball. I'll bet they're both hiding bulges right now. A shiver went through Olympia. *They've got beautiful cocks. I never thought I'd ever crave such wicked, wicked things!*

Olympia smiled as she passed from a drawing room into a library. It was the third library she'd found in the renovated castle, leading her to wonder just exactly how many libraries a person needed. And, to her enormous dismay, Mable Kennerly was in this library with three middle-aged women.

"There you are, dear!" Mrs. Kennerly said with a flourish, extending her hand in greeting when she saw Olympia. "Come here, dear. We're discussing the complete elimination of vice and why we need it now more than ever in this great empire of ours."

Olympia had no choice but to stop and listen to Mable's lecture. There was nothing more that she wanted to avoid than the old woman's sanctimony.

The Foundation for the Suppression of Vice? Olympia thought as she looked at the organisation's most determined member. *Would you have invited me if you knew that, at this very moment, I'm trying to find a place in your own home and during your fashionable banquet to give blowjobs to two men? And if you're so involved with ridding society of vice, why is it you've invited Prince Mallory and Lord Beldon? They're both notorious for their total, hedonistic embrace of vice.*

After having lectured for a couple of minutes, Mrs. Kennerly's voice lowered slightly as she concluded, "Of course, to enact these worthy programmes for the lower classes, we'll need money. Good intentions are all well and fine, but without finances, vice will flourish among the lower classes whose lives are so riddled with deficiencies."

And that's why Colby and Leland are here, Olympia thought savagely, her full-lipped mouth curling into a condescending smile. *I'll bet they both gave you nice, big endowments, and that's why they got the invitation. They've fucked a thousand women between them, and that's not even counting the men Leland's entertained. Its not vice among the Ton that scares you, it's vice among those not borne into the peerage.*

"Dear, are you feeling quite well?" Mrs. Kennerly asked, breaking into Olympia's thoughts. "You seemed faraway."

"I was just thinking of something, that's all."

I was thinking that you're a hypocrite, Mrs. Kennerly. And I just realised that Colby and Leland have fucked a thousand people...but the only woman they've made love to is me!

"But dear, I was speaking." There was mild reproach in her tone. The notion that Mrs. Kennerly could speak, but not be listened to, seemed to be a concept difficult to register in her brain.

Before Olympia could reply, an aged butler with a fringe of white hair encircling his head just above the ears stepped forward, holding a silver tray in his right hand. On the tray was a small, cream-coloured sealed envelope.

"Mrs. Whyte?" the butler asked.

"I am she."

The butler held the tray out to her. "This is for you. I received it only moments ago."

Ignoring the inquisitive look she received from Mrs. Kennerly, Olympia picked up the small envelope and opened it. She recognised Lady Darcia's handwriting immediately. She had written, "Dearest Friend, what you're looking for is in the carriage house. Ironic, don't you think, since it was a carriage house where all this started? D."

"Pardon me, there's something I must attend to," Olympia said to her hostess, ignoring the questioning look she received in return.

She walked as quickly as she dared, hoping to not draw attention to herself. Every nerve in her body was ready to give and receive pleasure.

This time, all they have to do is stand there and enjoy themselves, Olympia reminded herself. *I can't believe I'm going to do this…and I can't believe how much I'm anticipating getting on my knees to suck their cocks!*

* * * *

Lady Darcia's lead coachman, Abbott, was a cousin through marriage to Mr. Kennerly's lead coachman. Under the duchess's insistence, three quid went from palm to palm. The money guaranteed the carriage house's waiting room would be undisturbed for a period of thirty minutes.

The room was austere in the extreme, with only three simple, straight-backed chairs for seating, and a small cast iron stove to ward off the chill. Evidently, the Kennerly's weren't very generous to their household staff, Colby mused as he shifted his weight from one foot to the other, anxiously awaiting Olympia's arrival.

To the duchess's coachman, Colby asked, "You're sure we won't be disturbed for thirty minutes?"

Abbott nodded. "The Kennerly man's a good man. If he says we've got privacy in this room for thirty minutes, he'll make good on his word."

"Especially since we gave him money for his silence."

Jacob, the handsome, younger coachman, stepped forward and said, "Can't blame a fella for wanting to line his pockets a little, now can you?"

Lady Darcia, who had been watching for Olympia's arrival, stepped up to the four men and closed a fan attached by a slender cord to her left wrist with a distinctly annoyed 'snap!'

"What in the world can be taking that woman so long?" There was a jittery quality to all of her movements that signified either great anxiety or anticipation. As she fidgeted, Colby watched her breasts trembling above the half-cups of her corset, exposed by the low-cut bodice. To Abbott, she asked, "How much time is left."

He extracted a heavy silver pocket watch. "Exactly twenty-one minutes, Your Grace." For a man about to get his cock sucked by a very attractive woman dowager duchess, he was remarkably formal.

She placed her gloved palm lightly against his cheek. "Be patient, my dearest. I'll make you happy. I promise."

"Don't wait on account of us, Lady Darcia," the Duke of Tasley said, keeping his voice low as he struggled to ignore the throbbing bulge inside his breeches. "I'm sure Olympia will get here as quickly as she can."

The duchess turned sharply towards Colby. "You're sure? You're absolutely sure?"

Leland stepped forward and answered, "Yes, we're sure. For all that you've done for Olympia, Colby, and myself, acting as lookouts for you now is the least we can do."

Lady Darcia let out a soft squeal of joyous approval as she grabbed her servant lovers and pulled them closer. Standing only a few feet away, Colby had a perfect view as the coachmen made quick work of unbuttoning their breeches. It took only a few seconds for two erections to be exposed, pointing straight at the duchess.

"This is what I want," she purred, wrapping her fingers around both throbbing columns of manly flesh.

The men pulled her into their arms, taking turns kissing her mouth before they both pushed against her bare shoulders. Lady Darcia sank willingly to her knees. Yards of billowing ivory muslin crumbled around the duchess as she positioned her men so that they were directly in front of her, Abbott a little more to the right, and Jacob a little more to the left.

It was a lurid, visual aphrodisiac for the duke, an enticement to sensual excess that sent blood coursing straight into the shaft of his cock. When the duchess began lavishing the crowns of her lovers' erections with swipes of her tongue, Colby wondered whether he could continue watching the spectacle without going quite thoroughly insane.

"That goddamned Olympia had better get here in one hell of a hurry," the duke muttered under his breath. He tried to adjust his erection inside his breeches to make himself less uncomfortable. It didn't work.

Leland touched his forearm and whispered, "I could take Olympia's place...at least until she gets here." He winked saucily. "As I recall, you had me on my knees on that fateful night the three of us, even though we didn't know it at the time, all got together."

Colby shook his head. "The offer is tempting as hell, but she's worked up her courage to do this, so now we'd better let her have the chance to complete what she started."

The sounds of a man in his very early twenties groaning with pleasure, and a woman in her middle thirties moaning with desire, drew Colby's attention away from Leland's handsome face and kissable mouth.

Lady Darcia was on her knees, her lips pink and moist as she nibbled down the shaft of Jacob's erection. When the young man put a hand to her hair, she quickly batted his hand away, though she did not remove him from her mouth. The duchess obviously didn't want her coiffure disarranged.

Though Jacob was not nearly as endowed as Colby, the duke was still a little astonished when the duchess slowly swallowed every inch of the boy's arousal. The sight of Lady Darcia taking all that the coachman had, prompted another groan from the duke. His cock literally ached.

The sounds of hurried, kidskin-slippered feet against the marble floor drew Colby's attention, and he stepped quickly to the side, turning so that he could block with his body the approaching person's view of Lady Darcia on her knees. But it wasn't an intruder, it was his own lover, Olympia, and as she hurried through the darkened room towards him, the taut rise and fall of her mounding breasts was so visually erotic it was nearly enough to make the duke release his semen right then and there.

"What took you so long?" the duke demanded.

"Please don't be mad at me." Olympia was a little breathless. It was clear to Colby that she'd hurried the entire way from wherever the butler had found her. "I'm here now, and that's what's important."

Colby grabbed her by the shoulders and pulled her in tight against his body, desperately needing to feel those firm, extravagant breasts against his chest. He slanted his mouth down furiously over Olympia's, forcing his tongue between her lips, giving her a barbarian's kiss, angry that he needed her with such complete desperation.

After a full twenty seconds, she twisted her face sharply to the side to end the kiss. "We have no time for that," Olympia said in a hushed flurry of words. "Get them out for me."

The duke grabbed Olympia by the shoulders, turned her so that she was positioned directly behind the kneeling Lady Darcia, then pushed her to her knees. The women were now back-to-back, each with two men in front of her.

The duke had witnessed many, many wildly erotic things in his life, but nothing could compare to seeing Olympia—in her exquisite baby blue Grecian gown with her pale breasts full and round and on display, her coiffure perfectly arranged atop her head with auburn tendrils curling down her temples, and two strings of diamonds woven into the strands—on her knees in front of him. When her small, gloved hand wrapped around the hard shaft of his cock, the duke knew immediately that he would not withstand much pleasuring before he released his sperm.

Time away from Olympia and Leland, along with this unplanned tryst in the ancestral castle of a member of Parliament and his busybody wife—where the chances of getting caught were very real—had turned a burning lust into a raging conflagration that would not be dampened by a mere single orgasm. He'd need several climaxes before this night could be said to have come to a successful conclusion.

Of that, the Duke of Tasley had no doubts whatsoever.

It was strangely bewitching to feel the texture of Olympia's glove on the shaft of his cock. As she pushed her lips over the crown of his erection and he felt her slithering pink tongue work against the underside of his cock, Colby wondered if part of the reason he was so aroused was because his lovers were entirely clothed, and there were other people similarly engaged and very nearby.

With the women quite literally back-to-back, there was an ocean of priceless fabric billowing around their kneeling bodies. If either had any qualms about satisfying her lovers while being in such a position and with so many people in attendance, their actions certainly didn't show it.

"Kiss me."

It took the duke a moment before becoming aware that someone had spoken to him. Turning his gaze away from Olympia was not an easy feat, and certainly not at a time like this. He looked at the prince and, discordant with what was at that moment being done to him, asked in a rather casual voice, "Pardon?"

"I said, 'Kiss me.'" But an instant later, when Olympia's lips surrounded the head of his cock, Leland's long, dark lashes fluttered like butterfly wings against his pale cheeks for a moment. Then his startling silver-blue eyes opened, and looking straight at Colby, he repeated firmly, "Kiss me, damn it."

Colby put a hand around the back of Leland's neck and pulled him to the side to feast upon his pink lips. He kissed the prince firmly, deeply, his tongue dancing with Leland's as the sounds of Olympia's enthusiastic fellatio drifted upward like an erotic minuet.

Time was critical and discovery a very real danger. And so it was that when Jacob whispered, "Oh, God!" and then groaned rather loudly, it preceded Lady Darcia's satisfied moans by only a few seconds. The instant that young coachman's passion had been completely satisfied, she turned her full attention towards seeing Abbott's desire was similarly attended to.

Whether it was because she could hear that her friend had already brought one of her lovers to climax, or if she was simply determined to see to it that Colby and Leland experienced the ultimate sensation before all of their reputations were ruined on the *Ton* by an unfortunate witness, the duke couldn't say. Whatever the reason for her feverishly delivered fellatio, Colby didn't care because Olympia was sucking and licking and nibbling on him with greater skill and enthusiasm than ever before. With his nerve endings overloading with both the visual and tactile sensations, the Duke of Tasley clenched his jaws, forced his eyes to remain wide open throughout his orgasm so that he could see Olympia the entire time, and unleashed a torrent of semen against the kneeling woman's tongue.

Olympia swallowed, coughed slightly, and swallowed again. She looked up at Colby only briefly and flashed him a quick wink to let him know that everything was fine. Then she started sucking on Leland as though the completion of his passion was her lifeline to happiness.

* * * *

Col. Newton's smile was charming despite the fury blossoming in his chest. In his hand was a glass of champagne that had long since become room temperature. He was in full, formal uniform, complete with the ceremonial British sword in a scabbard on his left hip. Several women that evening had already made it clear — subtly, of course — that they were willing to share a bed with him that evening…but the colonel wasn't interested in any of them.

All women paled in comparison to Olympia Whyte. The colonel had long ago set his sights on her, and he hadn't bedded her yet. He was a man accustomed to having what he wanted, and he wasn't going to let Olympia escape. No matter what.

"A dance, my dearest?" It was a request, but as usual, he'd delivered it as a command. "I've been waiting all night, and you can't expect me to be patient."

Olympia took a sip of her champagne, her violet eyes alive with mischief. "Oh? Why can't you be patient? Mr.

Kennerly's in Parliament and he said he'd wait all night just to have one dance with me."

The colonel smiled, but inwardly he seethed at this widow's cheekiness. He was *never* the object of jokes.

"Patience is something other men need, I suppose. As for myself, I can take whatever I want." He smiled to soften the effrontery of his words, but Col. Newton saw the sudden flash of fear in Olympia's eyes, and he knew she'd received the appropriate message. "Now please. Mrs. Kennerly has hired a full orchestra. They're playing wonderfully, and I love to waltz."

When Olympia didn't move, the colonel took her by the wrist and wrapped her arm around his, then escorted her to the middle of the dance floor. As they walked between couples dancing, he was aware of the stiffness of Olympia's body, but he was also aware of the plush softness of her breast against his biceps.

He turned into Olympia, and when he took his first step, she was instantly in rhythm with him.

"That's better," he said, looking down. Unsmiling, she was staring at his chest. He had an unhurried and close-up view of her cleavage, and it was enough to make his penis, which paid so little attention to other women, awaken to the possibilities of carnal attention. "I didn't know you were such a skilled dancer." He waited for her to respond, and when she didn't he added, "Your husband never told me about your dancing abilities. Pity he had to die. You must be very lonely."

She looked up then, quickly and with obvious surprise. "What do you mean by 'he had to die?'"

"It's just a turn of phrase. A fairly common one at that." He pulled her in just a little tighter as they moved to the music, enjoying the contact of her breasts against his chest. "I didn't mean anything by it."

He waited for her to join in the conversation, and the longer she refused, the angrier the colonel got. The waltz ended and Olympia began disengaging herself from his arms, but he continued to hold her firmly.

"No." The single word was softly spoken, but its impact was sharp. "I'd like another dance."

She said nothing. The orchestra paused only long enough to receive a spattering of polite applause before starting into a waltz by Hurstmann. This time, when the colonel started dancing, Olympia was a half-step behind for several seconds before she finally timed her movements properly.

"Olympia, where were you earlier tonight?"

She shrugged her shoulders, and though she hadn't intended for her breasts to wiggle because of the gesture, they did, and the effect upon the colonel's flaring senses was instantaneous. He smiled. With Olympia, his penis behaved the way he wanted it to—it responded. With all other women, the organ was flaccid and useless.

"Listen to me carefully," he continued, directing the two of them through the crowd on the dance floor. "I don't want you leave privately with other men. That's disrespectful to me, and I won't allow it."

Olympia's mouth opened for a moment, then closed quickly. She was clearly affronted by the colonel, and her feistiness made him want her all the more.

"I mean it, my dear. I've waited a long time for you, so you can hardly expect me to sit around idly while you flaunt your charms and waste yourself with men like Lord Beldon and Prince Mallory." At the mention of the names, she looked up swiftly—and Col. Newton knew he had picked the right two names to speak. "You've behaved foolishly, but I'm willing to forgive."

Olympia stopped dancing so quickly the colonel stumbled for a moment.

"Just who the hell do you think you are, giving me orders?" Olympia hissed through clenched teeth, keeping her voice low but still drawing attention to her from the dancers nearby. "I'm not a child, Colonel. And I'm not a soldier under your command."

Only a single muscle twitching in his jaw displayed the colonel's fury. With controlled might, he pulled Olympia into the waltz, forcing her to keep time with him. After several seconds, she resumed dancing properly, just as he knew she would. However angry she might get, she was a woman of the *Ton*, and as such, she would never create a scene of hysteria. Hysterical women have an impossible time finding a wealthy man in the *Ton*, and as everyone knew, a single woman in the *Ton* was a woman waiting to become a bride. Of this, the colonel had no doubts.

"You're allowed your little spiff," the colonel said, bending so that he could speak directly into Olympia's ear. The move had the added advantage of allowing him to inhale her perfume, which was a narcotic to his senses. There was nothing about this woman — not even her anger — that didn't arouse his passions. "I won't begrudge you that. But don't think you're not mine, Olympia. You're a widow, after all, and you could do *much* worse than being married to an officer with connections to the highest offices in the land."

His hand tightened at the small of her back. Though his body posture suggested he could be whispering love words into her ear, the colonel then said, "And bad things happen to people who think they can fuck with me. Think about that, Olympia. A lot of good things can come your way when you're on my arm in public, and in my bed in private." He smiled, but it wasn't a friendly expression.

"Where did you go tonight with Lord Beldon and Prince Mallory? You all seemed to disappear at the same time, and that displeased me." The fingers of his left hand tightened around Olympia's right, causing her to wince in pain. "Now tell me, what were you doing with those disreputable rakes?"

In a voice that held the trace of a quiver, Olympia replied, "Nothing. Seriously. Nothing at all."

"Good," the colonel replied. "I intend to see that it remains that way."

Chapter Fourteen

"It really was quite frightening." Olympia, sitting in Lady Darcia's flower room, was casual inspecting a rose, though her thoughts were on Mrs. Kennerly's ball the previous evening. "Colonel Newton seems to think that just because he had the power to order my husband around, he has the same power over me."

The duchess, busy with a scissors snipping off dead leaves and pruning her much-pampered flowers, replied, "At first I thought the colonel was just another pompous military man. So many of them are all a lot of huff and puff but nothing else. But he seems more dangerous than that. Let me make some inquiries. Perhaps there's a way of keeping him away from you without causing a scene."

"The last thing in the world I need right now is to draw attention to myself."

Delicious memories flooded her consciousness of what it had been like to be on her knees, feeling Lady Darcia's back against her own, as together they pleasured their men. Though Olympia blushed at the thought, she wouldn't have changed a single thing about the encounter. And afterward, when they all returned to Mrs. Kennerly's lavish ballroom, her duke and prince were the epitome of charm, cordiality, and wit.

They made sure she always had champagne or punch, and volunteered to go get her the cakes that Mrs. Kennerly's numerous servants had brought out late in the evening. Though politesse dictated that the men dance with other women—it would have been entirely rude for them to refuse—they always returned to Olympia, allowing others to have a single dance, but nothing more than that.

And that night, in the simple flat in London that Leland kept exclusively for his more daring trysts—he kept not a single servant there—the Duke of Tasley and Prince Mallory made love to Olympia for hours, using their hands, their lips, their tongues, and their cocks to eke out every possible bit of pleasure from her ripe body.

"And you said that the colonel mentioned both the duke and the prince?" Lady Darcia inquired. "You're sure?"

"Yes. Very. I remember thinking, 'Oh, God, he knows!' when he said their names."

"He doesn't know. He's just guessing." Lady Darcia set her scissors aside and turned towards Olympia, putting her fists on her hips. "We're going to have to do something about Colonel Newton. I get the feeling that simply ignoring him isn't going to be enough to dissuade him from further advances."

"Do you think I should tell Leland and Colby about the colonel?"

"Good Lord, no!" Lady Darcia said emphatically. "Those men worship the ground you walk on. If they find out the colonel spoke that way with you, they'd call him out.

There would be a duel—even though they're outlawed—and I have no doubt that Colby or Leland would be victorious. We must find a way of ridding you of the colonel without your men knowing. If they get involved, there will be bloodshed."

"Blast and damn," Olympia muttered.

"Blast and damn, indeed," the duchess replied.

* * * *

Francesca looked at the big man seated in the chair across from her, and wondered once again why so many women wanted to have sex with him. Others might have been impressed with the breadth of his shoulders. but Francesca wasn't. And she'd heard that his erection was most formidable. No matter how much time she spent thinking of it, Francesca couldn't imagine a situation where she would want a man's cock inside her body. And if she *had* to accept such a disgusting thing, wouldn't it be best if the man's cock was very small instead of just the opposite?

It was all an unfathomable mystery to Francesca.

"You've considered my offer?"

"Yes, Colby, I've considered it. And since you're being so ungentlemanly about this, I've decided to accept your offer. In exchange for twenty-five thousand florins in gold, I'll release you from your promise to marry me."

She saw the duke react to the monetary figure she had demanded, and it took all her willpower to keep from smiling triumphantly.

"Francesca, I knew you were a greedy bitch, but I didn't think even you would ask that much." He scratched his chin, looking out the windows. "That's enough to keep a dozen families in food and shelter their entire lives."

"Don't be small, Colby. You've got plenty of money, so don't tell me you can't afford it. Besides, you're the one who wants to break a promise of marriage, not me. I've told you repeatedly, I've got my heart set on becoming Lady Beldon." She leant back in her chair, pleased to see the shock on her fiancé's face. If she was going to face temporary embarrassment on the *Ton* because he wanted to break off the marriage, at least she was going to have a tidy sum of gold for her troubles. "I'm to be paid in gold, not with a bank draft."

The duke looked at her, the smile on his face nasty. "Smart move. You wouldn't want anyone to know how you've extorted from me, would you?"

"I want the money within three days. After that, I'll announce the end of our engagement in a manner I feel is appropriate."

"Once I give you the florins, I want the announcement put in all the newspapers immediately." He rose to his feet. "Good day, Francesca. I'll be back soon with the gold."

"Good day, Your Grace," Francesca replied. "I look forward to our next visit."

"It'll be our *last* visit, you bitch."

Francesca merely smiled, immune to the insults of others.

* * * *

Col. Newton looked at the sign above the pub's entrance and grinned. *The Crippled Cow?* he thought with a grin. *Who in hell would want to meet at a pub called The Crippled Cow?*

He stepped inside. Though the sun was high in the sky and it was quite bright outside, the pub's few windows and low ceiling allowed for little illumination. This was the kind of place where people went to remain anonymous.

He found Claude LeMorneau sitting in a heavy wooden chair at an even heavier table. The scarred table and chairs were built solidly enough to last through a hundred years of service. There was another man at the table with Claude, a swarthy man wearing business clothes that had seen better days. London was filled with once-fortunate men whose luck had vanished. With a motion of his hand, Claude sent the man scurrying away. When the man walked past the colonel as he headed for the door, he never once raised his eyes.

"Thank you for coming," Claude said, raising from his chair with hand extended.

The colonel shook hands, sat, and made a point of ignoring the looks he received from other patrons. Officers in uniform were a novelty at *The Crippled Cow*, it would seem. Toward the back of the room, he saw a couple of women. Each wore a low-cut evening dress even though it was only a little past noon. The dresses were several years out of style, but they were very revealing, which the colonel suspected was their main purpose. Idly, the colonel wondered what the cost of their services was, then with a shrug realised that he didn't care. Col. Newton now accepted as indisputable fact that Olympia was the cure to all his afflictions.

"Who was that man who was just here?" the colonel asked.

"I make a little money as a lender," Claude replied. "A pleasant little sum to supplement my other income. He came to make an interest payment."

The colonel nodded thoughtfully. "It's always the interest that does them in, isn't it?"

Claude smiled. "Always."

"And you have money for me?"

Claude nodded. "Yes."

"Excellent, my friend."

"But I'd like to see the books once again, the leases and the schedules for the arrival of product from India." Claude held his hands palms outward, a gesture of innocence that the colonel didn't believe for a second. "I haven't seen the books since I first agreed to be an investor."

For a moment the colonel, who was never without words, could think of nothing to say. He smiled graciously and looked away, but he felt as though Claude had given him a sucker punch to the solar plexus.

Has this little prick grown a spine? Fucking Frenchman! How dare he question me?

"I'm sure everything is fine," Claude continued, "but I'd like to see how my investment is faring. Surely, you can understand that Colonel, can't you?"

Col. Newton cleared his throat, struggling for his brain to come up with a believable excuse for refusing to release the company ledgers.

"Can't you, Colonel?" Claude's tone had lost much of its friendliness.

"Yes, that will be no problem. No difficulty at all." He leant forward, his eyes alight as a new idea, not yet fully formed, began taking shape in his mind. "But how would you like it if you didn't have to make any more payments into the British-India Tea Company?"

Claude's eyes narrowed suspiciously. "And I remain an investor? I lose nothing?"

"Better than that. I'll cover your future payments for you, and you'll still be considered a full investor with equal shares of stock in the company."

"Why would you do that?"

"For money, my good fellow." The colonel could always count on the greed of his fellow man. "The best of all possible reasons — for money."

Claude was confused, and it showed in his expression. The colonel wanted to keep him that way. At first it had seemed like the world was about to drop out from beneath the colonel's boots, and now he realised that he was smarter, more clever, than all of his adversaries. Nothing would defeat him. He would always survive, always flourish, always come out victorious.

"I have been in negotiations with several businessmen for quite some time now, and they're very interested in developing a partnership with men of connections. Without using your name specifically, I have informed them of your daughter's upcoming nuptials. Well, you can imagine how enthusiastically they received that news." The colonel crossed his legs, putting a boot up on the opposite knee. "I've taken the liberty of negotiating on your behalf. You'll get twelve percent on all transactions where your royal connections are used. Twelve percent for doing nothing other than making an introduction to your son-in-law, the Duke of Tasley."

"And what do you get? I'm no fool, Colonel. You must get something."

"I get three percent. These businessmen think a fifteen percent mark-up is a small price to pay for access to ducal authority."

Claude smiled. "Colonel, you've got yourself a deal."

"The sooner that daughter of yours marries Lord Beldon, the sooner we can all begin turning a profit."

* * * *

The next day was entirely overcast, the clouds hanging grey and menacing, seemingly only a few yards above the heads of the people scurrying about on the crowded London streets.

Colby's mood was distinctly the opposite of the gloomy weather. The same could not be said for Sir Malcomb Westridge of London Bank West, who had looked on disconsolately as the duke withdrew twenty-five thousand pounds in gold florins. The coins had been put into a sturdy wooden box and, with an armed escort, brought from the bank to Colby's offices.

There's freedom in that ugly wooden box, thought Colby as he looked at the crate carrying enough gold to allow Francesca to live fashionably and leisurely the rest of her life. *As soon as Francesca is permanently out of my life, all I'll have to do is figure out how to arrange it so that I can be with Olympia and Leland…without causing a scandal the likes of which the Ton has never seen.*

There was a knock at the door before it opened just enough for the duke's secretary to stick his head into the room. He was a slender, bespectacled man in his early fifties who took his job terribly seriously.

"There's a lady here to see you, Your Grace," the secretary said. A glance at his face informed Colby that the good man had been having a difficult time with whoever had arrived. He suspected that Francesca was too greedy to wait until later in the day to take custody of the gold. "She insists that she see you."

"It's all right. Let her in."

The door was opened wide when Baroness Marion von Mecklenburg barged into the room. Tall, blonde, svelte, she was English by birth but had married into a family of German aristocracy. After having given her wealthy and titled husband a son, the baron promptly went on a world cruise—without either wife or son aboard. In the two years since his departure, the baroness and Colby had been frequent lovers, though both professed to having no designs on the other. It was "just sex," they liked to say, though the duke was beginning to have his doubts regarding Marion's veracity on the subject.

"Where the hell have you been, Colby?" the baroness demanded.

"At least you waited until the door was closed before talking to me that way."

Marion rolled her eyes expressively. "The old man's your secretary. What do you care what he thinks or what he hears?"

"He's been a faithful employee to my father and me for decades."

Looking at Marion with all her sleek sophistication, tall and slender, her features whispering of a thousand years of English aristocracy, Colby began to wonder what he ever saw in her. She was the antithesis of Olympia, who never lorded her money and power over servants and staff. And whereas Colby used to think of the baroness's breasts as small ripe apples made by Nature to be nibbled on, he now envisioned her bosom as unripened fruit not ready to be tasted. Compared to Olympia, the baroness's body was boyish.

And if Colby was interested in a boyish body, he had to look no further than Prince Leland Mallory to find sheer perfection.

"I want to know why you haven't come to see me," Marion stated. She began crossing the room, her hips moving with a subtle sway with each step. Her pale blue eyes were still angry, but beneath the anger was a smouldering passion. "It's been more than a month."

"You have lovers other than me."

"Yes, but they don't satisfy me like you do."

"I've been busy."

A flinty hardness came into her eyes. The baroness thought nothing of taking on new lovers and discarding old ones at a whim, but she loathed it whenever a lover bedded another woman.

"Busy? With who?"

"It's 'with whom?' And I don't see how that's any of your business."

The baroness half-sat on Colby's desk, her eyes evolving slowly from cold hardness to a flirtatious warmth.

"Let's not argue," she said after a moment, slender fingers toying with the top button of her blouse. "I came here to fuck, not fight." She unfastened the small, cloth covered button, then another. "You're right, of course, in not telling me her name. I wouldn't tell you of my other lovers." Her eyebrows danced for a moment with naughty amusement. "Guess what I've learned to do?"

Colby made a passing motion with his right hand, and replied, "Don't unfasten any more buttons, Baroness. This isn't the time, and my office sure as hell isn't the place."

"I've been going Greek." She saw his reaction. "Seriously, I met this thoroughly fascinating man about five weeks ago—"

"Does 'thoroughly fascinating' mean that he's got a fortune, and he doesn't mind spending it on you?"

"Precisely," the baroness replied without rancour. "See, nobody understands me quite like you do. We're perfect together. Anyway, he positively adores me, but he's got the smallest penis you've ever seen. Well, I don't suppose you've seen a lot, but I have, and I can tell you he's got nothing."

You'd be surprised, baroness, of the changes in my life since last you crawled between the sheets of my bed. Prince Mallory could teach you all sorts of tricks. He's certainly taught me more than a few.

The baroness angled her head slightly to the side, looking at Colby crossly. "Are you listening to me?"

"Of course I am."

"Anyway, he has this small penis. Nothing at all like that stallion's cock you keep inside your breeches. Well, he wanted to put it in my ass. I don't really know why I let him. Maybe I was just bored and thought I'd try something knew with him, and he had just given me these gorgeous two carat diamond ear bobs from that jeweller on Bond Street, so I thought I'd give it up to him." Her hand drifted up to her breast, and she pinched her nipple gently. A breath caught briefly in her throat. "You've been a very naughty boy by not coming to see me, but I'm here now. Maybe...just maybe...if you promise to stop if I can't take it, I'll let you have my ass."

"Thanks for the offer," Colby replied, a full measure of nonchalance colouring every word, "but my schedule is full up."

"Don't tell me that. I know from personal experience that you can fuck for days on end."

"I'm serious, Marion. I'm not interested."

It took several seconds for the stone seriousness of the duke's statement to make it past the barricades of the baroness's overblown ego to reach her consciousness. When it did, the blood drained from her face.

"I'm offering you my ass, and you're turning it down?" The words came out as an incredulous whisper. Colby simply looked straight into her eyes. "You prick." Hardly more than a whisper. "You vile bastard."

"I admit to having a prick, but I'm more than just that. And as for my birthright, as the Duke of Tasley, being called a bastard seems more foolish to me than anything else."

He saw the confusion going through Marion. For her entire life, men had thrown themselves at her, had promised to do whatever she wanted them to, had always given her everything she asked for. To offer herself sexually, but then get turned down, was for the baroness akin to discovering that the magnetic poles had shifted. North was no longer north and south no longer south.

Momentarily staggered, the baroness was not yet willing to admit defeat.

"I'll suck your cock," she said, speaking as though she had just played a winning trump card in a poker game with very high stakes. "I know it bothered you that I refused to do that, but I'm willing to do it now."

"I'm still not interested." The invitation was without intrigue now, with Leland and Olympia more than willing to satisfy that particular sexual desire for Colby.

Marion got up off the desk, taking slow steps backward away from the duke. She seemed to be having difficult refastening the buttons of her blouse.

"Do you really think you can walk away from me?"

"Actually, it looks like you're the one walking away from me."

"You haven't heard the last of me, Colby. People just don't do this to me."

She slammed the door as she left. Colby waited, knowing what would happen next. After thirty seconds, as expected, the door opened and the duke's secretary stuck his head into the office.

"Is there anything you need, Your Grace?"

"No. Everything is fine." Colby gave his secretary a benevolent smile. He had forgotten that Baroness von Mecklenburg was in his life, and he felt rather good now that she no longer was. "Go back to your desk. Thank you for your concern."

* * * *

"This is where you wanted me to take you, isn't it, m'lady?" the coachman asked.

Olympia sat in the open rented carriage, her mind in a whirl, hot unshed tears of anger and hurt pooling in her eyes.

The carriage had just pulled to a stop when she saw Baroness von Mecklenburg ascending the steps of the brownstone building. Olympia thought it was very strange for the baroness to be visiting a business office, since she was worth several fortunes, and she refused to do even the most innocuous of charity work for those less fortunate than herself.

Happiness had caused suspicion to be slow to take hold in her thoughts, but once green jealousy had insinuated itself, it went straight to the marrow of her bones and turned poisonous in seconds. She gave the coachman an additional half crown and told him to keep the carriage right where it was. Paid rather extravagantly to do nothing at all, the coachman was quite content to sit and smoke his pipe.

Olympia watched as, some time later, Baroness von Mecklenburg exited the building. She had the flushed look of a woman who had just been well-loved. Olympia recognised the look because she'd seen it on herself many times over the past weeks.

In a dull voice, Olympia said, "I've made a mistake. A terrible mistake. Would you please take me home?"

"Of course, m'lady. Whatever you wish."

Chapter Fifteen

To say that Francesca was in a good mood on the afternoon she was to receive the Duke of Tasley would be an understatement of galactic proportions. For the occasion she had all three of her personal maids with her to see to her every need. She tried on four different sets of clothing before settling on a white silk blouse with the finest stitching, and a light grey skirt and matching waist-length jacket. Her hair was wound into a chignon at the base of her skull that was so tight not a single strand had come free. Dangling from her earlobes were the pearl ear bobs that her father had purchased for her on the day she was born. Though she was still in morning attire, she had chosen to roll on her silk stockings instead of the customary daytime cotton stockings.

When one was about to become independently wealthy — with the key word being *independent*, a rarity in the Regent Prince's England — it seemed appropriate to dress with care for the occasion.

"There is a gentleman here to see you," the butler said, standing at the doorway to the sunroom. "Shall I allow his entrance?"

"Yes," Francesca answered, feeling her heart accelerate in response. "It's Lord Beldon. Please, show him in. And then close the door. I'll want privacy."

She saw the faint look of disapproval show in the old man's eyes, but Francesca didn't care. As all well brought up young women of the *Ton* knew, it was inappropriate for a single and unescorted woman to be in a closed room with a man, as such privacy might allow for sexual impropriety. Though she normally didn't care what the servants overheard, since she really didn't give a damn about their personal attitudes anyway, she couldn't risk their gossiping about what she and the duke had to say.

She heard the heels of Colby's boot clicking against the brightly polished wood flooring, and she straightened a bit in her chair, quickly adjusting the hem of her skirt so that it draped her legs properly. She wanted to present an attractive imagine for the duke to show him just what a fool he was being for breaking his promise of matrimony.

When he stepped into the room, she was surprised at the size of the wooden crate that he carried. Though he was a very powerful man, it was evident that the small box was quite heavy.

That's to be expected. Gold is very heavy…and the gold that's in that box is mine to do with whatever I want.

"Good afternoon, Colby. Thank you for arriving as scheduled." She gave him a sweet smile, which he completely ignored. "Is there anything I can get for you? A libation of some sort?"

"Only my freedom, Francesca. That's all I want."

"You needn't be brusque. You're getting what you want. As usual, you're getting everything you want."

"But at a price, Francesca." He set the box down at Francesca's feet. She enjoyed the solid 'thump' as it hit the floor. "At a very steep price."

"Please, take a seat. Let's discuss arrangements."

"I'd rather stand. We don't have that much to discuss."

She leant back in her chair to look up at him. He hated her now because she had extorted so much money from him, but that was of little concern to Francesca. From the very beginning, her relationship with the Duke of Tasley had been based solely on finances. She had very few illusions as to the type of woman she had grown into.

"I want the dissolution of our engagement in all of the major newspapers. Every newspaper that ran notice of our engagement should be contacted," Colby stated flatly. "You can tell them anything you want. Make me the big, bad villain. I don't care. Just make it clear to everyone in London that you and I are *not* getting married during the Little Season."

"Anything else?"

"That'll do it." He kicked the box lightly with the toe of his boot. The box did not move. "Twenty-five thousand florins in gold. Delivered, as promised and on time."

"You do understand that it's going to be difficult finding a proper bride after this, Colby. Whoever becomes your wife is going to be laughed at on the *Ton*." Her lashes lowered for a moment before she raised her gaze to the duke's. "Everyone will know she was your second choice. People will talk about her behind her back."

"You weren't my first choice, Francesca. Our marriage was arranged by my mother and your father. Everyone already knows that." He grinned and shook his head in bitter amusement, running fingers over his blond hair. "What in hell my mother saw in you I'll never know."

Though she tried to pretend that Colby's contempt was of little concern, she was prickly about insults. "Don't be nasty. Just remember, I can say a lot or a little about why we're not getting married."

"I don't care what you say. Just get the information in the newspapers, and do it right away."

As she watched the duke stride purposefully out of her sunroom — tall, broad-shouldered, and gorgeous to look at — she wondered whether she had made a lifelong enemy, and whether her victory now might not come at a price higher than she had calculated. Lord Beldon had a history of defeating all those who challenged him, and he could be especially vengeful to those who publicly defied him.

Whatever concerns Francesca had about making enemies vanished when she opened the lid to the box and looked inside. Twenty-five thousand florins in gold! A fortune in gold, and it was all hers to spend on herself, buying all the lovely things that she deserved! The sensation she received from looking at the gold, feeling the coins in her cupped hands, was as close to a sensual feeling as Francesca had ever known.

* * * *

As he left Francesca's home and stepped up into the saddle of Thunder, the six-year-old black Arabian gelding that was his favourite, the Duke of Tasley knew it wasn't *literally* true, but it still felt as though a thousand pound weight had been lifted from his shoulders. He was, at last, a truly free man. There never had been any barriers between himself and Leland, and now there were no barriers between himself and Olympia.

A thousand chaotic emotions began bombarding him now that the prospect of having Francesca as a wife, even if the whole world knew she was a wife in name only, was no longer hanging over his head. How would he and Leland arrange their worlds to suit Olympia's wishes? With approximately two thousand families in the *Ton*, how would the duke be able to be seen in public with his lovers and not have people guessing that they were in a permanent *ménage a trios* love affair? While it was undoubtedly true that people preferred turning a blind eye towards sexual indiscretion, especially by members of the aristocracy towards other members of the aristocracy, a *ménage a trios* love affair was treading into taboo territory.

So what would he do?

The Duke of Tasley decided the best way to make some order of this sudden flurry of questions and insecurities was to have a drink at one of his gentlemen's clubs, White's. Colby believed a good glass of whisky always helped soothe a troubled mind. Besides, he wanted to get the awful taste of Francesca out of his mouth before he went to see Olympia and Leland, and the all-male bastion of a gentleman's club seemed perfect for the occasion.

"Come on, Thunder," Colby said, patting the gelding's sleek neck. "Let's go to St. James's Street and have ourselves a whisky."

With a touch of his heels, Thunder started off through the streets of London at a canter, his iron shoes clacking loudly against the cobblestones. Since most of the best gentlemen's clubs in London are on St. James's Street, White's being just one of them, the animal could practically find his way there without assistance from his rider.

"My God, is luck ever with me!" Colby exclaimed upon entering White's and finding Prince Mallory seated in one of the heavy, wine-coloured leather wing-backed chairs.

When Leland bolted to his feet, there was a moment of awkwardness as both men clasped arms and were about to kiss before protocol, and a dozen witnesses in the all-male establishment, stopped them. For several seconds they simply looked into each other's eyes, then Colby smiled, gave his lover a quick, mischievous wink that only Leland could see, and took chairs facing each other with a small table between.

"What's going on?" Leland asked under his breath.

Colby waved off the question when a rotund, ancient man in immaculate livery stepped up. His name was Joshua, and he had been serving drinks to members of White's for more years than Colby or Leland could remember.

"I'd like a whisky, and please bring Prince Mallory another of what he's having. Make sure they're on my chit."

"Of course, Your Grace," Joshua replied. There wasn't a man in the *Ton* who he hadn't served a libation at some time or another. He knew everyone's name, everyone's title, and nearly every skeleton in the closets of club members.

Colby looked around. He recognised half a dozen of the men in the club. None of them were good friends of his, and for that he was grateful. He didn't need anyone horning in on his conversation with Leland.

"Wait 'til we get our drinks, then I have the best news to tell you." Though a big man and not given to silly flights of romantic fancy, the duke could hardly sit still in his chair. He felt positively boyish with happiness. After Joshua had served their drinks, Colby leant forward in his chair towards the prince, and kept his voice low. "I've just paid Francesca her blood money. The dissolution of our engagement will be in all the newspapers tomorrow. It was twenty-five thousand florins in gold, but now Olympia will be happy. That's what really matters."

Leland nodded. "Yes, that's the way I see it, too. Her happiness is all that really matters."

Colby sipped his whisky. It was the best liquor he'd ever tasted. Everything seemed better to him now that there was nothing standing between him and the people he loved...nothing, that is, except a British aristocratic society that condemned virtually everything about the love that he had at last found with a man and a woman.

"With Francesca out of the way, you and I have got to start thinking about how we're going to live our lives." He made a circular gesture with the hand that held his whisky glass. "I mean the three of us. We can't come right out and let everyone know how we're living. In fact, that's the *last* thing we can do. So what you and I have to do is figure out how the three of us can be together without any of us creating grist for the over-active rumour mill here in London."

Leland nodded, looking into the nearby flames of the fireplace. Colby looked at his profile, marvelling at its refined perfection, at the line of the jaw and the even, straight line of the nose. Prince Mallory was masculine beauty itself...and this awareness caused Colby to feel as though his heart had suddenly swelled in his chest.

Tamping down gentle feelings of love, and rather baser feelings of lust, Colby said, "I want to tell her the good news right away. Can you come with me?"

The prince made a sound in his throat and shook his head, and combed fingers through his long, wavy black hair, brushing the locks back off his forehead. "Wish I could, but I can't. Maman's got me seeing some barrister in less than an hour. Something about my aunt's will that I need to sign off on. Seems the ol' bird has always had a soft spot for me, and she wants me to oversee some investments she's made here in England while she takes a trip abroad. She's going to India to inspect her holdings there."

"Do you mind if I see Olympia alone?"

Leland shook his head. "This news is too important to wait. Go, my friend. Tell her the news, and perhaps I'll see you back here later this evening, when my work for auntie is finished." He smiled, and Colby remembered once again why he had always been so fascinated with the young prince. "And perhaps by then I'll have figured out some scheme where the three of us can be together in public and not cause the Regent Prince to have a royal hissy fit."

Colby chuckled. "Like he'd give a damn, the old reprobate. He's been spreading his sperm far and wide for a long time now."

"Yes, but now he's on the throne, and that makes all the difference in the world," Prince Mallory said.

"Indeed it does. Indeed it does."

* * * *

It was risky to simply go to Olympia's door and knock on it. The proper way to go about seeing a woman was to have a gentleman's gentleman deliver a handwritten message requesting the pleasure of her acquaintance for tea, a day or two in the future. A gentleman simply didn't show up at a woman's doorstep and expect to see her. To simply arrive at a woman's door and get admitted displayed a familiarity that would undoubtedly cause the tongues to wag on the *Ton*, and cause a stain on the reputation of the woman.

The duke knew all this, but he was still exhilarated with the successful conclusion of his engagement. Being free to pursue Olympia made him bold. He simply couldn't wait to tell Olympia the good news.

"I'm sorry, sir, but m'lady does not wish to see you," the tall, elderly butler said, standing firmly in the doorway.

"What do you mean?" It was unfathomable to Colby that Olympia wouldn't see him. They loved each other, and he had critical news for her.

"Your Grace, the lady of the manor does not wish to see you." He looked Colby directly in the eyes, secure in his position and duties. "I don't know how to say it more clearly."

Colby sized the old man up. He could, with very little effort, simply knock the butler to the floor, find Olympia, and demand that she explain herself. Such swift, bold action was what his nature demanded, but it was also what would most infuriate Olympia. And however much he wanted to see her, inciting her anger wouldn't do him any good.

"Did she say why she didn't want to speak to me?" He had to ask, though he knew no one in her employ would honestly answer.

"No, sir."

"Very well. Thank you."

Colby turned away as the old man closed the door. The lock sliding into place seemed ominous somehow.

He looked up and down the street. There were carriages rattling along, carrying society's elite. A crew of workers manning the manure wagon was laughing over some joke as, with shovels and brooms, they cleaned up after the horses. Women with parasols walked in pairs, talking quietly, their lives isolated and insulated from worries or concerns.

Everything was as it should be on this busy street in London's tony Kensington district.

Everything...except for the wildly unsettling fact of Olympia's refusal to see him.

Feeling his anger rising, since the duke had *never* been refused entrance into a lady's home before, Colby decided the small pub just around the corner on Freemont Boulevard should have some of his business. Another whisky might be just the ticket to calm his anger.

Maybe it's because I'm not with Leland. She probably wants to see the two of us together.

But the only rule the three had all agreed upon was that none of them would get intimate unless all three were together.

Does she really think I can't speak with her without wanting to seduce her? I'm not the barbarian she and Leland frequently and annoyingly accuse me of being.

* * * *

"He's gone now, m'lady," Missy stated quietly. She said the words in the same way a concerned mother might say, 'Your fever's broke, my child. You'll feel better soon.' The concern she felt showed plainly in her expression. "Can I get you anything? Something to make you feel better?"

Not knowing how to respond, Olympia nodded and tried to smile but failed miserably. Part of her had wanted to confront Colby, to demand that he explain why his lover had visited him at his office. More importantly, Olympia wanted answers as to why the baroness had that rosy-cheeked, well-loved look to her. Olympia had looked in mirrors and seen that identical look on herself, and it was always after making love with Colby and Leland.

Olympia could not remember a time when Missy wasn't in the household and on the staff. The woman could read her thoughts as well as anyone — and that's why Olympia needed to be away from her.

"I'll by fine," Olympia explained. "In fact, what I would like you to do is to make me a nice pot of tea, then you and the rest of the staff can have the rest of the day and evening off." When Missy started to protest, Olympia raised her palm to silence her. "I'll be fine. Right now what I want most is privacy. So I'm insisting that you and the rest of the staff leave within the half hour." She put her fists on her hips, elbows akimbo. It was a posture she only adopted when she was determined to get her way. It was the same posture she'd used since she was five years old and the light of her father's eye. "Now do I make myself clear?"

"Yes, m'lady." It was clear that Missy wasn't happy about the orders she'd been given, but she would not disobey them. "I'll see to your tea, and tell the others of your wishes."

When Missy left the room, Olympia sat down in her favourite rocking chair and quietly began to cry. The Duke of Tasley was notorious throughout London as the resident stud for the ladies of the *Ton*. Everyone new that. So why did Olympia foolishly think he would be faithful to her?

She had to talk to him, but she couldn't talk to him until she had regained her emotional strength. If she challenged him in her current weakened state, he would twist and distort her words, and she would end up believing all of his lies. She was certain of it. When he turned on the charm, the duke was amazingly persuasive.

"What a fool I am," she murmured, blinking away tears, determined to not let her foolish and wayward emotions get the better of her.

Chapter Sixteen

The Duke of Tasley was only a little intoxicated when he left Thunder at the stables off Sutton Street, and began walking the remaining three blocks to Olympia's house. He had just enough good whisky in his blood to make him unpleasantly belligerent. A lifetime of ducal privilege meant that he didn't have to beg to be seen by anyone. Women sent him perfumed notes asking for him to visit them. Mothers plotted for their daughters to marry him, even while they themselves were sleeping with the duke.

So, as a matter of fact, he *wasn't* going to allow some servant to tell him that the lady of the house would not see him. And he wasn't going to simply turn on his heel and walk away. He was going to talk to Olympia, and he was going to talk to her now, damn it.

He was a half block from the front gates to Olympia's when he saw what appeared to be all of the servants leaving at the same time. They were smiling and talking among themselves. He recognised Molly, even from a distance, and immediately crossed the street, weaving between passing carriages, and stepped into a doorway where he was out of sight.

Could his good luck have returned? Had Olympia dismissed the servants for the afternoon? Perhaps even for the entire evening?

Alcohol and a foul mood made Colby impatient, but he refused to act on his own intemperate feelings. Ducal privileges were extensive, particularly in London—but they didn't extend to breaking into someone's home.

He waited until Molly and the others had passed before he stepped out of the doorway. The sun was no longer high in the sky, but there was still at least a couple of hours before sundown. Too much time for Colby to give serious consideration to waiting for the cover of darkness.

He felt the excitement go through him like electricity from a lightning bolt. The last time he experienced this kind of thrilling danger, it was when he'd followed Olympia out through the back doors of Lady Darcia's estate...on that fateful night when he took his pleasures with her, and set in motion a series of events that had completely changed everything of importance in his life.

Feeling very much like a burglar, Colby didn't even bother with the front door to Olympia's house. Too many potential witnesses at this time of the day, and the door would undoubtedly be locked. He chose instead to walk to the next cross street then doubled back by way of the servants' alley to the neighbourhood stables. The horses were always housed where they wouldn't be glaringly visible to the gentry.

In a faintly intoxicated fashion, it occurred to Colby, as he walked slowly up the alley, that Olympia had inadvertently introduced him to the art of back alley stealth. He wasn't certain if he should thank her or criticise her for her influence.

Somewhere past Olympia's house he could hear a hammer striking an anvil. He was surprised to hear a blacksmith plying his trade in this section of Kensington. To his left a washerwoman was hanging up cotton undergarments on a clothesline, and humming a pleasant tune as she worked. The only time the duke had ever experienced back alleys was when he was sneaking out the back door of his lover's home while the husband was walking in the front.

Then he was at the back of Olympia's house…and there wasn't a soul around to see him!

The back gate was locked. Colby cursed under his breath but didn't hesitate. He quickly scaled the brick and mortar surrounding wall, avoiding the metal gate altogether. When he jumped down from the wall, his hat fell off and landed in a small, muddy patch of water.

"I'm a goddamned duke," he muttered angrily. He picked up his hat and flipped it over the wall. Perhaps someone else could clean it and use it. "I shouldn't have to lurk in back alleys to get invited into a widow's house."

Calmed by the sound of his voice, and realising that he was being entirely reckless and selfish in refusing Olympia's obvious desire to be left alone, he hurried to the rear doors and tested them. As expected, they were locked.

For an instant Colby considered the possibility that Olympia had given the servants the afternoon off because she herself had left the estate. He did not consider this possibility for long. Having spent his entire life getting whatever he wanted, he decided that, through sheer force of will, Olympia would be home because he wanted her to be there. The arrogance and selfishness of this mindset was not lost on the duke, though he had no intentions of changing anytime soon.

He found an unlocked window, but it was for the ground floor laundry room. Though the window wasn't locked, it would only raise six inches, and the duke wasn't as yet inclined to break a window to get entrance. Sneaking into Olympia's house was one thing, but to be quite literally breaking into her home was something else.

Stymied by the locked windows, feeling entirely incompetent as a burglar, Colby put his hands on his hips and simply looked at the rear of Olympia's house. There had to be some way in? How else could thieves make a living?

The rain downspout leading from the roof to the ground seemed like the easiest way for Colby to get up onto the second floor balcony. Who would lock the doors to a second floor balcony?

Though a big man, Colby's strength and athleticism were evident as he wrenched himself hand over hand up the downspout, his fingers gripping the pipe tightly as the toes of his boots sought purchase in the marble exterior. By the time he reached the second floor of the three-story estate, he was breathing harder than normal, though only a little.

The door from the balcony led to a billiard room, dominated by a large table covered in green cloth. Now inside Olympia's home, in a room he'd never before stepped foot, the feeling of being a burglar was exhilarating in an oddly sexual way.

He made his way slowly through the house, careful to keep the heels of his boots soundless against the flooring, listening intently for any sound of Olympia's presence.

She wasn't in the sunroom, nor in the library. A half-dozen guest bedrooms also proved to be empty.

Like a slow-moving nightmare, Colby considered what the ramifications would be if someone had seen him climbing the downspout. How long would it take for the news to race through the *Ton* that the Duke of Tasley had sunk so low that he'd actually broken into Olympia Whyte's home simply because she had refused to see him when he came calling? As a member of the peerage, he wouldn't suffer for the transgression with time in prison. It was unthinkable that a duke should be sent to prison. But he would surely be banished from all the most prestigious gentlemen's clubs. And in the financial sectors of London, where a man's word was either good as gold or utterly worthless, he would be seen as a bad risk. That would effectively put an end to generations of the Beldon name being as prestigious in business as any family in England.

It was just when the sheer foolishness of Colby's enterprise was beginning to overwhelm him that he heard the sound of a spoon briefly tapping against fine china. His spirits instantly elevated. Three more steps and he was able to peer through the slightly opened door.

And there she was, sitting at an ornately carved table, a teacup and saucer on the table, along with a plate of sliced and toasted bread, and a small bowl of caviar. Colby smiled. Olympia may spend much of her time concerned with the plight of those less fortune than herself, but that didn't mean she avoided the luxuries a certain amount of wealth provided. He made a mental note to always have caviar in the larder to satisfy her craving.

Knowing he would scare her, and hoping to mitigate this as much as possible, he opened the door wider, then rapped his knuckles gently upon it. Olympia flinched, but did not scream.

She said, "Molly, I wanted *all* of the servants to..." Then her eyes widened in shock and anger as she saw that it was Colby standing in the doorway. "And just how in hell did you get in here? Did someone on my staff let you in?"

"No. And they locked all the doors and windows, too. I had to shimmy up the rainwater downspout in back and came in through your billiard room." When he started to cross the room, Olympia bolted to her feet. "I need to talk to you, Olympia. I don't understand why—"

"Don't come any closer!" Her voice was desperately strained. He'd never seen her quite like this. "I didn't let you in through the front doors because I don't want to see you right now. Is that so hard for you to fathom?"

"Yes, it is." He stopped a dozen feet from her. "If I've done something to make you angry, please tell me and I'll make amends immediately." His smile turned faintly roguish. "As I recall, you enjoy yourself immensely when I'm doing my best to win your good graces."

Colby was shocked at the flash of contempt he saw in his lover's violet eyes. Despite his best intentions of being contrite and conciliatory, a spark of anger came to life in his breast. No one had been foolish enough to look upon him openly with contempt since his early teen years. Even as a young man, Colby had been bigger and stronger than his peers.

"It didn't take you long to fall back on your old ways, *Your Grace*, did it?" The inflection she used when addressing him formally was like a slap across the face. "I saw the Baroness von Mecklenburg leaving your office." Her lips curled with utter disdain. "She had that well-loved look your lovers all have when they leave you."

Several seconds ticked by before Colby understood what Olympia was talking about. So completely had she bewitched him that Baroness von Mecklenburg's visit to his office, her offer of sex, and his summary dismissal, had been completely forgotten.

"This is silly. You can't think that—"

"The hell I can't! I can think whatever I want!"

The scope of her fury startled Colby, and the words 'Hell hath no fury' danced tauntingly in the back of his mind. His eyes narrowed. He'd had countless women furious with him in the past, but it was always because he was ending their relationship quicker than they wanted. With them, some lavish gifts were usually his ticket to a peaceful departure. But he had no intentions of ending his affair with Olympia. Not now, and not in any foreseeable future.

"Wait a minute. You've got to let me explain."

"No!" She stomped her foot, her small hands clenched into fists. "I don't want you to explain because I know how persuasive you can be. In ten minutes time you'll have me believing that I was seeing nothing but a ghost, or some such other bit of nonsense." She issued a short, harsh laugh that wasn't at all mirthful. "So did you just have to give the baroness one last good fuck for old times' sake?"

"Listen to me, goddamn it!"

"No! No! No!" Olympia shot back, placing her hands over her ears and turning her back on the duke. "I will not listen, and you can't make me!"

What happened next was not a blind rage by the Duke of Tasley. Quite the contrary, in fact. Women did not scream at Colby, nor did they turn their back to him. In Lord Beldon's world, such things simply weren't allowed. And the most ridiculous thing of all was that he was being accused of a sexual indiscretion…when for once in his life he wasn't guilty!

"The hell I can't," he stated flatly as he crossed to the bank of high windows. Grabbing the long braided cord for the window curtains, he gave a single hard tug. The cord came free in his hand. When he turned towards Olympia, she still had her back to him with her hands over her ears, oblivious to what he had in mind for her.

The Duke of Tasley made his move.

She struggled with all her might, trying to claw, kick, and even bite Colby. All to no avail. Within seconds he had her sitting on the divan at the foot of her large, four-poster bed, with her arms outstretched, her wrists tied with the long curtain cord to the two bedposts of the footboard.

"Damn you, Colby!" Olympia hissed through teeth clenched in anger, fighting against the bonds holding her.

She tried to kick him in the groin, and would have succeeded if his reflexes weren't so swift. Her effort to injure Colby where she clearly felt would do the most damage or good, depending upon one's viewpoint, only brought a chuckle to her intended victim. Another long curtain cord was ripped from its moorings, and soon Olympia's ankles were tied to the heavy, ornately carved feet of the divan.

"There, now you're going to listen," the duke said, taking several steps away from Olympia so that he had a better view of her.

Her hair had gotten mussed with their struggles, and somehow the strands having pulled free of her chignon made her look even sexier. She was breathing deeply, and even though her white blouse buttoned to her throat, the sight of her bosom rising and falling agitatedly made the duke's libido awaken. Her billowing skirt covered her to the ankles, but her legs were spread wide apart, her ankles tied to the divan's legs. Shapely calves in the white silk stockings were visible.

She was completely helpless, totally assailable, and mad as hell. There was nothing about her that didn't excite Colby's passion. The duke's cock was growing at a furious pace, but before he could act on his lust, he had to retrieve Leland.

"I didn't cheat on you," he said, moving closer slowly. It wasn't that he was fearful she might strike out at him. She obviously couldn't. But the closer he got to her, the more forcefully the predator in Colby's nature screamed that he should pounce while he had the chance. "Baroness von Mecklenburg and I have been lovers in the past, but I told her that we're finished. If she was flushed upon leaving my office, it was because she was at me. It wasn't fucking that put the colour in her cheeks, I assure you."

Olympia tried to pull her hands free from the cord tying her wrists to the footboard. Her struggles were in vain, but not without effect. Seeing her complete vulnerability, watching the taut sway of her breasts inside her chemise and blouse, added the last bit of stimulation necessary to bring Colby's cock to full attention. He was long, hard, and frighteningly thick in just seconds, his erection creating a portentous bulge in the front of his black breeches.

"I'm the one who writes the rules," the duke said quietly, but with dictatorial authority. "And you're about to get a few lessons that have been a long time in coming."

Chapter Seventeen

Olympia twisted her head sharply to the right, then left, looking at her hands. It was strangely and intensely erotic to see the braided cord from the bedroom window curtains wrapped around her wrists and the heavy, carved posts of her footboard. Though she was sitting on the divan, because her ankles were tied to the divan's legs, her pelvis was provocatively thrust forward so that her bottom was barely on the seat cushion. With her arms wide apart and her legs spread, she felt terribly vulnerable.

When she took one look at Colby, standing so near with his bulging crotch just below face-level, a shiver of fear and excitement went through her. She closed her eyes and tilted her chin down, fighting to keep at bay the mental image of his swollen erection straining against his breeches. Her traitorous libido was stronger than her sense of moral outrage. In her mind's eye, she could see the duke's cock, long and pale with veins running just beneath the surface of the skin, its girth impressive to the point of being intimidating, the crown plump, taut, and dusky-hued. Her pussy was creaming, becoming slick, the pink lips slightly swollen, her femininity preparing for the hot, lusty loving that she wanted with all her heart and soul, even if she could never make such an admission to the Duke of Tasley—or even to herself.

"I didn't make love to her."

The duke's words came out cold, flat. Olympia was unimpressed.

"Would you fucking listen to me?" he said. Then, "I said I didn't make love to her."

Finally, Olympia tilted her chin up and opened her eyes. The allure of his straining erection beneath the fall of his breeches was powerful, but she kept her eyes only on his face. She wouldn't give him the satisfaction of know that, despite her anger towards him, her body still reacted with blatant approval of his sensual allure.

"Is this another one of your word games?" she asked. "You're so good at them." Against her wishes, her eyes darted down to his crotch before she forced them back up to his face. "What about fucking, Colby? If you say you didn't make love to the baroness, I'll believe you. But what about fucking? What about that raw, barbarian fucking you throw into me sometimes?"

An eyebrow arched above an emerald green eye. "The ones that make you come time and time again?" His smile was roguish, which did absolutely nothing to dampen her rage towards him. "No, I didn't even do that to her. I'm done with other women. Finished once and for all." His tone dropped to nearly a whisper. "You're the only woman in my life now. You're the only woman that matters. All other women are..." It was a pregnant pause, and Olympia held her breath, waiting for the duke to finish his sentence. Finally, he said slowly and distinctly, as though he had taken careful consideration of the word, "superfluous."

Olympia closed her eyes once again. She made an effort to block his words from her consciousness. He had spoken *precisely* the words that she had wanted to hear. But wasn't that *exactly* what she had expected of him? Hadn't she been suspicious, from the very beginning, of the duke's facility with words? She needed time away from Colby, and even Leland—time away from everyone, in fact—if she was ever to think clearly. Wasn't that why she had refused to see him earlier in the day? Hadn't that been the reason she had dismissed all her servants for the remainder of the day?

She turned her face up once more, opening violet eyes that sparkled with defiance. "You have to untie me," she said, her tone imperious, in stark contrast to her splayed-out and trussed-up posture. "When you finish untying me, you have to leave my house."

Olympia had been quite pleased with both her tone and delivery...right up to the time Colby's grin spread across his face, causing that damnably adorable dimple to form in his cheek. To be laughed at when she was trying her hardest to be as authoritative as the duke always sounded infuriated Olympia to the marrow of her bones, the tips of her toes, and through every auburn hair on her head.

"Leave?" the duke asked, both hands beginning to free the twin vertical rows of buttons securing the fall of his breeches. "Perhaps soon, because Leland should be here...but I'm not leaving just yet."

The glint in Colby's eyes told Olympia everything she needed to know. The glint, and a formidable erection he was in the process of freeing.

"No!" she hissed through teeth clenched in rage.

It was a rage at her own inability to maintain a perfectly justifiable anger at a man who simply took what he wanted from life, and didn't give a damn what anyone else thought. She raged at her traitorous body's wanton receptiveness to the unspoken promise of sexual fulfilment that seemed to hover around the duke like an erotic ghostly aura. But most of all there was rage at a world that looked upon a rich man's sexual excesses as simply aristocratic privilege, but upon a sexual woman, no matter what her economic or social status, as dissolute and despicable.

"Please, m'lady, give this reprobate a chance to change your mind." His words were like fine silk sliding across her breasts, caressing her nipples. There wasn't a single sharp edge to any syllable…and Olympia felt herself being drawn into an inviting earthly abyss she desperately wanted to avoid. "Kiss my lips, and you'll know for yourself they speak only the truth."

At hearing the duke's words, Olympia felt the rapid beating of her heart pulsing madly in her clitoris. The slick nectar of her pussy moistened tingling labia, readying for the duke's heroic dimensions. A sob of frustration and desire caught in her throat.

"Don't say another word!" Her whispered words were the plea of a woman about to be entangled in Colby's seductive web of carnal fulfilment. "You can't!"

As he straddled Olympia's hips with his knees, the duke chuckled softly and replied, "Oh, my love…but I *can*!" He chuckled. "And so can you."

He cupped her face in his palms, bending low to kiss her lips. Knowing her own weaknesses towards the man, realising a tongue-entwining kiss would end any hope of defiance she still possessed, she wrenched her face sharply to the side.

"Why fight the inevitable?" Colby murmured, transferring his attention from Olympia's full-lipped mouth to her smooth, perfumed throat.

He kissed her throat, moaning when her feverish pulse throbbed against his lips. After several seconds, he bared his teeth and nipped at her neck, and though Olympia made high-pitched sounds of protest and squirmed beneath him, there was nothing she could do to avoid his tantalising love bites...similarly, she couldn't stop the rush of heat to her pussy, or stop the slick honey of her excitement from making her labia achingly ready for the duke's cock.

He tried to kiss her mouth, and Olympia avoided his kisses by thrashing her head from side to side. Though he always towered over her, now that he was straddling her hips with his knees, leaning over her as he tried to capture her mouth with his lips, the duke seemed gigantic in size, intimidating and dominating in ever possible way.

"Kiss me, Olympia. My lips speak only the truth."

His hands slid from her cheeks down the front of her body until he held her breasts lightly in his hands. When his fingers pressed into the mounds, a sob caught in Olympia's throat, and her nipples tightened even more. His lips were at her throat, warm and moist, his tongue playing over the surface of her skin. The abyss now seemed so close. All Olympia had to do was let herself be swallowed up by it.

Colby caught her nipples between his fingers and thumbs, and even through a blouse and chemise, the intensity of the feelings that he evoked when he pinched the erect nubs was shocking to Olympia. Moments later, she felt the row of pearl buttons, starting at her throat, coming unfastened beneath the duke's skilled fingers. She realised, at that very moment, that if she allowed the duke to continue caressing her traitorously responsive breasts, she would be begging for his cock within seconds.

And Olympia Whyte just wasn't ready for such an abject defeat. Not without a fight, she wasn't.

She began twisting her torso as far to the right and left as the ropes around her wrists and ankles would allow. She couldn't avoid Colby's cresses, but she could move erratically enough to prevent him from unbuttoning her blouse.

"Damn it," he growled, the sound of a man unaccustomed to being thwarted. "Stop fighting, Olympia."

"Never!" she shot back, an elated sense of victory washing over her.

She expected reprisal, just not one so swift or so final. The duke grabbed Olympia's silk blouse between the breasts and pulled apart. Pearl buttons clattered on the polished wooden floor, scattering in every direction on the compass. An instant later, his powerful hands shredded her chemise, exposing the entire front of her torso to his heated, hungry gaze.

Olympia closed her eyes, feeling Colby's carnivorous gaze on her naked breasts, feeling her nipples tingling, too, as tantalising exhibitionism entwined itself into her libido. The sound of her chemise being ripped in half echoed in her mind, touching her aurally, caressing her burgeoning fascination with the forbidden. Suddenly, the feel of the braided curtain cords around her wrists and ankles was as evocative as the duke's most skilful caresses. She tried to close her legs, and fresh nectar oozed from her pussy when her efforts were in vain.

"The most beautiful woman in the world," Colby said, scraps of fabric in his fingers.

Olympia opened her eyes. The duke still hovered over her, but now the buttons of his breeches had been unfastened, and though he was still completely dressed, with the front flap down his arousal was at last freed. His cock was frightfully hard, and a blue vein, running an uneven path along the broad upper surface, throbbed visibly with his heartbeat.

"The most beautiful," he repeated, "and the most frustrating."

Turning her gaze from his erection up to his eyes, Olympia said with as much saucy defiance as she could manage, "Good. A little frustration in your life might do you a world of good. Your character needs improving."

He moved away from Olympia slowly, putting one booted foot on the floor then the other, appearing to be careful to not put too much of his weight on her. Olympia looked down at her own breasts, watching their slight tremble as the duke eased away, shocked at the taboo eroticism she took in seeing her blouse and chemise torn apart by brute masculine force.

For several seconds, Olympia refused to look up at Colby, afraid that being watched was what he wanted. Finally, though, whether driven by her own escalating desires, her burgeoning fascination with voyeurism and exhibitionism, or simple curiosity, she turned her gaze to him as he stood before her.

Being fully dressed, it made it so much more lurid to have his cock sticking out, long and hard, filling his big fist as he stroked himself slowly.

"Why me?" Olympia asked. She watched as a droplet of pre-cum formed at the slitted tip. It was with some difficulty that she forced her gaze back up to his face. "You could have any woman in London. Hell, any dozen women. Why me?"

In a tone that was both gruff and soft, he replied, "You've bewitched me. You've entranced me. There's no other woman but you."

He moved closer, and the breath caught in Olympia's throat. Colby bent at the waist without straddling her body, reaching for her heavy breasts, his mouth opening wide. Olympia started twisting and shaking her torso, as she had done earlier with success. But not this time. Colby wound his powerful arms around her middle, holding her very tightly, and began feasted on her lush breasts, sucking as much of her brown areolas and nubby nipples into his mouth as possible.

"Oh God!" Olympia gasped as the heated wetness of the duke's mouth engulfed her senses. Being bound and utterly vulnerable, somehow made her extravagant breasts even more responsive than they usually were. "Colby...Colby...." Her words died away when he transferred his attention to her other breast, sucking avariciously, drawing such a tight suction it bordered on the painful.

Then, quickly and without warning, he lifted his head and shoulders and straddled her body once again with his legs. The swollen crest of his erection tapped against Olympia chin, and she instantly turned her face aside...though the urge to taste that part of Colby which had given her such pleasure was nearly overwhelming.

"You know you want to, Olympia..."

It was his endless confidence that made Olympia *refuse* to open her lips. Yes, he was right. She *did* want to take his cock deep into her mouth to feel him throb with lust and hear his moans of pleasure. She wanted to drag her lips over his crown and shaft and feel his powerful body quiver from head to toe because of the pleasure she could provide. When she sucked on him, she felt an overwhelming sense of feminine power at being able to turn a hulkish barbarian like the Duke of Tasley into nothing more than a quivering mass of over-stimulated flesh. She wanted to do exactly that.

But she wouldn't.

"Just a taste," the duke continued, tapping the crown of his cock against Olympia's cheek, sliding the bulbous head towards her mouth.

She turned her face to the other side quickly. The heat of her lover's erection tapping against her lips, cheeks, and chin seared her soul. Her mouth literally salivated with want for the taste of him…but still she refused because she had yet to be convinced that the baroness's flushed and flustered demeanour wasn't the result of the duke's exquisite lovemaking.

"Stubborn woman," the duke said, without rancour. "Well, perhaps I can change your mind and your mood."

For a fleeting moment, Olympia considered reminding Colby that they had all made a promise to never make love unless all three were present. Was it cheating on Leland, she wondered, all her thoughts in chaos, if she climaxed with Colby? If Colby climaxed with her?

Feeling her skirt and petticoat being lifted up her wide-spread legs brought Olympia away from her troubling thoughts and back to the very real here and now. The duke sank to his knees before her, and though Olympia used all her strength in an attempt to close her legs, the cords around her ankles attached to the legs of the divan, held fast.

"Struggle hard, my sweet," Colby said as his palms slipped over her silk stockings, then caressed her bared pelvis. She felt his thumbs gently pry apart the lips of her pussy to more completely expose her clitoris. "The harder you struggle, the harder my cock gets."

She wanted to look away. She wanted to avoid feeling even the slightest bit of anticipation. But knowing that she was about to be on the receiving end of the Duke of Tasley's cunnilingus made a tremble work through her voluptuous body.

But what Olympia wanted most of all was to come. To experience a fierce climax because of the devilish oral talents that Colby possessed.

Flesh is weak. Olympia's wish to avoid feeling any pleasure evaporated the instant Colby's slick tongue slipped between the pink lips of her cunt. By the time he reached her clitoris, she couldn't remember ever wanting anything other than her next climax.

"Oh God!" she cried out.

The duke brought his lips from her pussy and replied conversationally, "Not God, just me. But I'm hoping that'll be good enough to make you feel heavenly."

She would have given a saucy reply, but Colby immediately resumed his oral caresses, and when he delivered them, Olympia simply wasn't capable of proper diction for individual words, much less having the intellectual capacity required to formulate an entire coherent sentence.

His sucked on her clitoris while easing a single finger deep into her pussy. His tongue whipped for a while, then leisurely licked, always concentrating on the very tip of her clitoris. Time became distorted. The room suddenly seemed to lack oxygen, because no matter how fast or deeply Olympia tried to inhale, she couldn't seem to get quite enough air. When Colby removed his finger completely from her pussy, a sobbing sound got caught in Olympia's throat.

But a moment later, when she felt his slick fingertip against her tight, forbidden entrance, the soft moan she made was one of supreme gratification. Simultaneously, as his middle finger slipped past her resistance and pushed up into her anus, and his thumb separated the lips of her cunt, his lips captured her erect clitoris and began a rather intense suckling.

Though she did not like to swear, the words "Fuck!" and "God!" and something undecipherable that may or may not have been an actual word bounced off the walls as a wrenching climax jolted her trussed, bound body. And when the last of the spasms had finally subsided, and it seemed as though the entire top of her head had simply exploded, Olympia's body went slack, her hips sliding down a couple of inches on the cushion of the divan, her downward progress not stopping until the cords surrounding her wrists went taut.

Colby rose to his feet and began wrestling his iron-hard erection back into his breeches.

"And now, if you'll excuse me, I've got to get Leland."

Even in the delirium of her past-orgasmic lassitude, Olympia's jaw dropped open and she asked incredulously, "You're going to leave? You're going to leave me here like this?"

"Yes. But trust me, knowing that you're here waiting for me is going to make me the fastest man in London. Guaranteed."

Chapter Eighteen

Col. John Newton had just discovered his timetable for withdrawing all his money from various bank accounts, and secretly boarding a ship bound for India, had to be altered significantly. This discovery made him so angry he could hardly contain his rage.

"I want all my investment back," Melvin Steglien said, his face almost white with fury. "And I want to see the books. I want to see the signatures for the leases. The British-India Tea Company sounded like a solid investment a year ago. Now it sounds like I'm being swindled, and if you think I'm going to just let you steal my money, you're a lunatic, Colonel. I've got friends in London, friends with influence. Don't goddamned think that I don't, or that your commission in the military somehow scares me."

"Melvin, this isn't the time to get cold feet. We've gone too far together for you to turn back now." He was trying for a soothing tone but having only limited success.

Leaning back in his chair in the pub, the colonel put his ankle up on the opposite knee. A military man through and through, his boots were immaculately polished, but that didn't stop him from wiping away an imaginary smudge from his toe. "If you really want to back out on your obligations, I'll see that you get back every shilling that you've invested in the company. But before we do that, why don't we let you have a good, long look at the company ledgers. I'm sure that once you see exactly how your investments have been used, you'll see that sound business judgement will tell you to keep your money in the company."

Melvin Steglien tossed back the last of his gin before rising to his feet. He didn't appear in the least bit mollified by what had been said, but Col. Newton wasn't dismayed. He had already decided on the necessary course of action to deal with the cantankerous—and now dangerously suspicious—London entrepreneur.

"If you'll just follow me, I'm sure we can alleviate all your worries," the colonel said, adjusting the sword and scabbard on his left hip. "There's a shortcut we can take." He picked up his tricorn hat from the small table they'd shared. "The sooner we get you going through the books, the sooner you'll feel confident that your original decision to be an investor was the best business decision you've ever made."

The back door of the public house led to an alleyway which, judging by the unsettling odour that assailed the colonel's senses the instant he opened the door, was often used as a toilet by the pub's patrons. Being surrounded by four-story buildings allowed little sunlight to reach the straw-strewn, muddy alley.

"Good God, man, it bloody stinks back here!" Melvin Steglien declared the instant he stepped out of the back door of the well-kept pub. "Why in hell couldn't we have left through the front?"

The colonel closed the door and made sure that the metalwork locked into place. He glanced up and down the alley. As expected, there was no one milling about. Melvin Steglien's back was towards the colonel. He was already walking towards the mouth of the alley, mumbling beneath his breath something about being a gentleman unaccustomed to being assaulted by the stench of peasant urine.

It was the sound of the colonel's sword being drawn from its scabbard that first alerted Melvin Steglien. He stopped walking and started to look back over his shoulder. By the time he saw the colonel, his fate had already been sealed.

The first strike had to be the killing strike, and Col. Newton knew it. With all his might, he raised his sword high before slashing down at an angle. The long, finely-honed blade caught Melvin Steglien beneath his jaw, on the side of the neck. The blade sliced through soft flesh, not stopping its lethal charge until striking the victim's vertebrae.

As blood sluiced from the wound and Melvin Steglien crumpled almost straight down to the muddy floor of the alley, the colonel took swift, nimble steps backward. He always kept his uniform immaculate, and severing a carotid artery caused a wound capable of squirting a yard or more.

Dispassionately, the colonel watched as one of the first investors in the phantom business known as the British-India Tea Company twitched twice as blood fountained from his deep wound before his body went completely slack. The colonel cleaned his blade on the leg of the corpse's clean breeches.

"Happy now?" he asked the corpse. "Glad you decided to call me a lunatic?"

He saw two eyes inside a face obscured by a wild mane of matted hair and an unkempt beard so overgrown the man's mouth was invisible. The man was huddled beside a wooden crate, squatting on the ground, clutching onto a porcelain jug that, if the colonel's guess was correct, contained gin.

Col. Newton looked up and down the alley, satisfied that he was still unseen despite the dozens or even hundreds of people who were just fifty yards away on the street. The sword was still in his hand, its blade clean.

"I didn't seen nothin'," the old man said. "I won't say nothin'."

When he was in fencing training during his early days with the military, the colonel was, at best, a middling student when it came to his sword. Looking at the old man huddled at his feet, his eyes wide as saucers, his body already ravaged by great quantities of alcohol and very little nourishing food, the colonel hesitated a moment, then tauntingly sliced a perfect X through the air with his sword. The old man flinched. The colonel smiled, then lunged into a perfect thrust. The blade went through the drunkard's heart.

Col. Newton cleaned his blade and was out of the alley without being noticed.

* * * *

Prince Mallory gave the Duke of Tasley a sidelong glance and asked, "Why are we going in through the back door?"

"It's the only door that's unlocked." Colby grinned and added cheekily, "I thought you liked going through the back door."

"Not funny. You want to give me an explanation that's actually relevant?"

"Not really."

"Try anyway."

"Let's get together with Olympia, then maybe things will be a little clearer for you."

Despite himself, the prince smiled. When Colby had met him at White's, the duke was adamant that they return to Olympia's house with all due haste—though he promised that there was absolutely nothing wrong. Then, riding double on Thunder—the duke explained that a carriage would be unconscionably slow—they raced at dangerous speeds through London to Olympia's Kensington estate.

As they approached the servant's entrance, Leland said, "I'd love to tell you I've never had to used the back door to see a mistress, but the truth is I have. Quite often, actually." They stepped into the estate, and he felt the hair rise at the back of his neck. "Where are Olympia's servants?"

"We'll have the estate to ourselves for the evening. That's what I'm hoping, anyway."

"Oh? Doesn't that seem a little strange to you?"

The heels of their boots clicked ominously against the floor, echoing through the empty rooms as they made their way to Olympia's bedroom. When Leland stepped into the bedroom and saw the woman of his life sitting on the divan at the foot of the bed with her arms outstretched and tied to the bedposts and her legs spread wide and similarly bound to the divan legs, the breath caught in his throat. Her breasts were visible, her blouse torn in two. All that remained of her chemise was strips of tattered cloth.

"Leland, thank God you're here! That barbarian's tied me up!"

But as Prince Mallory approached the bed, it wasn't Olympia he spoke to. "So, you tied her up and ripped off her clothes." It was a statement, not a question. "And you wonder why we call you a barbarian?"

"I can explain."

"This ought to be good."

With an exasperated sigh, Olympia exclaimed, "Damn it all! Will one of you pay me a little attention over here?"

Colby pulled loose his cravat, then sat in a chair near the windows and began pulling off his boots. Picking up on the unspoken cue, Leland stripped out of his cutaway coat, sat in a nearby chair, and started removing his boots.

"The Baroness von Mecklenburg came to my office, irked at me because I haven't been seeing her lately," the duke explained in a calm tone, tossing a sock into the shank of his black boot. "She wanted sex, but since I've been with you and Olympia, no one else holds any interest for me. I told her she had to leave."

"And she didn't take rejection very graciously?"

"You could say that. As she was leaving her face was the colour of a ripe tomato." He shrugged the suspenders off his shoulders. "And that's how the trouble started."

Leland looked at Olympia, and felt his cock begin to grow. Her nudity and anger, combined with her obvious complete vulnerability, was a powerful aphrodisiac for the prince, heating his blood despite his outward appearance of calm.

"Olympia had been coming to see me at the office when she spied the baroness leaving, appearing, if my memory of exactly what Olympia had said is correct, 'flushed' and looking 'well-loved,' or something like that. Anyway, our darling lady assumed that the baroness's high colour was the result of some rollicking sex from yours truly. And when I tried to explain the truth, to explain to her my complete innocence — "

"I have a very difficult time believing you to be completely innocent, no matter what the situation."

"Your humour is misplaced, my good fellow."

Colby unbuttoned his breeches, and they fell down around his ankles. When he stepped out of them, the front of his drawers was showing the effects of a rapidly-forming erection of prodigious dimensions. Seeing the bulge, Prince Mallory felt an electrical charge of raw lust go through him.

The duke said, "When she wouldn't listen to me, I tied her up. A simple kiss was all I wanted, but I'm afraid I really am the barbarian I'm accused of being. I gave our lady a climax, but I did not climax myself. Remembering our vow for the three of us to all be together when making love, I reined in my desire, hopped onto Thunder, and made with all due haste to White's."

Leland pulled his shirt over his head, and let his breeches drop. Unknotting the drawstring of his drawers, he stepped out of them. His arousal was on display as he walked barefooted towards Olympia.

"And that," he asked, "brings us to the present?"

"Precisely."

"You men are *sooo* frustrating!" Olympia said, her anger unabated.

When she pulled at the cords surrounding her wrists, her breast swayed tautly, the sight of which caused a drop of pre-cum to form at the tip of the prince's cock.

"It's a miracle I fell in love with you two!" Olympia said.

* * * *

The instant the words were out of her mouth, Olympia's jaw dropped open. Leland and Colby, realising the significance of what she'd spoken so heatedly, both smiled.

She'd said it. At last, Olympia had admitted her love for them. They had given her their vows of love, but she had never returned them.

Until now.

"So then you believe me when I say I'm innocent?" Colby asked as he eased down onto the divan to her left.

"No. As a matter of fact, I don't know what I believe. All I am certain of is that I wanted some bloody time alone to think."

Leland sat on the divan to her right. The men were magnificently naked, and close enough for her to feel the heat emanating from them. He said, "You just admitted that you love us." His tone was silky, an aural guarantee of trustworthiness. "But since you have your doubts about Colby and I, it seems what we need to do is love you and love you and love you some more until you're finally convinced that you're the only woman we need."

The men moved even closer, and the breath caught in Olympia's throat. She pulled at the cords surrounding her wrists, to no avail. When Colby took her by the chin and tried to turn her face towards him, she wrenched her face in the other direction — only to be held tightly, and kissed firmly, by Leland.

The prince was nibbling at her lips when Olympia felt Colby's mouth fasten onto the crest of her left breast. A strangled sound of surprised passion was trapped in her throat as a myriad of emotions and sensations went through her. Though it hadn't been touched, her clitoris throbbed with need, her pussy creaming in licentious anticipation. When Leland's tongue touched her lips,

Olympia wanted to resist him, but her good intentions were of little influence on a libido that never failed to respond to these men. Just moment's later, when the duke's tongue slithered between her lips, she moaned soulfully, her lush, curvaceous body quivering as she tugged against the cords keeping her in bondage.

Unseen hands touched, caressing with consummate skill. Whose? Was it Leland who was pulling her petticoat higher up her body to expose legs sheathed in silk stockings, and a pussy hungry for attention? Was it Colby whose fingers were tracing light, expanding circles on her thigh, touching her lightly through her white stocking? Not knowing the answer heightened Olympia's passion.

Turning back to the prince, she sucked his tongue deeper into her mouth. The memory of being grabbed from behind by Colby during Lady Darcia's banquet slithered across the surface of her mind, heightening her passion. The orgasm she'd experienced when the duke thrust his big cock into her from behind while she didn't even know his identity had changed the way she looked at herself. That unplanned encounter had been her first experience with the forbidden, and once the duke had given her a taste of the taboo, she hadn't been able to think of anything else for long.

She finally turned her face aside, ending the kiss with Leland. Olympia was breathing deeply by this time, her passions escalating meteorically. She looked into the prince's startling silver-blue eyes, and saw the lust smouldering there. Then, as she looked at him, he dipped his head down and sucked her right nipple between his lips.

"Ohhh! Oh, God!" she sighed, her breath coming in uneven gulps as her handsome lovers sucked and nibbled on both her breasts. "I feel like I'm being eaten alive."

It was impossible for her to stay angry at these men. Even if it was entirely reasonable and rational for her to be suspicious of Colby after seeing the baroness's frazzled condition as she left his office — his past profligacy a matter of record and good grounds for giving any woman pause — her body couldn't maintain the objectivity of her rational mind. Her body responded to these men romantically, erotically, with an anticipation of the multiple climaxes they never failed to deliver.

Colby lifted his face from the plush pillow of her breast, took her chin in his hand, and slanted his mouth over hers. The kiss was hungry, heated, demanding that Olympia respond. He was kissing her when he caught her saliva-moistened nipple between his forefinger and thumb and pinched hard enough for the sensation to dance on the tightrope separating pleasure from pain.

She felt Leland moving, but when she tried to look, Colby merely tightened his hold on her chin and continued feasting on her mouth. Olympia felt her skirt and petticoat being pushed higher, and she unconsciously tried to close her legs. The cords surrounding her ankles stopped her efforts, and the reminder of her own bondage caused fresh cream to seep to the lips of her cunt.

The prince's soft declaration of "Precious pussy!" drifted to Olympia's ears an instant before his lips captured her clitoris. She cried out, shocked at the jarring eroticism of having her clitoris sucked on by Leland, her exclamation being swallowed by Colby's kiss.

Seconds passed, and the pre-orgasmic pressure built upon itself inside Olympia. When Colby finally ended the kiss, she opened her eyes and looked down between the mounds of her breasts at the kneeling prince. His mouth was pressed tight against her pussy, his nose buried in the soft auburn curls above her entrance. In his right hand was Colby's cock. The prince stroked him slowly, running his fist up and down over its entire length. Though she couldn't see the prince's left hand, she could see his shoulder moving, and she knew he was stroking himself.

Colby leant into her, his teeth tantalisingly sharp against her throat, his big hand closing over her breast, the fingers burying deep in the pliant mound.

"It's...not...fair," Olympia whispered, her runaway senses charging headlong towards an orgasm. "I feel like...I'm on...fire."

She would have said more, but the duke suddenly bolted to his feet, straddled her as he had before with his powerful thighs, then wrapped her silken tresses around his left fist.

"Suck!"

It was a command, and Olympia had no choice but to obey. Without protest, she opened her mouth and the duke's enormity pushed between her lips, its initial thrust not stopping until the crest of his cock was pressing snugly and a bit uncomfortably against the opening of her throat.

"Awww!" the duke groaned, fully a third of his erection buried in Olympia's mouth. "Give me that mouth! I want to fuck that beautiful face!"

With the back of her head against the footboard, Olympia had no way of relieving the pressure against her throat, so she felt no small measure of relief when he finally retreated, pulling back until only the tip of his arousal remained between her lips.

Too much! Too much is happening to me all at once! I...I'm going to come!

She flicked her tongue against the slit at the tip of his cock, then drew a firm suction on the lusty flesh. Colby worked his hard cock back and forth between her lips, but

Olympia could not concentrate on giving him pleasure. Not when her own passions were only seconds away from reaching the summit.

Such a wanton I am! I've got the duke's cock in my mouth, and the prince's mouth on my pussy...and I'm going to come!

The orgasm was powerful in the extreme, the spasms quaking through her split-seconds apart, one after the next. As she shivered, tugging at the cords binding her wrists and ankles, her opulent breasts quivering with her contractions, she tried to turn her face aside, but Colby wouldn't allow it. Her hair was wrapped around his fists as he pumped his hips, fucking his cock deep into her mouth, his rapid breathing a roar in the spacious room.

When the last of her orgasm had been eked out by the prince's slithering oral caresses, Olympia let out a soft, weary sigh once Colby had completely withdrawn from her mouth.

"That was only the beginning," he said, his emerald green eyes aglow with raw lust. "You're in for a night you'll never forget!"

They're going to fuck me to death.

Curiously, though she felt more alive than ever before in her life, the thought was not entirely without its appeal to Olympia. A woman, after all, had to die somehow.

* * * *

Francesca looked at the small wooden box that Colby had delivered, and was amazed that she had needed to call two butlers to carry it to her bedroom. Once in the bedroom, she tried to move the cashbox to her closet, but could only manage to lift one end of it. Not a woman given to physical exercise of any kind, and monumentally averse to doing anything that might make her perspire,

Francesca chose instead to simply sit on the floor and caress the gold florins.

It was then, as she was letting the small coins filter between her fingers to fall back into the box with a pleasing, metallic sound, that she suddenly realised her vagina was creaming, getting warm, and starting to tingle. It was an unprecedented sensation. She had never before had a sexual response to anything.

It's mine and I don't have to share it with anyone.

The thought prompted a small sob of gratitude to catch in her throat. She filled her palms with the gold, and once again let the coins slip through her fingers. As the coins fell, clinking against other freshly minted coins, her pussy grew just a little wetter.

Colby's going to be furious when he finds out I'm not calling off the wedding. I don't care if he hates me. I'm going to be the Duchess of Tasley, I'm going to live in Beldon Manor, and he's never going to shove that foul penis of his in me.

She smiled. Her life was playing out even better than she had planned.

* * * *

Olympia, rather deliriously, was wondering exactly how much hard cock her lovers thought she could accept at one time.

The answered seemed to be—all they possessed.

Colby was on his knees between her spread thighs, rubbing the conical crown of his erection up and down over her tingling sex lips. Leland, was standing on the divan, his slender fingers entwined in her hair, pumping his hips with increasing speed as he fucked her mouth.

"Look at me," the prince demanded, his silver-blue eyes shooting flames of desire when Olympia turned her gaze up to his. He filled her mouth with his erection, his fingers tight in her hair to hold her steady. "You're ours now. Ours forever and always. The three of us. Always. There'll be no one else. Just the three of us." Then his demeanour changed, and rather than fiery intensity, she saw his eyes soften. "I know what you want. I know what you need."

Hardly had his words finished than Colby's arousal forced the petals of her pussy to separate as he entered her slowly, with controlled force. Leland moved off the divan, his slender, naked body gracefully leonine, in sharp contrast to the duke's ostentatiously muscular one. Colby's hands were on her hips, his fingers tight against her flesh.

"He's right, Olympia." He withdrew, then thrust hard into her, not stopping until his pelvis slapped against hers. The heavy, jostling sway of her breasts drew his gaze like a magnet. "Every word he spoke was the truth. You're the only woman we want. There's no one else, and there never will be."

"Lean back a little," Leland said to Colby, getting down on his knees beside him. "I know what will make her come again."

Without slowing the steady rhythm of his powerful thrusts, the duke put a hand to the back of Leland's neck, kissed his mouth hard, then forced him down. The prince's long, ebony hair spread out on Olympia's belly, black against the pale flesh. An instant later, she felt his frisking tongue slither against her clitoris as Colby's pumping arousal filled her completely.

It was not a gentle experience. But it was the sheer physicality of the loving, the nearly brutal force exerted by *her men*, that elicited another orgasm from Olympia. Leland's quicksilver tongue and Colby's brutish, bludgeoning cock were a combination that unleashed an unquenchable passion in Olympia.

This time when she came, she did so at high volume, her cries of ecstasy ringing through the nearly empty mansion.

Hardly had Olympia finished her climax when Leland resumed his position above her. Her eyes were clouded over with an excess of sensuality, when she looked up at the prince and whispered, "I...need...time."

"Don't worry, love," the prince said as he lowered his hips until the shaft of his cock was between her trembling breasts. He grabbed the pliant mounds, squeezing them together around his erection. "I've a thousand ways of loving you."

Olympia found it bawdy but flattering as the prince worked his slick cock back and forth through the unnaturally tight cleavage of her breasts. Tilting her chin down, she licked at the crown when it appeared between the firm flesh, and she tasted a salty drop of fluid. It wouldn't be long. She knew her lover. More importantly, she knew what he tasted like moments before he came.

"Look at me," Leland growled.

The instant Olympia tilted her face up to look into his eyes, she felt the first slick, heated eruption of cum strike the underside of her chin. She kept her eyes open, loving the fierce intensity in the prince's eyes as he unleashed his desire on her breasts and throat. And through it all, she was rocked and pummelled by Colby's hard-charging thrusts.

A low, growling groan of desire preceded Colby's climax by a mere instant. His torrent splashed on Olympia's stomach, skirt and petticoat, and mingled in her pubic curls.

Their passions spent, the men moved away from Olympia.

With her arms bound and outstretched, she looked down at the pale, cum-bespattered globes of her breasts, her stomach, and her pubis.

They always remember, she thought with a sense of pride and relief. *How lucky can one woman be?*

Chapter Nineteen

As the Duke of Tasley's carriage rattled through the streets of London on his way to Francesca's home, he felt a white-hot fury inside him burning more intensely with each passing second. Scattered around him in his private coach were the torn and crumpled remains of nearly a dozen different newspapers. He had been searching in vain for the newspaper accounts that his engagement to Francesca LaMorneau had been called off. He was more curious than concerned as to what would be written about him. He was assuming that Francesca would concoct a juicy story, making herself the innocent victim and him the calloused aristocratic cretin who had chosen the cowardly route and run from marriage.

Newspapers such as *The Scuttle*, and *Our Times* had already printed numerous stories through the years regarding his intemperate lifestyle, endlessly suggesting — and not without some basis in fact, usually — that the Duke of Tasley had seduced this unnamed woman of the *Ton*, or that one. What the newspapers never printed was that there didn't seem to be any complaints by the women he had seduced.

When he couldn't find a single story regarding the dissolution of his engagement in the first two newspapers, the duke got a little concerned. By the time he had gone through the fourth newspaper, something akin to controlled panic had set in, and he shouted for his carriage and driver to be brought around immediately.

By the time he reached the ninth newspaper, and not so much as a single word regarding the cancellation of his wedding plans had been printed, he knew that something had gone terribly, horribly wrong. And he was pretty goddamned sure who was responsible.

He picked up his walking stick, resisted the urge to tap on the roof of the carriage and shout for his coachman to hurry. He twirled the stick in his gloved hands, looking at the silver handle. The round knob was solid silver, heavy, unadorned by any carving or engraving. It had been his father's, a gift to Colby for "becoming a man." It was a heavy stick, and in a pinch he could use it as a club. Weird, distinctly violent fantasies of revenge wriggled across the surface of his subconscious.

What the Duke of Tasley couldn't possibly tolerate was being a man married to Francesca LaMorneau.

Colby wasn't inclined to wait for an invitation to be formally greeted. When Francesca's butler opened the front door, the duke pushed it open and stepped around the old man.

"She's in the sunroom, right?"

"But, sir – "

"No need to announce me," Colby said, already taking long strides down the hall. He reminded himself that his problems were with Francesca, not with the old man. "I'll introduce myself."

She was in the sunroom, sipping hot chocolate and eating strawberries and blueberries with whipped cream, just as she did most mornings of her indolent life. When the door swung on the hinges and banged loudly against the wall, she was startled, but only for a moment.

"Good morning, Colby. Do have a seat."

Her hair was pulled back in her typical severe chignon, and she had the appearance of a woman freshly bathed and clothed and just beginning her day. It was nearly one o'clock in the afternoon. She seemed a little too poised, and the duke began to get an empty feeling in the pit of his stomach, that dull ache he got when he was at the poker table and suddenly realised he's got a lot of money riding on the hand, and he's probably not holding winning cards.

"Why didn't you make the announcements?" Colby asked, crossing the room. "I checked nearly a dozen newspapers, and not a word was printed about our wedding being cancelled."

Francesca smiled indulgently, and waved a hand towards the empty chair. "Take a seat, my dear, and let's talk about this with civility."

"We have nothing to say to each other, civil or otherwise. Why didn't you make the announcement?"

"Because I didn't want to."

She spoke the words with a certain simplicity and childlike honesty, the way a young woman who had never done anything for anyone out of obligation or even gratitude. Her mind simply didn't work that way. Never in his life had Colby resorted to violence with a woman, but his hands clenched into powerful fists, and he took a step away from her as though needing the extra space to keep his temper in check.

"I paid you in gold, Francesca. You gave me your word."

She smiled sardonically. "My word? You left me no choice. I did what I had to do."

To repress an urge to violence, the duke turned his back to Francesca. What options for action did he have? He could unilaterally decide to not marry her, but that would create a world of headaches for him, and it would also bring shame to the Beldon name.

No, he couldn't be the one to break the promise of marriage unless Francesca agreed to accept the change in plans. Would it be so bad to have her as his wife? Many, many men of the *Ton* married for convenience or for social connections, had sex with their wife until they had the suitable male heir, then went back to their mistress to live as they wanted to. The men and women of the *Ton* did not look down their aristocratic noses at these men. They had shown the wisdom to marry within their ranks and insure the bloodline, so a measure of forgiveness was given to them if they decided to have a mistress or two.

The duke forced his jaws to unclench. "What *exactly* are you telling me?"

Francesca was toying with him now, secure in her knowledge that no matter what, he wouldn't resort to violence. Never in his life had he felt quite so powerless, quite so mocked. He felt like a mouse being toyed with by a sadistic cat before being eaten. "Just for the novelty of doing something you've never done before, tell the whole truth."

"You want the truth? Fine. Because I want to live in Beldon Manor, that's what I'll do." An eyebrow arched in mockery of the duke. "And I want to be a duchess, so I'll be Francesca Beldon, Duchess of Tasley. I want many things, and in exchange, I'll give you a male heir. Or…maybe not." She smiled in malicious triumph. "Either way, I'm not saying one word to the newspapers. If you try to put a premature end to my marriage plans…I'll go straight to my uncle. He's in Parliament, you know, and he's got the ear of the Prince Regent."

"Half this fucking country has the ear of the prince. He's damned near as crazy as his father."

"True. But he does have an overweening sense of decorum — for others, that is, not for himself. Your ducal powers extend to the King…but not beyond him. So, you see, I've got you by the testicles. Unless you marry me, I'll fuck over that family name of yours." She issued a short, barking laugh. Her voice was quite loud as she continued. "And then where will you be? A fucking duke without connections, disgraced, without all that power and influence that you inherited from your father, and he inherited from his, and so on, and so fucking forth!"

The Duke of Tasley had to leave. He had to leave Francesca immediately. He no longer trusted his ability to keep his temper reined in like a gentleman. He started walking briskly towards the door. He was in the hallway when he heard Francesca's taunting, cackling laughter. She was torturing him, delighting in having secured wealth and privilege for herself for the rest of her life.

For the first time in his life, Colby ran from a fight.

* * * *

Col. John Newton was not ready to give in to full-scale panic. Not yet. He was a military man, after all, and he'd been through plenty of tough fights in his life on battlefields and back alleys — and almost always he'd come out victorious.

But this fight was significantly different than the military battles he'd been in. This time, should the King's men discover how he had bilked thousands of pounds from some of the wealthier members of polite society's upper crust, they'd put a rope around his neck and hang him. Or, even worse, he could be hanged, drawn and quartered — in the colonel's opinion, the most sadistic of all possible means of execution, though some soft-hearted politicians were trying to abolish that particularly gruesome form of execution. He'd watched a man get drawn and quartered several years earlier, and it was the single most barbaric thing he'd ever witnessed. The man's hideous screams, before death finally put an end to his horrific suffering, still rang in the colonel's ears.

He looked at Sgt. Rogers, dressed for the occasion in a crisp cutaway jacket of royal blue, with a high-collared white shirt, and striped breeches. Tucked into the waistband of his breeches was a pistol, and in his hands was a long-bladed dagger.

"Don't use the pistol unless it is absolutely necessary," the colonel said.

Sgt. Rogers met his gaze, then nodded. "I know what you expect of me, sir. We'll get the girl and be on *The North Queen* 'afore a soul in London is the wiser." The side of his mouth quirked up in what might have been a smile. "This dagger'll do the deed, and be right quiet about it, too. I only wish we could wait until dark. This sort of thing is done best under cover of darkness."

The colonel shook his head. "No choice but to make our move now." He flashed the smile that never failed to instil confidence in his men, no matter how dangerous the orders were that he gave them. "Before the sun comes up again, we'll be at sea and on our way to our new life. In India, we can start our lives all over again."

Sgt. Rogers's grin had a greedy quality to it. "But we'll be much, much richer this time around, won't we, sir?"

"Rich as Midas." He turned to the other four soldiers, all in civilian clothing, standing near their horses. "Look alive now. The carriage should arrive soon."

* * * *

The news hit Claude LeMorneau with the delicacy of a sledgehammer blow to the solar plexus.

"It's true, then?" he asked, standing in the sunroom.

Francesca smiled sweetly, seated near the windows. "Yes, Daddy, it's true. Lord Beldon was here, and he gave me twenty-five thousand in gold coin to call off the wedding."

Margaret, an elderly maid, sat in a corner of the room, knitting. She had been with Claude for decades, and she knew when it was time to give him privacy. She gave him a look.

"Yes, you can leave," he said, answering the unspoken question.

"No. I forbid you to leave this room." Francesca always used a sharp tone with the servants, but her voice was particularly lacerating on this afternoon. Everyone knew that Claude was too concerned with appearances to really chastise his daughter if the servants might hear. She often kept them near to blunt her father's criticism. To her father, she used a conciliatory tone. "Daddy, trust me, you don't have a thing to worry about. I've thought the whole thing through. And let's face it—twenty-five thousand florins is a fortune."

"I've got my future riding on you become the Duke of Tasley's wife." His tone hinted he was on the verge of hysteria. "Now what agreement have you reached with Lord Beldon?"

Francesca, infuriatingly, took the time to sip her tea before responding. "Daddy, let me tell you how it is. I've received a payment of twenty-five thousand in gold from Colby to call off the wedding. But in matters such as these, you can't really write anything down, now can you? So the gold is my personal payment for agreeing to bear him a son." She smiled in feline fashion. "Of course, there will be other monetary benefits to being Lady Beldon, but the gold is mine and mine alone."

"But you agreed to call off the wedding." His brow furrowed in confusion.

"Yes, that's what I told Colby to begin with." She laughed softly. "What a fool he is. I was supposed to have announcements put in all the major newspapers, and even several of those gossip sheets the lower classes like to read." She sighed. "But I've decided I want the gold *and* the title, so I'm keeping the gold and I'm going to marry Colby during the Little Season, just as planned. He can have my pussy, since it seems so dreadfully important to him, but I get the title and a pleasant sum of gold for..." her lips curled disdainfully, "spreading my legs."

It was scary to look at his own daughter and realise just how cold-blooded and mercenary she really was. Though Claude prided himself on being a cutthroat negotiator, Francesca's deceitfulness, her unhesitating willingness to lie, cheat, and steal just to get whatever she wanted, put her in a league of one.

"You idiot. You little fool," Claude said quietly. "Nobody steals from the Duke of Tasley and gets away with it. You'll get your gold, and you'll get your title, but he'll have me blackballed. There won't be a financier in England who will come near me once he puts the word out on what you've done."

Francesca smiled. Claude realised then that his personal agony meant nothing to his daughter.

"Well, it *is* my pussy," she said pointedly, "So it's obvious that I'm the only one who can decide what it's worth. What have you contributed? Why should you get even a single shilling of my money?"

He put a hand to his throat. For several seconds it seemed as though all the air had been sucked out of the room. "But I'll be ruined...completely ruined. And you...you'll have all that gold. That's not fair. I had *plans*."

"Plans! Plans! Plans! Oh, Daddy, you've always had plans, and they've never come through for you, have they?" The scorn in Francesca's flinty eyes was undisguised. "You met with Colby's mother and thought that you could line your own pockets by selling me off to be his wife. He's a duke and he needs someone to be his broodmare so he gets a male heir, someone who understands what's expected of the wife of a peer. There's no woman of the *Ton* more qualified than me. I'll be the most gracious hostess in Kensington, and he can fuck me until he gets his son." She crossed her arms over her small bosom and narrowed her eyes in critical assessment. "Frankly, Father, the simple and sad truth is that I don't need you any more. If Colby gets angry because he's got to marry me to save face in society, then he can get angry. And if you get blackballed from the best gentlemen's clubs — and we both know that's where all the deals really get finalised in London — I still don't see how that's any problem of mine."

"You bitch." Claude's breathing had become laboured. "You lousy, rotten, cold-hearted bitch. You'd ruin me like that?"

"You've ruined yourself," Francesca said dismissively. "You've been doing it for years. I'm just the person to finally put a knife in you."

A thought came to Claude, and it was just as jolting to his senses as it had been to discover what his daughter had blackmailed and then lied to the Duke of Tasley. It took a few seconds, but a smile slowly formed, beginning with his mouth before moving upward to put a gleaming light of approval in his eyes as he formulated his plan.

"The gold...where is it?" Claude demanded.

He was looking directly at his daughter when he asked the question. Had he not been paying such close attention, he would have missed it when Francesca's eyes flicked towards the windows before moving back to fix on his face.

His smile broadened. "The gold is mine, Francesca."

"It's mine!" was her quicksilver response.

He strode quickly to the window, tossing the heavy curtain aside. There on the floor, against the wall and behind the curtain, was a squat, oblong wooden box. There was a latch on the box, but no lock. He had already gotten down on one knee and had grabbed the box by the two rope handles on either end when Francesca hit him from behind, her small fists ineffectually striking his shoulders and the back of his head.

A rush of adrenaline went through Claude when he tried to lift the box. It wasn't a large box, but it was *very* heavy. He hardly noticed his daughter as she continued to pummel him with small, white fists ill-suited for being used as weapons.

"Goddamn it, Daddy, that's my gold!" Francesca screamed.

Without looking over his shoulder, Claude twisted his upper body and shot his elbow straight backward. His elbow connected solidly with Francesca's chin. He heard her startled cry of alarm, immediately followed by the sound of her knees striking the floor. He smiled. He'd been waiting a long time to teach his daughter some life lessons — with his fists, elbows, and boots, if necessary.

Knocking Francesca to the floor seemed to give Claude a burst of both strength and confidence. He lifted the gold-laden box, groaning a little under the weight, the smile on his lips one of pure elation.

"You bastard!" Francesca screamed. "That's my gold! That's mine!"

Claude kept walking towards the sunroom door. Her gold? No, it was *his* gold. He deserved it because he'd swallowed a thousand insults from Francesca without ever insulting her back. He'd listened to her prattle on about her life as though she really had problems, when in fact she didn't really have a legitimate care in the world.

Margaret's scream startled him. She had been with the family for years, and it was the very first time that Claude had ever heard her raise her voice, much less actually scream.

He turned just in time to see Francesca's arm begin its downward arc.

Claude might have been able to defend himself against the attack, but he refused to release his hold on the cash box. When she had hit him, her small fist had done little damage to him. But now there was something in her fist. He recognised Margaret's knitting needle inside his daughter's fist an instant before it buried into his neck just above his cravat.

He watched his life's blood shoot onto Francesca's pristine white blouse, and heard Margaret's horrified cry as she shouted, "She's killed him! Dear God, the girl's killed her daddy!"

It wasn't the weight of the cash box that toppled Claude over, it was loss of blood. He rolled onto his back as darkness closed in around him.

Francesca moved so that she stood over her father. She bent at the waist to look into the dying man's eyes, and said slowly and triumphantly, "It's my fucking gold, Daddy!"

Chapter Twenty

Dennard sat in the carriage's front seat, holding the reins to the twin Belgian mares loosely in his hands. Lately, the prince had been assigning him to serve Olympia—a duty Dennard found entirely to his liking. She had a pleasant disposition that was nearly always very cheerful—especially when she was near Lord Beldon and Prince Mallory. She was as hesitant to make a frivolous request of him as she was generous with her compliments. She had made it abundantly clear that she adored the way he prepared her coiffure, and she let Colby and Leland know of her opinion. And best of all, she thought she knew of a few nice, young men who might be interested in making his acquaintance.

Since Dennard had not had a love interest in well over a year, the prospect of meeting someone pre-selected and deemed suitable by Olympia—and therefore a gentleman, since she'd made it quite clear that he would not be a consort to riffraff—had been playing pleasantly on his mind.

He was driving her home now from another tryst at Prince Mallory's estate outside the city, trying to concentrate on properly driving the Belgian team and being mindful of the foot traffic, but it was difficult to concentrate when there was the distinct possibility that he would soon meet a gentleman who would want him for something more than just sex.

"You need a young man of culture and learning," Olympia had said to him the previous evening. "You need a man who wants you for everything that you are, not just for that glorious body of yours." Her gaze had been critical as she looked at him through the reflection in the mirror. "I believe the prince is requesting my presence tomorrow morning. Let me see if I can make up a list of suitable names by then. My standards are high for you, but there must be some men who are worthy."

"You needn't put yourself out, m'lady," Dennard had replied.

"It's the least I can do for a man who is a genius with hair. You've spoilt me forever, you know. No one can do my hair like you can," Olympia had said.

Dennard was so distracted by thoughts of Olympia's previous conversation, and of a possible romance in his near future, that he didn't notice the four men dressed in fashionable cutaway jackets of navy blue satin standing at the side of the road, paying careful attention to his carriage. Not at first, anyway. As he drew nearer, the men stepped into the street and motioned for him to bring the carriage to a stop, though none said a word. Their mouths were curled into smiles, though their eyes showed no pleasure.

And then, from across the street, a man in a sergeant's uniform called out, "Hail, there, good fellow!"

Two of the men in the street reached for the horses, one going for the left horse's bit, the other for the right horse's collar.

Dennard was just about to ask the men if they'd lost their senses—gentlemen simply didn't stop another gentleman's carriage without extreme provocation—when he met the eyes of one of the men. He was staying back a little, watching the activities without being a direct participant—but his eyes were like a hawk's, missing nothing. It was his civilian clothing that had befuddled Dennard to begin with, he realised a split-second later.

It was the colonel! The one Prince Mallory found so detestable!

Dennard had never been a man of action, so it was inexperience and naïveté alone—and not cowardice—that made him pull back on the reins to slow his Belgians.

That was when he saw the handle of a knife sticking out of the colonel's belt, half-hidden by his coat. Gentleman often carried knives, but none carried them where honest people might see them. It was considered *gauche*.

The sergeant in uniform was rushing forward, and paying much more attention to Dennard than to the men grabbing the reins and collar for the team of horses.

Reality registered in his brain with the clarity of a lightning bolt cutting through midnight darkness. These men weren't stopping the carriage because they wanted to talk. Col. Newton wasn't in civilian clothes because he had decided to dress casually on that day, and the uniformed sergeant certainly wasn't rushing forward to find out what the civilians were doing by stopping the carriage.

"Bastards!" Dennard hissed, raising his hands and bringing them down furiously, sending the reins slapping against the backs of the Belgians.

It happened very fast, and Dennard was surprised at how little pain there was.

The horses started to bolt, but three men had them by the reins and were holding them back. Given time, Dennard could have urged his horses to run, even with the impediment of the men—but his time had run out. When the sergeant leapt up into the coachman's compartment, Dennard lashed out at him with a fist.

It was an ill-matched battle. Dennard was not a fighter, and the sergeant was a remorseless, experienced killer. The stiletto blade went into Dennard's body just under his right arm, buried to the hilt.

Dennard was tossed into the street a moment later. He did not actually feel his body hit the cobblestones, though he was conscious of it. The carriage sped away. As though from a great distance, he heard Olympia's high, panicked scream ring through the cool, early evening air.

His last thought was of the woman he served, and he felt sad and guilty that he had not been able to protect her.

* * * *

Standing in the entryway to Olympia's home, the Duke of Tasley looked down at the pale, lifeless body of Dennard. With a voice as controlled as he could keep it, he asked, "How long ago did this happen?"

Molly, Olympia's elderly maid, replied, "Less than an hour, m'lord." Her lower lip trembled. "They took my mistress, Your Grace." A sob caught in her throat. "They took my Olympia."

"And you saw it happen?" Colby asked.

"The poultry man down the way sent me a message that he had some fresh laying hens and fryers, and I thought I'd get some for my lady. She does so enjoy an egg in the morning. I stepped out and saw it all happen."

Time was critical, Colby knew, but he couldn't shout at this old woman because she was already on the edge of hysteria, and yelling at her to be concise wouldn't help her nerves any.

"Tell me once again what the men did." In her previous statements she said she had seen 'everything' but could remember 'nothing,' which didn't help the duke in the least. "Listen to me now, close your eyes, concentrate very hard, and then recreate what you saw for me."

He watched as Molly closed her eyes. Her concentration was palpable. She was a lovely old woman, and as a trusted servant she was completely dedicated to Olympia...but brilliant she wasn't.

"I remember now." Her eyes opened, and Colby felt his heart clench with anxiety. The thought of Olympia being under anyone's custody but his own created a horror in his soul more frightening than anything he had ever experienced. "That officer was there. I'm pretty sure it was him, but he weren't in his uniform. But I recognised his face. I recognised it plain as day cause he used to come calling on m'lady, only she didn't much like it when he came."

"Officer?" A chill went through Colby's blood. "Are you talking about Colonel Newton?"

Molly nodded vigorously. "The very same!"

He was headed for his horse an instant later, inadvertently knocking a young stable boy to the ground in his haste. He'd apologise later.

* * * *

Col. Newton looked at Olympia, seeing the fear shimmering brightly in her violet eyes, and felt a surge of desire go through him. He had wanted her for years. He had killed her husband to be with her. And for months now he had planned to take her with him to India, only waiting for his personal coffers to be sufficiently filled before making his escape from London.

Events had conspired to make him speed up his departure, and Olympia had proven to be recalcitrant — but that really didn't matter. He had her under control now, and by the time they had reached India, she would come to understand that she belonged to him. It would take some training, and assuredly some unpleasant lessons, but she would learn to follow his orders without question or hesitation.

"You've only yourself to blame," the colonel said, the dagger in his right hand as he ran the palm of his left hand over her knee and thigh, touching her through woollen skirt and cotton petticoat. "I told you long ago that you weren't to smile at other men, and yet you persisted."

Though the fear in her heart showed plainly in her eyes, her expression altered to one of defiance. "You'll suffer for this, colonel. Set me free now...or your fate is sealed."

The colonel laughed. "Spunk! That's what I first saw in you!" He laughed some more, and when Olympia slapped his hand off her thigh, he laughed even louder. But then, abruptly, his expression became murderously intense. "Listen to me good, Olympia, and remember what you hear. You're mine now. Mine alone...and there's not one fucking thing you can do about it. I played your little game and waited while you mourned the death of your husband, but I'm done waiting. You should have been mine from the very beginning, but that bloody beggar Arthur up and married you before I'd ever set eyes on you." His mouth curled unattractively. "But I got the better of him, didn't I?"

Olympia's eyes narrowed in confusion. "Got the better of him?"

"I jimmied the cannon that blew up in his face. I knew I could never have you as long as your husband was alive, so I made sure he got himself killed dead as a doornail." His voice softened with sincerity. "See what I'm willing to do to have you? You shouldn't have made me do that. You're just as responsible for killing him. Don't think you're not."

Olympia made a soft sound in her throat, her eyes rolled back white, and she fainted.

The colonel put his left hand over her breast and squeezed. Her breast was full and firm, and the delights that would be his once he had her safely locked up aboard *The North Queen* were almost beyond imagination. He was certain of it.

* * * *

"How long have they had her now?"

The question came from Sir Reginald Longley, Vice Chancellor of Maritime Commerce, and long-time member of Parliament.

Prince Mallory withdrew the gold watch from his waistcoat pocket and thumbed the catch. "Just over two hours."

"And you're proposing…?"

The Duke of Tasley put out his enormous hands and with controlled fury answered, "We need a blockade of the Thames. From everything we've been able to learn, Olympia's carriage was seen several times headed towards the waterfront. If Colonel Newton's kidnapped her, he can't stay in town."

"Yes." Sir Reginald contemplatively pinched his lower lip between thumb and forefinger, his gaze going back and forth between these two young members of the peer, clearly deliberating what next needed to be said. After several seconds of silence, during which both Prince Mallory and Lord Beldon fidgeted—he said, "As Vice Chancellor of Maritime Commerce, I have received some reports lately of nefarious criminal activity. We get them all the time, and usually it's rather petty crimes. But this time the reports involved someone in the military, and that's why the report made it to my desk. It seems that Colonel Newton created a company called the British-India Tea Company, or some such thing, and has been taking investment money from quite a number of our finest citizens. Nothing wrong with that...except the British-India Tea Company only exists on paper. It looks like he's been pocketing everyone's investment. If Colonel Newton has kidnapped Mrs. Whyte, then he surely intends to flee the country with her."

"We'll never be able to search all the ships if they make it out to sea," the duke said. "As long as they're on the Thames, we've got a chance."

"It would be unprecedented to blockade the Thames, Lord Beldon. It would require the instant mobilisation of hundreds of sailors and dozens of ships. On what authority could I do such a thing? It simply isn't done."

Colby bent at the waist, putting his nose very close to Sir Reginald's. "If you do not order a complete blockade of the Thames, and that bastard escapes with Mrs. Whyte, I swear on the soul of my mother that I will hold you personally responsible." His voice was nearly a whisper, yet it vibrated with a deadly intensity. "Do I make myself clear?"

Though a man of considerable power and influence in the British Parliament, Sir Reginald's smile was wan as he replied, "Frighteningly so, Your Grace."

* * * *

As *The North Queen* sailed away from its London dock, Col. Newton turned to the bearded man at the helm in civilian clothes and asked, "You have everything under control, Captain?"

"Aye, Colonel. We're on the water now, and that's where I belong. You and your men can just relax. I'll get you to India safe and sound."

Col. Newton nodded, and though he felt like smiling, he did not. He had procured the services of the captain, and his crew, at a hefty cost. Once they reached India, the sailors would be free to make their way back to England however they saw fit—leaving *The North Queen* for the colonel to sell to the highest bidder. His profit from the British-India Tea Company scam, as well as the theft of *The North Queen*, would set him up in luxury for the rest of his life.

The colonel said, "In that case, I'll go to my cabin."

The captain grinned knowingly. "That you should, Colonel. I saw that gel your men brought aboard. She loud and feisty, she is. Nearly gouged the eye out o' one of your men. She'll be a hard one to tame."

"I'll tame her," the colonel replied, his tone hard, as though he had been challenged. "Only a fool would think that I can't."

And since he didn't want to argue with the captain, as there was no profit to be made from it, Col. Newton made his way to his cabin, the one he would share with Olympia through the three to five weeks it took to sail the forty-two hundred miles to India.

His private cabin was not particularly spacious, but then, no cabins on the ship were. At least he had the fifteen-by-twenty-five-foot room to himself...and Olympia, of course. He had also paid extra to have a private supply of food put aboard, so he and Olympia would eat and drink well. His men would have to make do with significantly less tasty fare.

He took the key from his waistcoat pocket and quietly inserted it into the lock. The tumblers moved smoothly, unlocking without a sound. When the door was unlocked, he returned the key to his pocket, listened carefully for movement inside the cabin, heard none, then opened the door.

Olympia was standing in the corner of the room, apparently keeping as far away from the small bed as possible. The desire to rush across the small space separating them, take her in his arms, and throw her to the bed was very powerful. Very powerful, indeed. But the colonel tamped down this base, animal emotion. He would have Olympia—he would have her every way it was possible for a man to take a woman, whether she consented, or not—but he would rather she gave herself willingly. Ripping her clothes off the very first instant he was alone with her would not be conducive to connubial contentment in the future.

"Hello, Olympia." He leant back against the door, his eyes hooded, his breathing suddenly coming in quick, shallow inhalations. He pushed himself away from the door, took a step towards his captive, then promptly spun around towards the door. With a quick twist of the wrist, he had relocked the door, and returned the key to his waistcoat. "There," he said, turning once more towards the voluptuous woman trembling in the corner. "Now we won't be disturbed."

"You'll never get away with this." Olympia straightened her shoulders. It was such an obvious — and pathetic — act of futile defiance that the colonel almost chuckled. "You'll never *ever* get away with this."

"Silly girl, look around…I already *have* gotten away!" He waved a hand towards the small table with two chairs beside it. "Are you hungry? Thirsty? I've had special supplies stocked just for the two of us. There's a claret that will be especially nice after our evening meals." *And right before I take you to bed*, he thought, but did not say.

"You're insane, Colonel."

"Technically, I'm no longer a colonel, but you can continue to call me that." He sat in one of the chairs near the table. "You might say that I've resigned my commission. Please, have a seat and let's talk civilly. We have much to discuss." The colonel believed he was much too intelligent to ever be insane. His confidence had always been high, but now that he was sailing away from London and headed for India — with a fortune in gold, and Olympia in his cabin — he had never been more self-assured.

"Fuck…you."

He had adored Olympia from the moment he'd met her, and to hear her speak so bluntly, so crudely, was an insult to the idealised woman he had created in his fantasies. In an effort to control his temper, he cleared his throat twice before saying calmly, "Such base behaviour does not flatter you, my dear. Now have a seat. I have much to explain." His gaze turned cold. "Listen well, because you have much to learn." When Olympia didn't move, the colonel's hands briefly clenched into fists before relaxing.

"You're going to do as I tell you. The sooner you accept that simple fact of life, the happier you'll be."

"I'll be happy...when I'm dancing on your grave."

A tic in the colonel's jaw was his only outward sign of frustrated despotism. He again had to consciously tamp down his desire to pounce on Olympia. He envisioned her as he'd seen her so many times in the evening at Hyde Park, in a lovely evening gown, with a fashionably revealing neckline that displayed those alabaster breasts. Now, with her white blouse buttoned up to her chin, she looked perfectly proper...but he knew in his soul that once he had her naked and beneath him, she'd turn into a wildcat. He'd bring the sensuality out in her. Of that he was certain.

And he wouldn't have problems getting an erection, either.

He hoped.

"You'll be happy when we're in India."

"India?" Her mouth opened slightly, and she inhaled sharply. "My God, India?"

He nodded, smiling, and closed the distance between them. "You'll live a life of luxury."

"I'll live the life of a slave."

He reached for her shoulders, and she slapped his hands away. He smiled again. "Things have changed. You might just as well make the best of it."

"Never."

"Don't fight me. You can't win."

"Fuck you!" she replied, then spit in his face.

As though it was something distinctly physical, Col. Newton felt his patience snap. It was hearing his fantasy woman speaking so coarsely, more than the actual defiance, which infuriated him so. When he reached for her a second time, it wasn't her shoulders he sought to hold, it was her breasts.

"No! You bastard!" Olympia screamed slapping at his hands.

A black rage came over the colonel. He grabbed Olympia's throat with his left hand, pushing her against the cabin wall, as he caught her breast with his right, his fingers burying into delicate tissue with sufficient force to bruise. A curse Olympia tried to scream was suffocated in her throat. Aware that he was choking her so severely she couldn't breathe, the colonel loosened his grip on her throat, but tightened his hold on her breast. The garbled sound she emitted spoke of pain and rage. She tried to knee him in the groin, but he easily blocked her attack with his thigh.

In the back of his mind, where conscious, rational thought was still possible, Col. Newton heard the sound of running feet, both above him on the ships' deck, and outside his cabin door. Had he not been intoxicated with Olympia's beauty, or narcotised by his power over this erotic and defiant woman, an alarm would have sounded in his brain.

But all that mattered to Col. John Newton was Olympia. He wanted—no, he *needed*—to feel and hear the cloth tearing as he ripped the clothes from her body until she was naked. He wanted to feel her bruised breasts flattening against his chest as he crushed her body with his. He wanted to hear her soft, whimpering cries of defeat as he stabbed his cock into her.

He dug his fingers into the neckline of Olympia's blouse, and jerked down with all his might. Blouse and camisole gave way to brutish strength heightened by feral, sadistic desires. Olympia's heavy breasts, full and round with tan areolas and nipples elongated with fear, sprang free.

Seeing her breasts brought a cry of bloodlust to the colonel's lips.

The sight of her breasts was so bewitching to the colonel that he didn't even hear the sound of wood shattering as his cabin door was kicked in.

She's mine! She'll always be mine!

It was the last entirely coherent thought the colonel had before enormously powerful hands grabbed him from behind, spinning him around. Then he saw the Duke of Tasley and Prince Malley reaching for him. It was the duke's hands, like steel bands, wrapping around his throat that made breathing impossible.

The prince had a dagger in his hand. The colonel saw that dagger and knew that he was about to die. He grabbed Colby's wrists and tried to wrench the punishing hands from his throat, but the duke's strength seemed infinite.

As though from faraway, he heard Olympia say, "Don't kill him! Don't kill him!"

And then blackness swept over the colonel.

Epilogue

"However did you get so many boats looking for me in so short a time?" Olympia asked, sitting on the balcony off the bedroom she shared with Leland and Colby. She wore a sheer white silk robe that, though it covered her to her ankles, somehow enhanced the extravagance of her body by showing her form while simultaneously hiding it. There were newspapers scattered everywhere. "You say the Chancellor of Maritime Commerce was involved?" She watched as her lovers laughed softly and exchanged a knowing glance. "Come on, tell me the whole truth this time, and not the drivel that's been printed in all these newspapers."

"We knew that if you made it through the Thames and into open water, we'd never find you," the duke explained, the smile vanishing from his face. "Good God, Olympia, we were so scared."

"That's behind us now," Prince Mallory said quickly, sliding his hand over the duke's and squeezing it. Sitting at the table, he turned towards Olympia. "While it's true that Sir Reginald did activate the Navy on our behalf, there were really only a handful of ships available at a moment's notice." His eyebrows lifted in amusement. "That's when I got the idea of putting a bounty out on you. I said that whoever found you would receive a reward — a bounty, if you will — of five thousand pounds in gold."

"That's a fortune!" Olympia exclaimed.

"A fortune well spent," the prince continued. "The news of the reward went through the shipyards like wildfire." He smiled and gave Colby's hand another squeeze. "For all practical purposes, all work on the docks came to a complete standstill and everyone — and I mean *everyone* — was looking for you. It wasn't long before we got word of a screaming woman being hustled onto *The North Queen*. You can't imagine how many ships there were involved in stopping your boat."

Olympia poured tea for her lovers. They, too, were in their white silk robes, and though they were both in a relaxed sprawl, their musculature was on display. Though she'd thought her passions had been satisfied with them earlier in the day, she felt another fresh surge of warmth flow outward from her pussy.

"It's all worked out," the duke said. In his hands was a newspaper with the headline, 'She wanted to be a duchess. Now she's in the dungeon!' "I have been released from any obligation to Francesca, and have not blackened the family name in the process. Who would have thought she'd kill her own father? At least now the three of us can all be together."

"Secretly, of course," Olympia said, mindful of society's influence. She lacked the titles of her lovers, and was therefore more cautious. "But that seems a small price to pay for such bliss."

"Small, indeed," the duke said as he tossed aside a newspaper, revealing to both Olympia and Leland an erection sticking prominently out through the folds of his robe. "So how about we turn this conversation towards more entertaining topics."

Olympia and the prince exchanged a look, then both slipped off their chairs, moving towards the Duke of Tasley.

About the Author

Robin Gideon is the author of a dozen historical romance paperbacks. Robin is married and lives in the Upper Midwest. Robin's favorite cities in the world are London and Edinburgh. She was featured author on CBS Sunday Morning TV show. Her books have been translated into German, Chinese, and Romanian. Robin's novel "Cheyenne Desire" was named 3rd Best All-time for sexy romances by Amazon.com's Listmania.

Robin Gideon loves to hear from readers. You can find her contact information, website details and author profile page at http://www.total-e-bound.com.

Total-E-Bound Publishing

www.total-e-bound.com

Take a look at our exciting range of literagasmic™
erotic romance titles and discover pure quality
at Total-E-Bound.